THE MURDER THAT HAD EVERYTHING!

AN AMOS LEE MAPPIN MYSTERY

THE MURDER THAT HAD EVERYTHING!

AN AMOS LEE MAPPIN MYSTERY

HULBERT FOOTNER

COACHWHIP PUBLICATIONS

Greenville, Ohio

ISBN 1-61646-258-2
ISBN-13 978-1-61646-258-1

Cover: Hulbert Footner (George H. Doran Co., 1921)
Inside map from back cover of 1945 Dell Mystery reprint (not renewed).

CoachwhipBooks.com

CONTENTS

CHAPTER ONE
THE GLAMOUR GIRL

FANNY PARRAN CONTINUED up Madison Avenue, very businesslike with her heavy-rimmed glasses and bulging briefcase. There was nothing in the spectacles but plain glass; Fanny wore them on the street to discourage the young men. Fanny had no heart of stone; if the young man was personable and mirthful, the corners of her mouth would turn up when he smiled, and then it would be almost impossible to shake him off. As it was, the spectacles were only partly successful.

In the block between 38th and 39th Streets, she mounted the steps of an old brownstone residence that had been converted into offices. Her employer, Amos Lee Mappin, occupied the front half of the second floor. His name did not appear in the directory of tenants, nor was it painted on the glass of the entrance door; in fact, as an author he had no real need of a suite of offices, but he was well able to afford it, and it was convenient to have a place where he could meet the queer people with whom his affairs brought him into contact, without having them come to his apartment.

Entering the front office, Fanny found Judy Bowles so engrossed in the morning paper that her cigarette lay on the edge of an ash tray beside her, burning itself up unheeded. Judy never looked up. "You're late," she said.

"Well, I was taking dictation until 11:00 last night. I was entitled to an extra hour's sleep."

"Have you read the paper? Peggy Brocklin and René Doria are engaged!" said Judy impressively. "She announced it at a dinner at her house last night."

"It's nothing in my life."

"Come off!" said Judy. "You're just as excited about it as I am! When did an engagement ever make the front page before?"

"Why should it make the front page?"

"Because Peggy is the richest unmarried girl in the world, that's why. And the whole world is interested to know who she's going to marry! Why, she has $40,000,000 in her own right, her own right!"

"I'd be satisfied with less," said Fanny.

"Pooh!" said Judy. "Your cynicism doesn't fool me. You're just imitating Pop."

"Pop isn't cynical; he's humorous."

"Here are a lot of new photographs of her," said Judy.

"I'm sick of looking at that pinched little face!"

"Why, she's beautiful, Fan!"

"Beautiful, my foot! She looks both bad-tempered and frigid." Fanny tossed the briefcase on the desk that backed Judy's, and came around to look over the other girl's shoulder. They made a striking contrast. Judy was dark and statuesque, and just as many young men tried to make up to her on the street, but she didn't need to wear spectacles, for Haughty was her watchword.

"Look," said Judy, "here's one of the dinner table where the announcement was made."

"Fancy letting the photographers in at a family dinner!" said Fanny. "Publicity is like a drug. You've got to take it in bigger and bigger doses to get any kick out of it."

"Peggy's dress is orchid mousseline with a taffeta underskirt. Notice the cute way it's draped over the bust."

"She hasn't got any bust to speak of."

"She doesn't need any with forty million."

"I suppose all the reporters had been summoned in advance."

"Sure. They were waiting in the library. The second butler served them champagne. And then Peggy came in and they toasted her."

"My God!" said Fanny.

"There's René. You can't say that he's not handsome. I think he's the handsomest man I ever saw."

"He looks pretty dumb."

"No photograph could do him justice. His eyes are simply hypnotic. That doesn't show in a photograph."

"Have you ever seen him personally?"

"Sure. They go to all the first nights at the theater, and when 'Ravenel' was produced, another girl and I stood outside to see them come out. They were mobbed, Fan! The cops couldn't hold the crowd. I was pushed right up close to them. She was exquisite, Fan! Like a piece of hand-painted china!"

"That's just what I said—brittle."

"I could even hear what they said to each other. René said, 'What a lousy show!' And Peggy said, 'Putrid!'"

"Witty, what?"

"This is Peggy's father, Dexter Brocklin," said Judy, pointing; "such an elegant man!"

"The clerk who married the boss's daughter and never did another tap. He looks it."

"And this is Peggy's Aunt Clara, Mrs. Thorne, who lives with her and goes everywhere with her."

"She'll be out of a job now."

"And this is Eliot Brocklin, her cousin. Everybody thought she was going to marry him until René came along."

"He seems to be bearing up all right."

"Oh, you can't tell! And this is the famous Jack Vynson."

"What s he famous for?"

"As if you didn't know! After René, he's the most talked about young man in town. He married Myra Fitch, who inherited all the tobacco money."

Fanny returned to the other desk and Judy continued to stare fondly at the newspaper photographs. "Just think of having all that money to do what you liked with," she murmured, "and then getting the man that all women dream about."

"She can have his hypnotic eyes," said Fanny. "I prefer eyes with fun in them!"

"Oh, you always make out you haven't any soul!"

"Soul has damn little to do with this marriage," said Fanny. Opening the briefcase she took out a sheaf of opened letters and a stenographer's notebook; then, holding the case upside down, allowed a cascade of unopened letters to pour out on the desk.

"Boy! they're still coming!" said Judy.

"It's on account of the Gavin Dordress case," said Fanny. "People can't stop talking about it. And Pop insists on having every letter read, and all the sensible ones answered."

"What have you got there?" asked Judy, glancing at the notebook.

"About 60 letters, long and short. I'll read them to you from my notes while you type. That's the quickest way to get them out."

"Is Pop coming down?"

"I don't think so. No reason why he should."

"No hurry, then," said Judy comfortably. "Let's go to lunch first. I want to see the afternoon papers."

"They will say exactly the same things as the morning papers."

"Oh, in the news, maybe. But I want to read the columnists, Walter Winchell and Beau Gramercy and the others. That old Beau Gramercy is always taking nasty cracks at René. René and Peggy were going to Tiffany's this morning to buy a ring."

"Along with the reporters?"

"Well, this is Peggy and René's day in the sun. Why not let them enjoy it?"

"In the sun!" snorted Fanny. "Your head is turned by all this slop you read in the papers. This René of yours is just a common two-timer."

"Why, Fan, how can you say such a thing! He's a Count of Bessarabia!"

"Who says he is?"

"Everybody says so!"

"Well, Bessarabia is a long way off. Too far to check the story. There is another story that his father is a barber in El Paso."

"That's just jealousy. His family was ruined by the war."

"The great lover," said Fanny scornfully. "Casanova, Don Juan. All the women in New York running after him! The girl must be balmy to marry such a man! Women are not going to stop running after him just because he's married."

"They are going to Get Away From It All!" said Judy. "They are sailing on the 80th. The whole after-part of the top deck has been engaged."

"They'll be back," said Fanny. "New York is where the suckers are."

"You're not fair, Fan. Peggy hates publicity."

"Oh, yes? Said so herself, didn't she?"

"She's always saying it. She told the reporters last night that she and René were going to steal away to a quiet country parsonage for their wedding."

"The reporters will be there," said Fanny. "I'll lay you a dollar to a nickel they'll be there." She rapped the newspaper with her forefinger. "And all those grinning people at the table; the girl's family and her friends! If they had any sense they'd lock her up before they let her throw herself away like that!"

"Oh, her family are not any too pleased at this marriage," said Judy. "You can see that by reading between the lines. Because why? Peggy is their meal ticket, and they don't know where they're going to get off after she marries. But she's her own mistress—they can't stop her."

The telephone rang, and Fanny picked up the instrument. "Yes, this is Mr. Mappin's office. Who is speaking, please? . . . No, Mr. Mappin is not here. This is his secretary. Who is this, please? . . . I can't say, Madam. We have not heard from him this morning. . . . No, I am not permitted to give out the number of his private phone. But I can send a message. . . . Who is speaking, please?"

So far Judy had paid no attention. But now Fanny was oddly silent, and Judy saw that her blue eyes had become as round as saucers; her face had actually paled with excitement. "Did I get your name right?" Fanny stammered. "Miss—Margaret Brocklin?"

Judy simply gasped.

The color rushed back into Fanny's face and her eyes sparkled with indignation. "How do I know that you are Miss Margaret Brocklin? Mr. Mappin has had so much publicity lately that we are flooded with letters and calls. You'll have to identify yourself before I can trouble Mr. Mappin."

There was a silence. Judy could hear the voice on the wire, but not what it said. Fanny smiled tightly. "I'm sorry you consider me insolent; however, I have my instructions to carry out."

Another pause. "Is that number in the book?"

"No," said the voice on the wire.

"Then what good would it do for me to call it? I still wouldn't know if it was the real Miss Brocklin that I was talking to."

After a long pause Fanny said, "Mr. Mappin is not in business, Miss Brocklin—if you are Miss Brocklin, nor are his services for hire. He's a writer. . . . Certainly I will send him a message if you can satisfy me that you are really Miss Margaret Brocklin."

Judy signaled frantically to Fanny to hold the receiver away from her ear so she could hear, too, but Fanny, intent upon receiving some instructions, paid no attention.

Fanny finally said, "Very well, I'll come at once," and hung up. She dropped in a chair, and stared across at Judy. "You heard—Peggy Brocklin—just when we were talking about her!"

"Nothing very strange in that," said Judy. "Everybody in New York is talking about her at this moment. What does she want?"

"Wants to see Pop—very important—I told her he wouldn't fool with her. No matter—she's got to see him. She sounded half crazy."

"What do you suppose has happened? René has jilted her!"

"Jilted $40,000,000! Not likely!"

"Oh, my God, Fan! And we're the first to know!"

"We don't know it yet."

"You're going up to her house?"

"That's the only way I could satisfy myself it was really she."

"Take me with you!"

"We can't both leave. Pop might call."

"How can I bear it until I hear what's the matter?"

Fanny still looked a little dazed. "It may be only a hoax," she said. "But I don't think so. The voice sounded as if she were crying."

"Then René *has* run out on her!" cried Judy.

"How could Pop help her if he's run out on her?"

"Oh, hurry! hurry!" cried Judy. "You're wasting time—for the love of Mike, call me up the moment you leave her, or I'll go crazy wondering!"

Fanny pulled her little hat on with only half a glance in the mirror, picked up her pocketbook and left.

Peggy Brocklin lived in one of the last of the great palaces on upper Fifth Avenue to be occupied by a private family. The others have mostly become art museums or have been pulled down to make way for lofty apartment houses. The Brocklin mansion was a vast affair of brick and sandstone with a mansard roof, and alongside it lay the famous garden, one of the only two private gardens in the city. The plot comprised a whole block frontage on the Avenue.

Fanny Parran pressed the bell button feeling rather queer. *I'll look like a pretty fool if it's only a practical joke*, she thought. She glanced up and down the street, but there was nobody in sight except a taxi driver reading a newspaper and a messenger boy slouching along the pavement and whistling.

The moment the door was opened she knew there was more than a joke in it. "You are the young lady who is expected?" said the deferential manservant. Fanny nodded. "Step this way, please."

She entered a hall big enough for a railway terminal but much more luxurious. It ended in an immense glass bay filled with tropical plants and growing orchids. The manservant was leading her toward a wide sweeping stairway, and through open doors she had glimpses of a suite of drawing-rooms extending across the front of the house. On the second floor the man tapped at a door and without waiting for an answer opened it and announced, "The young lady."

And there stood Peggy Brocklin, the most be-photographed young woman in the world. Even the hard-boiled Fanny beheld her with awe, so great is the power of publicity to create a personality. Her slim figure was clad in a plain, straight slip of a beige dress, but around her throat she wore a string of pearls as big as blueberries. Her aspect was as rare and delicate and exotic as an orchid, but the keen-eyed Fanny perceived that this was mostly due to art. Nature had not been particularly kind to the glamour girl. Peggy's medium brown hair had been lightened a shade or two and her eyebrows darkened to make an effective contrast. The famous Sèvres-china complexion was mottled now, and her insipid features all screwed up like those of a child about to cry, but there were no tears. She had a lace handkerchief in her hand which she had torn to rags. Temper more than grief, Fanny decided.

As soon as she saw that the door was closed, Peggy burst out, "Are you satisfied now that I am what I say I am?" Her voice was sharp with hysteria.

"Why, of course, Miss Brocklin," said Fanny. "I hope—"

Peggy gave her no time to finish. "Then go and get Mr. Mappin at once," she commanded. "I must see him immediately. Or telephone him from here. That will save time."

Fanny was a bit overcome by the vast house, the deferential servants, and the slim young mistress of it all, who issued her commands so imperiously, but she stiffened her backbone. "I must know what you want to see him about before I can talk to him."

Peggy ran up her eyebrows like offended royalty. "Isn't it sufficient that I want to see him?" she demanded. "If you tell him that Miss Margaret Brocklin would like to talk to him, won't that bring him?"

Fanny faced her out. "I'm not sure that it will. Mr. Mappin is not the sort of man who can be sent for in that fashion."

Peggy climbed clown a little. "I want to consult him professionally," she said sullenly.

"Mr. Mappin's profession is that of an author."

"I know that, but he's a detective, too."

"I beg your pardon," said Fanny. "Nothing annoys him more than to be called that."

"Didn't he just solve the Gavin Dordress murder?"

"That was because Mr. Dordress was his most intimate friend."

"And the case of the Sultan of Shihkar just before that?"

"He was drawn into that through friendship also."

"Mr. Mappin can ask me anything he likes," said Peggy. "His fee is no object with me."

Fanny said quietly, "Since the Dordress case my employer has been offered hundreds of thousands of dollars in fees and has declined them all."

Peggy began to cry. "Oh, why are you so stubborn and insolent!" She put the torn handkerchief to her eyes, but Fanny couldn't see any tears. It was the hard, bad-tempered sobbing of a spoiled child who is denied what she wants, and Fanny couldn't feel very sorry for her. She merely waited.

"Do you refuse even to tell Mr. Mappin that I want to see him?" sobbed Peggy.

"Of course not, Miss Brocklin. It's my duty to tell him."

Peggy seized her arm. "Then lose no time! Lose no time! There's the telephone. Call him up now."

Fanny resisted her. "It would be useless to call him—I must see him. It's only five minutes from here."

"Where does he live?" Peggy eagerly demanded.

"I can't tell you that."

The penciled eyebrows went up again. "I could easily find out."

"No doubt," said Fanny, "but I can't tell you."

Peggy suddenly became imploring. "Go! Go! Don't say anything about a fee unless he brings it up, but tell him I am in terrible distress. I live in such a blaze of publicity. There is no one I dare trust!"

Fanny began to feel a little sorry for her then. She said, "It would help if you could give me some idea of what you want of Mr. Mappin."

Peggy pressed her thin painted lips together. "I can't tell that to anybody but Mr. Mappin himself."

Fanny started for the door.

"How will I know what he says?" cried Peggy, wringing her hands together. "The suspense is driving me out of my mind!"

"I will call you up just as soon as I have talked with him. Fifteen minutes at the outside."

"Oh, hurry! hurry! hurry!" She tore the lace handkerchief clean across without realizing what she was doing.

Point d'Alençon, thought Fanny. Would feed a poor family for a month. She hastened away.

CHAPTER TWO
THE FIANCÉ

AMOS LEE MAPPIN LIVED in one of the towering apartment houses that hang over the bank of the East River in midtown. The outer wall of this house rose sheer out of the water, and there was a yacht landing in the basement. "Very convenient," Lee was fond of saying, "if I had a yacht." His immense square living-room had a row of windows looking east over the river and another row looking south over the lower city. Outside the river windows ran a narrow terrace.

The little rotund Lee issued out of his bedroom looking and feeling in the pink of condition. In his own home he could to a greater extent indulge his idiosyncrasies of dress without attracting rude stares. Long ago an instinct had informed him that early 19th century was his period: tight trousers, lemon-colored spats and waistcoat to match, a brown cutaway that almost ran to tails, a soft collar of fine linen that turned over a marvelously tied black satin stock. All this was precisely right with his polished bald head and glittering spectacles, and he knew it.

In the living-room he stood looking out of one of the river windows, hissing softly between his teeth and tapping on the glass in a pleasant idleness of mind. His book was on the press and all the pain and the mess of the Dordress case cleared up, and on the way, he hoped, to be forgotten. What to take up next, he was debating, but there was no urgency in it. A little social relaxation would be pleasant before setting to work again As to his next book, he was a bit fed up with specific crimes. He rather fancied a general work on the psychology of murder. That would require many hours of

16

research in a quiet library, something that Lee fancied much more than the hurly-burly of police work.

His servant Jermyn, tall, angular, and homely, entered the room behind him and coughed deprecatingly behind his hand. Lee turned around. "Monsieur Cabanel and his assistants have come."

"Very good," said Lee. "Is there any change in the menu?"

"No, sir. Everything is to be as arranged."

"Good. I want you to oversee everything, Jermyn. You know the way I like things better than Monsieur Cabanel."

Jermyn coughed delicately again. "Yes, sir, quite. But if you'll excuse the liberty, the Monsieur does not take very kindly to suggestions, sir."

Lee grinned and Jermyn, much relieved, permitted himself to grin back. "Sure," said Lee, "great man and all that; his susceptibilities must be respected. But you are not without tact, either, Jermyn. You can flatter. Do I not have daily experience of it?"

"Oh, no, sir!"

"Make believe you are learning from Monsieur Cabanel, while you see that things are done the way I want."

"Yes, sir."

"All questions of food may be left to the chef. As to wines, while he is to be informed, and his suggestions listened to, the final decision rests with you and me. Have you the list there?"

"Yes, sir." Jermyn handed it over.

Reading from the list Lee said, "Mackenzie's grand reserve Amontillado," and sighed. "It's much too good for them, Jermyn, but I suppose I owe it to myself."

"Yes, sir."

"You must also have dry Martinis for the barbarians who know no better."

"Yes, sir. Very good, sir."

Lee read on: "With the terrapin, Le Chevalier Montrachet 1926. A good year—a very good year."

"Yes, sir."

"With the duckling, Château Mouton-Rothschild 1918—our last magnum, isn't it, Jermyn?"

"Yes, sir, the last."

"I can't bear to let it go! Substitute a burgundy; le Corton Grancey 1919."

"Very well, sir."

"And you can offer to substitute champagne for the ladies with the main course. They know no better, the darlings!"

"Yes, sir."

"And finally, with the truffles baked in oil paper, the Château Latour 1904." Lee kissed his fingers. "My mouth waters at the very sound of the name. Be sure you give me plenty of it, Jermyn."

"Yes, indeed, sir."

"And champagne for all with the dessert. Ice the Granité au Lanson."

"Very good, sir."

The sound of the doorbell was heard and Jermyn went away to answer it. He presently returned and announced at the door, "Miss Parran." Little Fanny ran in.

Lee's face lighted up. "Bless my soul! What brought you up? Why didn't you phone?" As she came farther into the light, he saw how big her eyes were, and his voice changed. "What's the matter, my dear?"

Fanny dropped in a chair. "Oh, Pop!" she stammered. "The most extraordinary thing—"

He held up his hand. "Wait! You need a drink!" He pressed the bell and toddled to the door "Ho, Jermyn!" he called down the hall. "Fetch Miss Parran a glass of Amontillado!"

"Coming, sir!"

When Lee returned Fanny said, "Have you read the morning paper?"

"More or less."

"About Peggy Brocklin's engagement to René Doria."

"Oh, that," said Lee. "I noted the fact without reading the details. What have those mayflies got to do with you and me?"

Jermyn entered with the wine, and Fanny waited until he had left before answering. She then told Lee all about the telephone call and her visit to the Brocklin palace. When little Fanny became excited she lisped, and Lee was really more interested in the play of her red tongue between her teeth than in her story. Before she got to the end Fanny knew from the quality of his grin that he was going to refuse all offers from La Brocklin. She was a little disappointed, for after all it was exciting.

"You acted rightly," said Lee, "Did you gather any hint of what the trouble was?"

"No."

"One of three things: (a) somebody is trying to blackmail her, (b) somebody has threatened to kidnap her or her precious René, (c) somebody has exposed René's past, and she wants me to prove or disprove it."

"I expect so," said Fanny.

"What did you think of the girl?" Lee asked.

"Not much," said Fanny. "Thin-blooded. She can't measure up to the big part the newspapers give her. Scarcely knows what it's all about."

"That's generally the way with world-shakers."

"What am I to say to her, Pop?"

"Need you ask? This crowd is too trifling for sensible people to fool with, Fanny. We'd only make ourselves ridiculous. And we're just coming out from the cyclone of publicity in the Dordress case. Do we want to expose ourselves to another?"

"That's what I thought you'd say, Pop." Fanny sighed a little. "Judy will be disappointed."

Lee pinched her cheek, "And Fanny too, I reckon. Never mind. I'll find an amusing job for you girls."

The bell had rung, and Jermyn entered looking disturbed. This was so unusual that Lee took instant notice of it. "What is it, Jermyn?"

"Beg pardon, sir. A young lady. She says she's Miss Margaret Brocklin. And I think it is, sir. Judging by the photographs."

Fanny flung up her hands and turned away. "I didn't give her the address, Pop."

"Oh, Lord!" groaned Lee. "We can't turn Peggy Brocklin from the door. Show her in, Jermyn." Lee took a pinch of snuff and tapped the box shut.

Peggy Brocklin came in. A veil hung from her hat partly hiding the shocking state of her complexion. Her lips were parted over her clenched teeth. Glancing sharply from Fanny to Lee and back to Fanny, she said unevenly, "I couldn't trust her! She was against me from the beginning. So I came myself. A friend told me where you lived."

"Won't you sit down?" said Lee mildly. "A cigarette? You appear a little upset. May I offer you a glass of sherry?"

Peggy dropped in a chair, but waved aside the offered refreshment. "What has she told you?"

"Miss Parran told me that you wished for my assistance. Apparently you believe that I am a consultant of some sort, but that is not so. I told her I was exceedingly sorry, but I could not act for you."

"Oh, you must! You must!" wailed Peggy, wringing her hands together. "You can't do this to me. I couldn't trust a common detective or any of that sort. They'd sell me out to the newspapers. But you're a gentleman. You can keep your mouth shut. And they say you're cleverer than any of them!"

Lee smiled without relenting. "You flatter me, Miss Brocklin. If I knew the nature of your trouble—"

"Send her out of the room and I'll tell you."

"Sorry," said Lee. "Miss Parran, as my secretary, is present at all interviews. I may say that she is even more discreet than I am. Otherwise she wouldn't be my secretary."

Peggy lowered her head. "I've got to tell you," she muttered. "I can't keep it in any longer." She raised her tormented face. "René— my fiancé—Count Doria—is gone!"

Fanny softly released her pent breath. Lee, making conventional sounds of sympathy, said, "How do you mean *gone?*"

"He never went home last night after leaving me," said Peggy hysterically. "He hasn't been home since! He has disappeared!"

"Isn't it a little too soon to make up your mind that he has disappeared?" said Lee soothingly. "Surely, for a young man to spend the night away—"

"No! No! Not under the circumstances! He was to come to me at 11:00 this morning. We were going to Tiffany's together. Something dreadful has happened!"

"Then why not go to the police?"

A dreadful wail escaped from Peggy. "The police! Oh, my God, no! Think of what the newspapers would say! It would kill me!"

"You think," said Lee dryly, "that the young man may have gone away voluntarily?"

"I don't think so," wailed Peggy. "But I must find out the truth before anything comes out. I'm sure he hasn't left me because—well, I have my reasons. I think something terrible has happened to him."

"He has enemies?"

"Well, there are jealous women—"

"And jealous husbands, perhaps?"

Peggy was silent.

"I am deeply sorry for you," said Lee, "but this is merely a matter of routine investigation. There is nothing that I could do to help."

"Oh, you must! You must!"

"I will give you the name of a man whom you can trust to keep his mouth shut. I have employed him—you can mention my name. It is Stanley Oberry—"

"I want you!"

"Sorry—" Lee happened to glance at Fanny Parran. She made no sound, but her blue eyes held so imploring an expression that he broke off what he was saying. "Excuse me a minute," he said to Peggy. He drew Fanny over to one of the south windows. "What's the matter, my dear?"

"Oh, Pop, you mustn't pass this up!" she whispered.

"But I thought you agreed—"

"I have a hunch that this is going to be the case of the century. It has everything—money, social position, sex interest. You are at the head of your profession and you simply can't afford not to be in it!"

"But, my child—"

Fanny would not be stopped. "Think of the advantage in being consulted beforehand! You have a free hand, Pop, before everything is messed up by newspapers and police. You may carry out your investigation in secret. It's the chance of a lifetime!"

Lee raised his shoulders and sighed. "Oh, very well, I give in." He returned to Peggy. "Miss Parran has persuaded me to conduct the investigation myself, Miss Brocklin—so you see she is not against you."

Peggy did not thank him; it was her nature to take everything done for her as no more than her due, but she broke down and wept unrestrainedly. Lee signaled to Fanny to go get her a glass of sherry. He glanced at his watch and lit a cigarette to give Peggy time to pull herself together.

After she had sipped the sherry, Lee said, "What can you give me to go on, Miss Brocklin? You said that Mr. Doria had enemies. Who, for instance?"

An ugly expression came into Peggy's face. "Mrs. Beekman Vosper," she said. "If you read the papers you must know about her."

Lee shrugged. "But I don't."

"She's been René's mistress. She won't leave him alone. The news of the engagement must have infuriated her. She's a poisonous woman."

Lee glanced at Fanny, who quietly procured a little book from her handbag, and made notes of the conversation. "Anybody else?" Lee asked Peggy.

She wept afresh. "My father."

Lee turned grim. "What about him?"

"He *hates* René," said Peggy.

"Why?"

"Well, my father is dependent on me. My grandfather didn't like my father, and he left all his money to my mother in trust for me. That's not my fault. My father manages my properly and I suppose he thinks that when I marry I'll take it away from him. And that's not all. Somebody has told my father horrible lies about René, and my father pretends to believe them as an excuse to separate us.

"Who told him?"

"I don't know. I don't think he knows either. I think it was an anonymous letter. He wouldn't let me see it." Peggy looked around, and Lee, guessing her need, calmly handed her a folded handkerchief. Peggy wept into it. "It said—it said, that René's real name was Pietro Bosi, and that his father was a barber—and that he had been married before—and that he was brutal to women!"

"Any place, names, or dates we could check?"

"No. There wasn't any proof. Just a lot of lies."

"When did your father get this?"

"Three days ago."

Lee rubbed his lip, "And the result was only to hasten your engagement?"

"Well—yes! I wasn't going to be influenced by a lot of lies!"

"Then the announcement at the party last night was in defiance of your father?"

"Yes, if you want to put it that way. I wanted to have others present when he heard of it, so he couldn't make a scene."

"Was anybody else at the party who might have taken it badly?"

"My cousin, Eliot Brocklin. He considered we were engaged though I never gave him a definite promise."

"Your father favored his suit."

"Why, of course! His own nephew—that would have kept the money in the family. My aunt, Mrs. Thorne, wanted it, too. She's a Brocklin. They were all against me!"

"When the other guests had gone were there any painful family scenes?"

"No. I gave them no chance. After dinner I took René up to my own sitting-room. He left early, 11:30, and I went to bed."

"At precisely 11:30? This may be important."

"Yes. I remember hearing the clock strike. Then René got up to go."

"Well, say 11:35 or 11:40."

"About that. I went down to the door with him. He said he was going straight home. I offered him my car, but he took a taxi."

"Did you notice what kind of a taxi?"

"Yes, a green taxi always hanging around our corner. I have used it. It comes from the Sherwood garage."

"Where does Mr. Doria live?" asked Lee.

"In the Carlton Tower on Madison Avenue. He has a small apartment there, and a manservant to take care of him. The servant's name is Baddely."

"You have talked to Baddely this morning?"

"Yes. He merely said that René had not come home and that he had heard nothing from him."

"Did the man sound distressed."

"Oh, you couldn't tell anything about Baddely. He's too smooth!"

"I take it you don't like Baddely," suggested Lee.

"I distrust him," she said nervously. "Oh, he's a perfect servant, English-trained; always so soft-voiced and obsequious. But there's something sinister about him. René almost seems afraid of him. I made René promise to discharge him when we are married."

"You are very strongly attached to Mr. Doria?" asked Lee, studying her face.

She lowered her head. "Of course," she said sullenly. "Why else should I marry him?"

Lee thought, *Well, some show feeling in one way and some in another.* He said, "There's one more question I must ask. It's a delicate matter. Have you and Mr. Doria discussed a marriage settlement?"

Peggy said defiantly, "I gave him a check for $500,000 yesterday morning—all I had in the bank. I shall make up the balance when I can sell some securities."

"The balance?"

"I shall settle $2,000,000 on my husband. I want him to be financially independent of me."

Fanny caught her breath, and slowly released it. $2,000,000! Peggy said two *million* as coolly as two *dollars*.

"I see," said Lee. He stood up. "You have given me plenty to start on, Miss Brocklin. I'll keep in close touch with you."

"What are you going to do first?"

"First, I'll have a talk with Baddely."

"Oh, lose no time!" she murmured. "The suspense is driving me crazy! I'll be waiting by the phone."

"But, my dear young lady! I'm having guests to lunch. They'll be here at any moment. I can't start to work until they leave."

Peggy made her way out. Lee saw her to the door. When he returned he and Fanny exchanged a glance. They understood each other pretty well, these two.

"This is going to be a particularly dirty mess," said Lee.

"Well, that's our business, Pop."

Lee telephoned to Stan Oberry to try to trace René Doria after he had left the Brocklin house on the previous night. He then glanced at his watch, "Quick, before we're interrupted. Tell me some other prominent women whose names have been connected with René Doria recently."

"These have been so many, Pop!" She named several which signified nothing to Lee. "And Delphine Harley the actress—"

"Delphine Harley! She's a good friend of mine. I'll ask her to lunch. I'll ask Houson Bell too. And Vida Cadbury. Those two between them know everything there is to know about that world. And Tom Cottar." He moved toward the telephone. "You'll have to stay to lunch, Fanny. I need a second observer."

Fanny flushed with pleasure. "But look at me, Pop. I'm a sight!"

"I am looking at you. I find it easy."

An invitation to one of Lee Mappin's luncheons was so highly prized that none of the four people thus included at the last moment were offended. Surely they'd drop everything. "I'll be there with my hair in a braid," said the sprightly Miss Cadbury. "Don't! I couldn't bear it," said Lee, hanging up.

"Houson Bell!" murmured Fanny. "Fancy meeting him! The number one society reporter. He goes all the way back to Mrs. Astor's plush horse. He must he near a hundred, Pop."

"Wait till you see him, my child."

"And Vida Cadbury. Somebody has called her society's Prime Minister."

"Court Jester would be nearer to it."

"I want to have a good look at that woman. She's old; she never had any looks or figure. She has no money, and she comes of the plainest sort of people. How did she ever get where she is, Pop?"

"Sheer determination. I suppose as a little girl she made up her mind to be a great social leader and she has never swerved. People with only one idea cannot be kept down. She started as a social secretary and she has cast all her former mistresses in the shade."

"But how, Pop?"

"By providing amusement to the idle rich. They are perishing for amusement."

"They say Vida Cadbury has the handsomest young men in New York on her string. An old woman!"

"Sure. Vida's in a position to get them invited to the smartest houses in New York. Not where everybody goes, but to the intimate little affairs where an ambitious young man can make hay."

"I see. . . . Who's Tom Cottar?"

"One of the stars on the *Herald Tribune*. He knows the town, too—from a wider angle. An up and coming lad. I'll put him next to you."

"Thanks."

Lee got up. "Now I have to go and smooth down a chef whose masterpiece for ten must be stretched to feed fifteen!"

CHAPTER THREE
A DEVIL WITH THE WOMEN

LEE MAPPIN'S GUESTS were seated at a large round table, banked in the middle with yellow roses and trailing smilax. "So much more cumsocious than being stretched out in two rows," remarked Mr. Houson Bell. Several personable young waiters moved around behind the guests, and the gaunt Jermyn hovered in the background watching over all. Fanny Parran, to her immense gratification, had been placed immediately opposite Lee, in the position of hostess. On her right she had the famous Mr. Bell, better known as Beau Gramercy, and on the left Tom Cottar of the *Herald Tribune*. The two most interesting men at the table, she told herself, barring Pop, of course.

Mr. Bell was a great surprise to her. He had become an almost legendary figure. Away back in the days of Ward McAllister and the Four Hundred, he had started as a mere society reporter and had been content to keep his humble place. With the disintegration of formal society and the huge growth of publicity, his power had grown until now they called him the king of the newer café society with the power of life and death over its aspirants; His column was syndicated throughout the length and the breadth of the land.

He was a tiny man with a long face that rarely smiled even when he was outrageously jesting. He must have been very old, but he looked neither young nor old, merely ageless. His still plentiful hair was dyed a jetty black and his battered complexion had been as carefully worked over as an aging actress's—and showed the

27

same unnatural bloom. He dressed in a style peculiarly his own, always a double-breasted coat reaching halfway down his thighs with the idea of giving him more height, and neat cassimere trousers. His shoes were built up to give him an additional inch or two, and a boutonniere flowered permanently in his lapel. A strange figure, with marked distinction. It pleased him to be stared at. One could not have had a better table companion than Beau Gramercy; for his fund of malicious anecdote was inexhaustible. Fanny was both attracted and repelled.

Tom Cottar was much nearer Fanny's own age—rather an untidy young man who looked clever. Fanny felt a little sorry for him because he had red hair. A red-haired woman may be ravishingly beautiful, but a red-haired man is always a little comic. Tom Cottar, however, obviously didn't give a damn how he looked. Fanny wished to hear him talk, but Beau Gramercy hardly gave him a chance.

The rest of the company included a Catholic bishop and a celebrated dancer; the president of a bank and a young clerk from the same bank whose father had been Lee's classmate; the lady author of a current best-seller and another lady who ran a department store; a painter who had shocked Boston by his too-faithful rendering of the human anatomy, a corporation lawyer and a beautiful girl who had been asked simply for the gentlemen to look at. Across from Fanny, Lee was flanked by the two most arresting women at the table. On his right sat the famous Miss Vida Cadbury, a short stout woman with a button nose and graying hair cut man fashion. She was wearing a masterfully tailored black suit with a man's collar and tie, and she too sported a boutonniere. She dressed in this fashion, she said, not because she liked it, but because such clothes were kinder to her figure—or lack of figure. Which may or may not have been true; Vida Cadbury was an expert show-woman. It was her line to be vivacious and indecent. Fanny noted that while her tongue rattled, her eyes never lost their watchfulness. She watched everybody at the table without giving anything away.

On Lee's left the scarcely less famous Miss Harley had turned 40 and didn't care, because she knew she had a gift of comedy that would serve her for years yet—or until she lost her figure. There were already wrinkles of good humor around her eyes and she wasn't afraid to open her mouth and laugh.

It wasn't at all difficult to get them talking about Peggy Brocklin and René Doria. In fact, if anybody changed the subject it soon came back to the much-publicized couple. Fanny observed that Pop was up to his old tricks, just letting them talk and occasionally putting in a sly question. Beau Gramercy was naturally the best source of information. In summing up René, he said, "He has the beauty of Apollo and the temperament of a he-goat."

"I've never met this paragon," said the authoress, "but of course one sees him everywhere about town looking down his nose. I've always been struck by the fact that he never appears to say anything. He lets women talk to him. I suppose he has worked up a great reputation for depth and mystery."

"Exactly," said Beau Gramercy. "He doesn't say anything because he has nothing to say. A compound of conceit and stupidity."

"If he is nothing in himself," asked the bishop mildly, "how is it that he has become so great in the news of the day?"

"We gentlemen of the press have inflated him," said Tom Cottar, grinning.

Beau Gramercy spread out his hands. "I must cry *peccavi*," he said, "yet my worst enemy must admit I have done what I could to arrest the phenomenon. I am only a chronicler, and as soon as René became a social figure I was obliged to record it. But I always disliked the young man, and have never hesitated to speak my real mind concerning him."

"True," said Tom Cottar, "and the worse reputation we gave him, the more famous he became. Times have changed. Nowadays heroes must be bad!"

"Incredible!" murmured the bishop.

"Is there anything known about René's antecedents?" asked Lee.

"Nothing is known," said Beau Gramercy, "but all kinds of stories are going around. For my part I am certain that there is no continental background. Whenever his smooth surface is scratched, you find a hard American commonness beneath."

"But if he's such a horrible creature, what's the secret of his attraction for women?" asked the lady author.

"That's easy," said Beau Gramercy. "René's bold and shameless glance strips a woman naked, and she likes it." As the women around the table bridled, he added with a smile, "That is, many women like it. He is as direct as an animal, and this to our women, over-civilized, over-sophisticated, given to playing with love, is devastating."

The ladies looked uncomfortable.

"How is it, with his extraordinary good looks," asked Lee, "that he has escaped Hollywood?"

"But he hasn't escaped. I remember hearing—I don't know who told me—that eight years ago as a youth of 18, he was hanging around the casting offices eking out a miserable existence as an extra. He was too crude and stupid to be trusted with a part. Then he drifted to New York."

"Who first took him up here?"

Beau Gramercy shook his head. "That is lost in the mists of time."

"Jack Vynson was one of his earliest associates," said Tom.

"That's right."

"Jack had just consolidated his position by marrying the Fitch tobacco millions."

"Right. And is still René's closest friend."

"If you can call them friends! It is more likely that they have to stick together."

"If René is so stupid," said Lee, "it must have cost somebody a lot of trouble to teach him how to dress and how to behave. Who could that have been?"

Beau Gramercy and Tom Cottar shook their heads. "I have no idea," they murmured.

Delphine Harley spoke up. "His fine manners don't go very deep. True, he has learned a few parlor tricks such as jumping up when a woman enters the room, bringing his heels together and bowing from the waist and so on. He kisses your hand with a simper that is positively insulting."

"That's it!" cried Tom, "He insults everybody and the poor worms fall for it!"

"But when he's not on parade," Delphine went on, "he drops his fine manners, and he is then capable of incredible coarseness of speech and manner."

"Very effective in our hothouse society," murmured Beau Gramercy, grinning.

The bishop shook his head sadly.

"To continue about Hollywood," said Beau Gramercy, "it has generally been forgotten, but about four years ago in the full tide of René's success here, a prominent producer offered him a contract and he went out to Hollywood. They put him in a picture specially designed with respect to his limitations as an actor, but it wouldn't work. He was too stupid. Production was suspended; René sued them; they settled, and he returned to New York."

"I heard a different version," said Tom, "René was stupid enough, God knows; still the producers felt they were getting his curious animal attraction across—that was all they wanted. But René walked out on them in the middle of the picture. It was the producer who sued him, and collected too."

"Where would René get the money?"

"Oh, some woman ponied up."

"Well, whichever it was," said Beau Gramercy, "René is too lazy even to be an actor. His life in New York, living on the fat of the land and selling himself to one woman after another, suits him much better."

"And this is the creature you newspapermen have made a hero of!" said the shocked bishop.

"Not me, sir," protested Beau Gramercy, holding up a beringed hand. "I am forced to report his doings, but I have never exalted him. The sobsisters of the press swoon when they write about him."

"But if the newspapers made him, the newspapers could destroy him. I mean if you acted together."

"You are asking too much of poor humankind, Bishop. This man is a gold mine of copy to us. Moreover, and our employers are well aware of it, the stories about him help to sell the papers. If we destroyed his news value, not only would we be flooding our own mine, but it would anger our bosses, and some of us would find ourselves out of a job."

"What a world!" murmured the bishop.

"It seems odd," suggested Lee, "that one so stupid as Rene should be able to think up the stunts that provide you with so many spicy paragraphs."

"What sort of stunts?" asked a lady.

"Well, I remember reading a few weeks ago of how he and several of the weak-minded young men who pattern themselves after him turned up in a fashionable night club wearing only their pajamas."

"I wouldn't call that very clever."

"Not clever, certainly, but rather surprising in one quite mindless. Another time I read how he and his friends, who had just bade farewell to a pal sailing abroad, called for deck chairs and set them up in front of a store facing the Plaza—in mid-afternoon. A great crowd gathered and the police came and begged them to go away. *Begged* them, mark you."

"What does this suggest to you, Lee?" asked Beau Gramercy.

"Nothing," said Lee innocently. "I was just wondering."

"Probably somebody else thought of it, and René was given credit for it simply because he was the most prominent member of the party."

"Then there is another kind of story—the principals are not named, but it is always told in such a manner that the reader could scarcely fail to identify them. Take the case of René and the lady who were discovered in a compromising position by the latter's husband and René contrived to persuade him they were rehearsing a tableau for the Beaux-Arts Ball. Who would start such a story as that, Houson?"

"Oh, one of the crew that surrounds René. Real men detest him, but he always has plenty of hangers-on among younger men who are hoping to share in the overflow of his publicity."

"I see."

It was fascinating to Fanny to watch the play of glances between Vida Cadbury and Beau Gramercy. These two were bitter rivals for the leadership of glamorous society. They were said to hate each other like poison, yet all their smiles and glances across the table were sweetness itself. Well, that was according to the rules. Perhaps each knew so much about the other that they were forced to act friendly in public. Vida let the Beau air himself on the subject of René without interrupting. When he had finished, she murmured:

"Poor René! Everybody feels free to take a swing at him. I suppose it's the penalty for having climbed to the top. What if he is a little on the dumb side? When did brains ever help a young man in the smart world? Youth, good looks, fire, that is what he needs, and that's what René has." Miss Cadbury pulled a demure face. "Of course I cannot speak of his *chief* attribute, but in other respects I know him as well as anybody, and I've never seen any sign of this brutality they talk about. To me he has always been perfectly charming."

"He would be," murmured Beau Gramercy.

"The extraordinary magnetism that he possesses is a curse to him," said Vida. "To me René is a misunderstood and rather pathetic boy."

"You are always so kind to the sinner!" put in the Beau.

What object has Vida Cadbury in making such a speech? Fanny asked herself. Vida, she judged, never said anything without having an object.

Lee Mappin was sufficiently expert socially to bring about the early breaking up of his party. He had dropped a hint to Delphine Harley to remain, and after the others had departed, he, Delphine and Fanny settled down in the big living-room, each with a demitasse and a snifter of old armagnac.

Lee remarked carelessly, "You betrayed considerable feeling in your reference to young René Doria at the table, Delphine."

"Did I?" she exclaimed. "You're too sharp, Lee. I must put a guard on my tongue."

"Gossip cannot hurt a woman like you. . . . I have an interest in this young man."

"Was that why I was asked to lunch today?" she demanded.

"Yes, it was," said Lee coolly. "I'm not going to lie to you. I have asked you plenty of other times merely for the pleasure of your company, and shall ask you again."

"That's nice of you. . . . What is the nature of your interest in René?" she asked eagerly.

"That I may not say at the moment. But I expect it will soon come out. Nothing can be hidden long. In the meantime you can help me if you will. You know you can trust Fanny and me."

"Surely. Anything I can do. But what gave you the idea that I could help you?"

"You must know that some months ago your name was rather freely connected with his."

"I didn't know it, but I'm not surprised." She shivered delicately. "Oh, Lee, that was horrible."

"Tell me what you can about it."

Delphine sipped her brandy. "There's nothing to tell, really, Lee. I escaped, through no virtue of my own. I don't know what saved me. I fell for him, Lee, that's all. A man 12 years younger, and a stupid animal to boot! I was never deceived. I tasted the very dregs of humiliation. Even now when I am forced to think of it, I blush all over my body. A woman like me leads too artificial a life. I kid myself along to make up for the absence of anything real. I suppose a psychologist would say there was something starved in me, and that through this frank animal, it turned on me. Lee, when he looked at me with his shameless eyes I went weak inside. It was as if heavy chains were laid on me. I felt incapable of resisting him."

She took a sip of brandy and continued, "I don't know what he saw in me—with a whole city full of women to choose from! I must have seemed like an old woman to him; but he did want me, at least as much as a man like that ever wants a particular woman. I suffered when I was not with him because, you see, even while he desired me, he despised me, and never troubled to hide it. That was his method with women. We never had much talk together. I chattered to try to keep my courage up and he just looked me over. One night without any warning he suggested that we go to his hide-out."

"His hide-out?"

"Didn't you know about that? I thought everybody did. Wonderful stories are told about René Doria's love nest. Oriental luxury and all that. I managed to stand out against him the first night, but that sort of temptation only grows stronger when it is resisted The second time he proposed it, I knew I was going; I was at the end of my string—and then suddenly he changed his mind and didn't want me."

"Didn't want you?"

Delphine nodded. "That was a fresh humiliation. I suppose he suddenly realized I was a working woman with no great amount of money. Or perhaps he saw somebody that appealed to him more. I connect it with a telephone call he had while we were in the Heron Club. When he came back to the table he was frankly anxious to get rid of me. He took me home and that is the last I saw of him. I thought I was going to die, Lee. And I'm supposed to be a comedian without any deep feelings."

"However, you have come through."

"Oh, yes. In order to get away from him, I took a summer engagement at half my usual salary. Once out of New York, I got a grip on myself. But I don't want to see him again, I—couldn't trust myself. I'm staying home nights for fear of an accidental meeting. Lee, he's like a disease in a woman's blood. If you could rid the town of him you'd be a public benefactor!"

"Perhaps his strength will fail," said Lee with a grim smile.

"Not for years to come. He has all the vigor of a peasant, and a devil's cunning! Some devil out of hell must have taught him how to trade on the weakness of women. It is much more likely that some woman will kill him."

Lee's eyebrows went up. "A woman, you think?"

"Sure. Even a woman like me. You never thought of me as a potential murderess, did you? But I dwelt on the thought of sticking a knife in his beautiful body. It gave me a voluptuous pleasure. Because, you see, he had enslaved me, and it seemed the only way to free myself. Believe me, Lee, since that time I understand crimes of passion!"

Lee smiled at her affectionately. "No, I never should have suspected it of you, Delphine. One lives and learns. However, you did get the better of it."

"Sure, in a way," she said somberly. "But I don't want to see him again."

"Can't you give me a clue to the location of the love nest?"

She shook her head. "Haven't the least idea. You'd better ask Mrs. Beekman Vosper. According to popular report, she's paying the rent at present. All René told me was that it was perfectly safe. A kind of maisonnette somewhere; no doorman or elevator boys; no danger of us being seen going in or out."

CHAPTER FOUR
THE LOVE NEST

As Delphine Harley was being shown out, the telephone rang. It was Stan Oberry calling up to report he had had no difficulty finding the taxi driver who picked up René Doria at the door of the Brocklin mansion the night before. René had had himself driven to an all-night drug store on the corner of Lexington Avenue and 59th Street, where after paying off the driver he had entered a booth to telephone. The driver had seen him make two calls. He was waiting outside hoping to get another fare when he came out, but René, with a suspicious glance, had passed him by and taken another cab at the corner of 58th Street. The driver had taken no particular notice of this cab, except that it was yellow, consequently the trail was lost here. Lee instructed Stan to put out a line to every yellow-cab garage in town.

Lee and Fanny then set out in a taxi for the Carlton Tower.

"What do you think, Pop?" asked Fanny. "He could hardly have gone away of his own free will."

"Not likely with a million and a half in the offing. Delphine Harley has supplied the most likely explanation. A woman has done him in—it might have been Delphine herself."

"Good Heavens! You're not serious!" said Fanny, making saucer eyes.

"Would you blame her? He richly deserved it."

"But what reason have you for thinking she—?"

"No reason," said Lee calmly. "I was just trying to put myself in her place. Delphine is an actress and very clever. If it was me and I had done it, I would have behaved and talked just as she did."

At the Carlton Tower René had a five-room apartment with windows overlooking every quarter of town. All very luxurious, but lacking in character: the big living-room and René's bedroom were furnished with all the correct things, just like hotel rooms. Another room was entirely given up to René's vast wardrobe; a kitchen and a room for the manservant Baddely completed the suite.

This servant was apparently an Englishman, still youngish, tall, muscular, with a pale face like a polite mask. Miss Brocklin had called him up again after seeing Lee, consequently Baddely took their appearance as a matter of course.

"Have you heard anything of your master?" asked Lee.

"No, sir," said Baddely, pulling a lugubrious face.

"When did you last hear from him?"

"At a few minutes before 12:00 last night, sir."

"You didn't tell Miss Brocklin that."

"No, sir. I didn't want to make trouble."

"What did Mr. Doria say to you then?"

"He merely said that he wouldn't be home until morning, and that I could go to bed."

"Did he sound excited or upset?"

"No, indeed, sir. Quite his usual self."

"Was that all the conversation?"

"I asked him what I was to say if somebody called up before he got home, and he said, 'Oh, I'll be home before anybody calls up,' and hung up."

"You have no idea where he was going?"

"None whatever, sir."

"Where's his other apartment?" Lee asked abruptly. The servant was taken aback. "I—I beg your pardon, sir," he stammered. "I don't understand you."

"Oh, yes, you do. It's a matter of common knowledge. He must have the place cleaned up and I don't suppose he does it himself. I am referring to the place where he goes when he has a date with a lady."

"I never heard of any such place, sir."

Lee was convinced he was lying, but he let it pass. "How long have you been working for Mr. Doria?"

"Upward of six years, sir."

"Did you accompany him to Hollywood four years ago?"

"No, sir, Mr. Doria dispensed with my services upon leaving for Hollywood, but he re-engaged me when he came back."

"Why did he walk out in the middle of the making of his picture?"

"He never said, sir."

"How did you get this position in the first place?"

"Through an agency, sir—Miss Blatchford's."

"Where had you worked before that?"

"Only in England, sir. I was own man to the Earl of Doncaster for six years, and with the Marquess of Salibury for four. Those were my only places."

"Have you a passport?"

"No, sir. That expired years ago. I am an American citizen now, sir."

"Citizenship papers?"

"Not here, sir. They are in a friend's keeping."

"Hm!" said Lee.

"Surely, Mr. Mappin," whined Baddely, "you have no reason to suspect me of—"

"I suspect you of nothing, but I find you singularly unhelpful."

"I'm very sorry, sir. I'm doing my best. Mr. Doria was very secretive. He never told me anything."

"Have you any objection to letting me search the apartment?" asked Lee. "There might be a letter which would give us a clue to his whereabouts."

"Certainly there is no objection, Mr. Mappin, since you represent Miss Brocklin. But there are no letters, sir. Mr. Doria is most particular to destroy everything."

"I find it difficult to believe that, Baddely."

"Look for yourself, sir."

While Fanny waited in the living-room, Lee, accompanied by Baddely, made a search. Whether René had destroyed everything, or Baddely himself had made away with it, not a scrap of hand-writing was to he found; nor any photographs or lists of telephone numbers. Neither were there any locked receptacles, except a wall-safe which Baddely opened for Lee. It contained only some male jewelry of no great value. It was as if René expected a search and had prepared for it. The only thing Lee found that might conceivably he of interest was a Yale key which did not fit any lock in the apartment.

"With your permission I'll take this," he said.

"Certainly, sir," said Baddely.

Returning to the living-room, they found Fanny poring over a scrapbook, one of three big volumes handsomely hound in morocco, which constituted a file of all the references to René Doria and the photographs of him which had appeared in the press.

"Anything of interest to us?" asked Lee.

"Not so far," said Fanny. "It would take a long time to go through it all."

"Baddely." said Lee, "if I am not successful in finding Mr. Doria within an hour or two, I will ask you to send these books to my office where I can study them at leisure."

"Very good, sir."

"Baddely," said Lee crisply, "if Mr. Doria had a date with a lady last night, who was it?"

"I have no idea, sir."

"You mean you won't tell me. Very well, I'll get the information elsewhere. Now I ask you for the last time, have you any statement to make that might throw light on his whereabouts?"

"I wish I could, sir. I wish I could!" said Baddely, affecting the deepest distress. It did not ring true.

"One more question. Where does Mr. Doria bank?"

"At the Corn Exchange Bank, sir. The 57th Street branch."

"Thank you for that piece of information," said Lee dryly. "Come, Fanny."

In the cab Fanny suggested, "But Lee, he may just have been trying to protect his master."

"I don't believe it," said Lee. "The fellow exuded a sliminess. I doubt if he is capable of any decent impulse. He is being paid to keep his mouth shut."

The bank was not far away. Banking hours were over but the staff was still at work. Lee presented his card to the manager, and they were led into a private office. "Do you know who I am?" asked Lee.

"Certainly, Mr. Mappin. Everybody knows you."

"I wonder if you are willing to give me a little information about one of your depositors, or must I first obtain police authorization?"

"It would depend on what you want to know."

"I want to know if Mr. René Doria deposited a large check yesterday. You needn't tell me the amount nor who drew it, because I know that."

"Yes, sir, he did make such a deposit."

"Has he drawn against it?"

"Yes, sir. He drew $100,000 at the time he deposited the check. The check was certified."

"Thank you. At what time was this?"

"Shortly before closing time. Say, 2:45."

"In what form did you give him the money?"

"In $1000 bills, sir."

"How did he carry it?"

"He had a briefcase. I happened to notice it because it was a very handsome article of pigskin."

"Have you the numbers of the bills?"

"Yes, sir."

"Very good. I'll let you know, should it be necessary to circularize the numbers."

"This morning," the manager volunteered, "a check was presented for certification which will use up the balance."

"Who presented it?"

"A firm of stockbrokers, Mr. Mappin. Mr. Doria has invested the money in government bonds."

"Thank you very much," said Lee. "Please do not mention my visit. There may be nothing in it."

"You may depend upon me, Mr. Mappin."

When they came out of the bank, Lee gave their driver a number in East 76th Street.

"Where are we going now?" asked Fanny.

"To call on Mrs. Beekman Vosper."

"That'll be exciting. Do you know her, Pop?"

"I've met her out at dinner occasionally."

"What sort of woman is she?"

"Little woman, raven hair, hot eyes, exaggerated nonchalance Must be near 50 but looks almost anything. Has a sort of candled look."

"Beautiful!'

"Oh, my God, no! Not by any stretch of the imagination. But very smart. She used to weigh about 160, and was fat and good-natured. She took some kind of cure and weighs about 118 now, and is as restless as an ant. An insatiable woman."

"Rich?"

"Her husband is in New York real estate."

"Something tells me this is going to be a difficult interview, Pop."

Lee shrugged. "Well, either she will tell us or she won't tell us. After all, it's nothing in our lives."

The Vospers belonged to the rapidly shrinking class who live in houses of their own in New York, Their house was a big double affair a few doors east of the Avenue, very plain to the street and unexpectedly magnificent within. Lee and Fanny were not required to wait long in the lofty drawing-room before the little lady herself entered briskly. She was the sort of woman who by sheer will-power forces the world to go on acknowledging her as young and attractive long after her natural charm has departed.

"My dear Mr. Mappin!" she cried. "To what do I owe this unexpected pleasure?" It sounded much the same as if she had said, What the hell do *you* want? She looked inquiringly at Fanny.

"My secretary, Miss Parran," said Lee blandly. "Mrs. Vosper."

Mrs. Vosper gave Fanny a mechanical smile and a cold shoulder. "Do you always go calling with your secretary?" she asked Lee lightly.

"This is not exactly a social call," said Lee. "I have a delicate matter to discuss with you. It concerns Mr. René Doria."

Mrs. Vesper was not to be caught napping. "Bless my soul!" she laughed. "What have I got to do with him? They say he's a terrible person."

"I throw myself on your mercy," said Lee, spreading out his hands. "You have been seen everywhere with him the past few months, and naturally people look on you as intimate friends. Will you help me?"

"How help you?" she asked sharply.

"Mr. Doria has disappeared. Help me find him."

She laughed very quickly, but Fanny had seen her sink her teeth in her lower lip. "Disappeared! You sound like a melodrama. How? When? Where?"

Lee disregarded her questions. "Did you see him last night?"

"No."

"Did you hear from him?"

"No. . . . If you told me the circumstances I might be able to answer more intelligently."

Lee told her what he knew.

"Lord! The girl must be out of her mind to want to marry such a man!" she said with a sneer.

He shrugged and waited.

Mrs. Vosper considered. She could not keep still. She went to the windows; she went out in the hall and glanced up and down as if she feared eavesdroppers. She glanced in a mirror to see how much her face might be giving away. She burst out:

"Doria is a liar and a cad! He's a thief—a crook!"

"A thief?" put in Lee.

"Oh, of course I have no proof of that. But it makes me furious that such a person should be allowed to associate with decent people!

"I quite agree!" said Lee.

"Common and cheap and ignorant!" cried Mrs. Vosper. "He hasn't a redeeming feature!" Whatever impression she might have wished to convey, there was no doubt that these words came from the heart. She realized she was giving too much away, and closed her mouth with a snap. She went out in the hall again. *Afraid her husband may come in*, thought Fanny. Returning, Mrs. Vosper said abruptly:

"Come up to my room. Mr. Mappin. There's no danger of our being interrupted there."

As Lee and Fanny prepared to follow her, she said over her shoulder, "Can't she stay here?"

"Please, Mrs. Vosper," said Lee, "Miss Parran is my memory."

She stopped short. "Then everything I may say is to be recorded?"

"Only in our memories," said Lee.

She went on and they followed her to a Marie Antoinette boudoir on the floor above. Here she impatiently bade them to be seated, but she couldn't sit still. She twisted the cuff of her dress, she fluffed out her hair, she went to her desk and fussed among the papers on it. Finally she said, "I'll help you all I can, if you'll help me."

"Anything in my power," said Lee.

"It is true, I did befriend this young man," she went on, nervously pacing the room. "I was very, very foolish—but no morel Why, René Doria was a mere child! He was very poor, and I gave—I mean, I lent him money. Worse, I gave him jewels to pawn. People would think the worst if that came out. You must protect my good name, Mr. Mappin."

"I will do my best," said Lee.

Rage overcame her again. "And now I've learned that all the time I was trying to help him, he was receiving great sums from that half-witted Peggy Brocklin! Just a common swindler!"

"Quite," said Lee. "About last night—"

"I've already told you I didn't see him. I haven't seen him since—since last week. We quarreled and I told him to keep away from me."

Lee couldn't very well call the lady a liar. His silence suggested it.

"I was deceived in him," cried Mrs. Vosper; "so terribly deceived in him!"

"Where did you spend last night?" asked Lee.

She was going to refuse to answer, but thought better of it. "I went to the ball of the St. Nicholas Society at the Waldorf," she said languidly. "It was a tedious affair; I didn't stay very late."

"How late?"

"Really, I never noticed the time I got home."

"Did Mr. Vosper accompany you to the ball?"

The sharp black eyes glittered. "Are you suggesting I'm a liar?" she demanded. "You have a cheek, forcing yourself into my house and assuming to put me through a cross examination!"

Lee's voice was as smooth as cream, but it held a threat, too. "My dear lady! I thought we were allies. I thought we were going to work together!"

"No, my husband wasn't there," she said.

"Do you know where Doria's second apartment is?" asked Lee.

She stared at him speechlessly.

"Everybody says he has two apartments," Lee went on. "I know his official address, but not the other—"

"Your question is insulting!" she said.

Lee faced her out. "It seems quite possible you have heard of this address, without having visited it."

"I never visited it and I don't know where it is."

Lee rose. "Well, that's all," he said.

"Oh, must you go?" said Mrs. Vosper with dry politeness. She pressed a button in the wall. "Humphreys will see you to the door. Do come again."

"Thanks," said Lee.

Fanny, Mrs. Vosper ignored entirely.

In the cab Lee philosophically took a pinch of snuff. "Well, we didn't get much. I had no standing in her house. Man! I'd like to pin her down!"

Fanny said, "Did you notice that she referred once to René Doria in the past tense?"

"I marked it twice, my dear."

Lee stopped at the first pay station to telephone Stan Oberry. He asked the detective to verify that Mrs. Vosper had attended the St. Nicholas ball, and to learn what time she left the Waldorf.

When they drove on, after a silence Fanny said in a small voice, "Pop, I have a confession to make. I have been a very naughty girl."

"What, again?" said Lee undisturbed.

"I stole something out of that house."

He looked at her sharply. "What are you talking about?"

"Well, when we first entered the boudoir I saw Mrs. Vosper pull a sheet of paper over a snapshot lying on her desk. And later I prigged it when her back was turned. It's important, Pop."

"You shouldn't have done it," said Lee. "We're supposed to be kid-glove criminologists, not crooks."

"I know, Pop. I'm dreadfully sorry, now. You'd better let me out and I'll take it right back. I'll tell her it was all my fault."

He rubbed his lip to hide a grin. "Well, you'd better let me have a look at it first."

Fanny handed over a photograph of the handsome René Doria clad in dressing gown and slippers, reclining in a deck chair on a balcony. His hands were clasped behind his head and his face bore a contemptuous smile. He looked as sleek and sated as a tomcat after lapping a saucer of cream.

"I think that must have been taken in the love nest we are looking for," said Fanny. "Since he's in his dressing gown. There are no balconies on the Carlton Tower."

"Quite," said Lee. "And in the background is a view of the Chrysler Building from the northeast, and quite close too, because the top doesn't get in the picture. With this it will be easy to locate the hide-out,"

"Shall I take it back?" asked Fanny slyly.

Lee tried to look stern. "That would only make the matter worse. But mind you, Fanny, you must never do anything of the sort again."

"Oh, no, Pop!"

Lee rapped on the glass in front of them. To the driver he said, "Take us to the Chrysler Building."

There was no use in ascending to the observatory because the observatory was out of the photograph, so Lee made believe to be looking for office space, and was shown a suite on the 50th floor.

He took one window, Fanny another, and after a little searching both located the corner of a little garden far below, with the rear of several houses facing it, each with a balcony. By counting the blocks it was easy to establish that the houses fronted on 46th Street, east of Third Avenue.

"Thank you very much," said Lee to the renting agent. "If I decide I want this space, I'll let you know."

CHAPTER FIVE
AT THE BOTTOM OF THE SHAFT

THE PLACE THEY WERE LOOKING FOR was called Lancaster Court, It consisted of 20 identical little dwellings with brownstone fronts in the old style, 10 fronting on 46th Street and 10 on 45th. Some astute operator had thrown the backyards together to create an attractive garden—a boon in midtown New York—and had turned each house into two modern maisonnettes; very smart, very expensive. The original stoops and doors on the street had been done away with, and one now entered the garden through a passageway from either street. Inside, a covered way around the garden carried the balconies overhead. Each lower maisonnette had a covered balcony, while that of the upper apartment was open, such as the one in the snapshot.

Lee and Fanny entered the garden and walked out into the middle where they could get a good view of the houses along the north side. The garden was charming, and the little houses with their double galleries hanging over the covered way had an old-world effect.

Lee consulted the photograph. "This shot must have been taken in one of the upper maisonnettes to the east of the entrance. But which of the five is difficult to tell from below. We'd better go to the office."

To the young woman in charge, Lee said affably, "You have a charming place here! Any vacancies?"

"Yes, sir, a few."

"I would prefer one of the upper apartments facing south in order to get the sun."

"Yes, sir, those are the most desirable. Number 4 is vacant, to the west of the entrance."

"Anything on the other side? The view of the Chrysler Building is so striking from there."

"Yes. Number 18 is available."

"Could you show it to me?"

"With pleasure, sir."

Each upper maisonnette was served by its own tiny automatic elevator. They found the elevator of Number 18 at the top. It did not answer the button and the young woman had to climb the stairs to bring it down. "The last person who used it left the door open," she said with annoyance. "It seems odd that they should prefer to walk down."

Lee spent no time in surveying the rooms, but made his way directly to the balcony.

"Charming!" he exclaimed, looking down at the garden and up at the Chrysler Building. It was obvious that the photograph had been taken from this very spot or close to it.

The balcony was divided from its neighbor on either side by a wooden partition. By climbing partly up the rail and leaning over, Lee was able to stick his head around the partition on the left. The young woman looked a little scandalized, but said nothing. The adjoining balcony was empty. Presently Lee repeated the maneuver on the right side, and on that balcony he saw the very steamer chair which appeared in the photograph. He could identify it by a leather-covered headrest tied to the back. This maisonnette, according to the way they were numbered, would be 16. Lee climbed down. Fanny guessed from his bland expression that he had made a discovery, and she took a look, too.

In order to avoid arousing suspicion, Lee allowed the young woman to take him on a tour of the rooms. The room with the balcony was a dining-room; the living-room extended across the front of the house, and there was a small kitchen between with a dumb-waiter from the service entrance below. Above were two bedrooms and two baths. Overhead in the upstairs hall was a scuttle leading to the roof. It looked as if it had been in the original house, and had been allowed to remain. Lee, whose sharp eyes missed nothing, pointed out to the young woman that the two hooks which were supposed to fasten it were dangling. She scampered up the ladder and hooked them.

"Very careless of somebody," she said.

As they returned to the elevator, Lee asked the rent. He whistled when he heard the answer. "I'm afraid that's too expensive for me. I should have asked you in the beginning.

"Always glad to show the apartments, sir."

"Who lives in Number 16?" asked Lee carelessly.

"Mr. William Forsythe."

"Bill Forsythe!" cried Lee, turning to Fanny with a glad smile.

"Fancy that!" said Fanny, playing up.

"Can you describe him?" asked Lee.

"I've never seen the gentleman."

"Bill's a friend of mine," said Lee. "It must be the same one. As long as I'm here, I must see if he's home."

"I understand from one of the maids that he's a traveling man, sir. Usually out of town."

"Of course. But he might possibly be at home."

Lee paused at the door of 16, and pushed the button. The young woman continued on to her office.

There was no answer to their ring. They didn't expect any.

Fanny said, "Won't you have to call the police to get in?"

Lee smiled at her. "I have one thing to try first." From his pocket he took the key he had found in the Carlton Tower apartment. It opened the door. Fanny's heart began to beat fast.

There was a short hall with a steep stair running up at the side and the automatic elevator at the back. As they rose in the elevator Lee said with a droll face, "Have you got a piece of string—or ribbon—or a strap? I can't spare my braces."

Fanny removed a narrow leather belt that she was wearing. "Will this do?"

"Just the thing." When the elevator stopped at the third floor he fastened the inner gate back with the strap. "Just to delay anybody who might try to slip out while we're looking around."

Fanny's eyes widened. "Do you think there's somebody here?"

Lee shrugged. "Who knows?"

"Oh, Pop!" She drew close to him.

This apartment of René Doria's had plenty of character—of a dubious sort. The furnishings were lush. Fanny, who considered herself broadminded, avoided looking at the pictures. Lee wished to make a quick tour of the rooms before pausing to examine anything in detail, and they entered the living-room. The principal furniture was a broad, low divan in the middle of the floor without any arms or back, and stuffed about two feet deep with feathers. There was a small grand piano in the corner and one of the rugs beside it showed a broad wet spot.

Lee knelt, rubbed the spot with his finger, smelled of it, tasted it. "Water," he said.

On the piano stood a photograph frame with, oddly enough, its back turned to the room. When Lee turned it around, it proved to be a picture of René himself clad in a leopard skin like a Roman gladiator. "Magnificent physique," said Lee dryly. The glass was cracked across. "I wonder how that happened." Lee took a quick look into the closet opening off the living-room. It was empty. He sniffed suspiciously.

"What do you smell?" asked Fanny.

"I don't know. It's like Harris tweed, but there's no clothing hanging here."

Back of the living-room the little kitchen was in a mess. Someone had prepared a meal, and had not troubled to clean up. Sausages, scrambled eggs, toast and coffee. For two people. Since the cream in the pitcher had not soured, Lee guessed it could not have been more than about 12 hours before. In a waste basket they found half a dozen roses not yet faded and some broken cut-glass.

"If I may hazard a guess," said Lee, "the flowers were in a vase and the vase stood on the piano. It was knocked off and broken;

hence the water on the rug. . . . Don't touch anything in here. The pots and pans ought to yield valuable fingerprints"

In the dining-room were more pictures which Fanny carefully did not look at. The balcony outside was empty except for the deck chair. One of the windows was open. Fanny stopped dead, feeling as if a cold hand had been laid on her breast. On the dining table lay a pair of women's brown kid gloves.

"Those are daytime gloves, Pop. They have not been here long. Look, there are crumbs on the table under the gloves!"

Lee put the gloves in his pocket.

"Pop, I'm certain there's somebody in this place."

"It is possible," said Lee calmly. "Naturally they wouldn't answer the bell."

"Are you armed, Pop?"

"No."

"Oh, Pop! Shouldn't I go for help?"

"Not necessary. If there is anybody here they are more afraid than we are."

Fanny followed him upstairs with heavy feet.

The principal bedroom looked out over the garden. Fanny gasped when they entered it. Walls and ceiling were paneled with immense mirrors, and she saw herself all around a thousand times repeated. It was like something out of the Arabian Nights. The enormous bed stood between the two windows; the bedclothing had not been disturbed—a satin spread was smoothly drawn over it. When Lee opened the door of the clothes closet they saw René's evening clothes hanging inside. The lapel of the coat still bore last night's gardenia, turning brown. On the floor was a pair of patent-leather pumps. Beside them lay a pigskin briefcase. It was empty.

"The dressing gown is missing," said Lee grimly. "He would hardly leave the place in that."

"He might—he might have had other clothes here," stammered Fanny.

"He might."

The bathroom opening off was done in black and silver. As they entered it they heard a sudden wild scurry on the stairs outside.

Somebody was leaping down several steps at a time—an extraordinarily light-footed person. Fanny and Lee ran for the stairs, but they were too late to catch sight of him. They ran on down. Judging from the sounds, the fugitive had made the elevator, and finding the gate tied, darted into the living-room. Lee and Fanny followed, but the room was empty.

They heard him running through the kitchen. Lee followed and Fanny ran through the hall to head him off. They met in the dining-room but it was empty. There was nobody on the balcony. As they stood at the open window, they heard glass shatter on the adjoining balcony, Number 18. "Trying to get out through the vacant apartment," said Lee.

There was no time to free the elevator gate, and they went pell-mell down the stairs—a long flight and a shorter flight. As they ran out onto the paved walk a little black-haired figure very smartly dressed burst out of the door of Number 18, and they found themselves face to face with Mrs. Beekman Vosper.

Her face was ghastly under its make-up and she was panting; nevertheless, she tried to carry it off with a polite titter, "Upon my word, Mr. Mappin! So you have friends in Lancaster Court, too. Charming place, isn't it? So unusual."

She made as if to pass by them, and Lee caught her arm. Her haggard face flamed. "Let go of me!"

"You can't get away with that," said Lee, blandly. "I want an explanation of your presence here."

"Who are you to demand explanations of me? Let go of me, or I'll call for help!"

Lee put his free hand in his pocket and produced the gloves. "Yours, I believe."

"I never saw them before. You're crazy!"

"Not wearing gloves today?" said Lee, glancing at her bare hands. She stood silent, breathing fast.

Lee put the gloves back in his pocket. She was sorry then that she had disowned them.

"I am no lover of scandal," said Lee. "I want to keep this as quiet as I can. But it is a serious matter. If you refuse to give me an explanation I must turn you over to the police, and then the *fat* will be in the fire."

"Where can we go?" she muttered.

"In here," said Lee, nodding toward 16.

The door had closed itself. "How can we get in?"

"I have a key," said Lee cheerfully, "and so, I think, have you."

He opened the door and she entered. She had courage of a sort; her back was straight and her black eyes glared defiantly, though she was shaking. She was in no condition to climb the stairs.

Lee said to Fanny, "Run up like a good girl and bring down the elevator."

Later Mrs. Vosper sat in a chair in René Doria's living-room looking straight before her. Hands and teeth were clenched in a desperate effort to control her shaking. Lee said to Fanny with a significant look, "Fetch Mrs. Vosper a glass of water."

Fanny got his meaning. She went into the kitchen and returned bearing a glass of water on a plate. Mrs. Vosper drank thirstily and put the glass back. Fanny carried it into the kitchen, and put it on a high shelf where it would not be disturbed.

Mrs. Vosper began to get a little control. "It is true, I came here this afternoon," she said with harsh defiance. "I was about to leave when you rang the bell. Then I was trapped." Her voice scaled up hysterically. "But I was not here last night! I was not! A week has passed since I was here before."

"What brought you this afternoon?" asked Lee.

"It was because you—you said that something had happened to René, and I was terrified that when this place was searched something might be found which would show I had visited him here."

"Letters, perhaps?" suggested Lee.

She smiled scornfully. "I'm not the letter-writing kind."

"What were you looking for?"

"I told you earlier that I had lent him jewels because he said he was in a jam. It was a necklace of emeralds. I came to look for that, or, if he had pawned it, for the ticket."

"And you found?"

"I found the emeralds." She thrust a hand in the bosom of her dress. "And there they are, if you don't believe me." On her hand was a chain of magnificent square-cut emeralds set in platinum.

"Exceedingly valuable," said Lee. "May I ask where you found them?"

"In the—" She suddenly thought better of it. "No, I won't tell you."

Lee shrugged.

"You said," she went on in a strained voice, "something had happened to René. Have you proof?"

"No proof yet," said Lee gravely. "But several things lead to that inference. For instance, your story about the emeralds."

She looked at him questioningly.

"If he had gone away of his own accord, he would not have left the emeralds behind him."

"But he—he is not here," she said huskily.

"I have not had time yet to make certain."

The woman's nerve began to break. "Oh, you must keep my name out of this! I have done nothing wrong—nothing criminal. Think of what this story would do to a woman like me—and to my husband! The punishment would be too great for my folly!" She added in a lower tone, "I have suffered enough!"

Lee was softened by the genuine cry of pain. "I can make no promises," he said, "but believe me, I'm not going to rush into print with the story."

She got up wearily. "Are you through with me?"

"For the present, yes."

"I feel absolutely desperate," she murmured.

"There is no need of it if you have no crime on your conscience," said Lee. "A scandal is very unpleasant, but it blows over."

She left the room without speaking again. They heard the elevator door close.

"Shouldn't you have kept her here?" said Fanny.

"I couldn't very well detain her by force."

"She may kill herself."

"If she's guilty," said Lee somberly, "it would be the best way out for her."

"Do you think—she killed him?"

"We don't know yet if there has been a killing."

"I don't think she was telling the whole truth," said Fanny thoughtfully. "A man like René Doria would not have kept the emeralds on him for a week."

"No. But you must bear in mind that she may have produced the emeralds just as an alibi."

"If it wasn't for the emeralds, why should she have come back here this afternoon?"

"To make sure she hadn't overlooked any incriminating evidence last night. I've got to go through the rooms again. You can wait here."

"Let me stay with you," murmured Fanny.

"Very well. We'll start at the top and work down."

Lee produced the magnifying glass that he never traveled without. In the room of mirrors above, there were plenty of indications that René had not been alone the previous night, but no positive evidence that his companion was Mrs. Vosper.

Lee, regarding the empty briefcase, said, "After all, my dear, it might prove to be simple robbery. It is possible somebody saw René draw $100,000 from the bank yesterday and trailed him waiting for a chance to strike."

"I don't see how he could have got in here. Pop, without breaking in."

"Well, neither do I."

"And why should René have carried the money around with him?"

"That is something we have to look into. Take a memo to call up Miss Brocklin and ask her if he had the briefcase when he came to her house."

The front bedroom apparently had not been used lately. There was no bedding under the satin coverlet; considerable dust lay on everything. Mrs. Vesper had apparently run into the room in a panic and locked the door; then, thinking better of it, had made a break for the stairs. The closet opening off was empty. When the water was turned on in the bathroom it ran rusty.

Then downstairs. Balcony and dining-room yielded nothing new. The dining-room closet was stored with liquors and expensive canned and bottled foods. Before entering the littered kitchen Lee put on gloves so he could move things around. "Don't touch anything," he said to Fanny. "We must come back to fix and photograph fingerprints. Where did you put the glass that Mrs. Vosper used?"

Fanny pointed to it. "I was careful not to touch it with my hand."

Lee opened the door of the dumbwaiter shaft and looked up and down. He pulled up the dumbwaiter. It was empty. "Why do you suppose they ran the shaft to the top floor when there's no opening there?"

"They may have had the possibility in mind of renting the two floors separately."

"Smart girl."

Lee picked up a curious little object from the kitchen floor. It was a flat disk of black glass less than an inch in diameter with a hole in the middle. It seemed to have had a bent hollow stem which had broken off. Lee found the rest of the black glass a yard or so away, but it had been ground to a powder under somebody's foot.

"Now what in the world would you call this?"

"It looks like part of a glass flower," said Fanny.

"Black?"

"A stylized flower. René seems to have fancied that sort of thing. There are two arrangements of glass flowers on the living-room mantel."

"I looked at them when we were in there. They do not appear to have been broken, and none were black. This disk is too flat and regular for a flower, and notice the curious angle of the hollow stem or spur. No flower is like that. Guess again, Fanny."

She shook her head helplessly.

"Well, time will tell," said Lee. "Fetch me an envelope off the desk in the living-room."

He stowed the disk in the envelope and gathered up as much of the broken glass as he could.

"There's something odd on the desk blotter," said Fanny. "I'll show you when you've finished here."

When they went on to the living-room, Fanny led Lee to the desk. On a clean green blotter somebody with a lead pencil had roughly drawn a circle and put four dots in it arranged in a square.

"Hm!" said Lee. "It may just be somebody's idle scribbling, but we'll remember it."

With his magnifying glass he was able to establish that a scarf had been thrown across the piano. Just lately (dust gathers quickly in New York!) it had been jerked off. That accounted for the vase of roses smashed on the floor and the cracked glass in the photograph frame.

Lee opened the closet door. "You've got a good nose," he said. "See if you can identify this smell."

Fanny sniffed. "Like Harris tweed, as you said, Pop, but a little different. Somewhere, and not so long ago, I have smelt that smell, but I can't place it."

Lee shut the door. "Well, let's cork it up, and recollection may come."

The bottom of the big divan was only a couple of inches above the floor. When Lee got down on his plump knees and put an eye to the crack, an exclamation of astonishment broke from him. From under the edge of the divan he drew another gardenia, bound together with a couple of glossy leaves for a gentleman's buttonhole. This flower was in a better state of preservation than the one in René's jacket upstairs. It had scarcely begun to fade.

"Well!" said Lee. "It would appear that René also had a gentleman visitor last night or early this morning. It puts a new aspect on the situation."

"Strange," said Fanny, "that it should be under the divan."

"Evidently kicked there without being noticed. Obviously there were some strenuous moments here last night. The vase of roses was pulled off the piano, and something was dragged across the floor. Fortunately, this room was not dusted every day."

"Well, that lets Mrs. Vosper out," said Fanny.

"Not altogether. However, it gives her a loophole." Lee studied the flower. "It is curious," he murmured, "a fashionable florist always winds a bit of lead foil around a boutonniere to keep the stems from staining the clothing, but this has none. Yet this came from a florist, too. It is arranged with the professional touch."

The gardenia was the last discovery they made.

"He couldn't have been killed here," said Fanny. "There's no blood."

"Mustn't jump to conclusions, my dear. The killer had plenty of time to remove the traces."

"But if he was killed here, how could the body have been disposed of?"

"It is useless to speculate. We will know when we find out. Let us go down to the ground level. I have one more place to look."

Each little building facing the central garden had three doors on the covered walk The ones on the right gave entrance to the upper maisonnette and the lower apartment, and that on the left was a service door for both apartments. The service door for 15 and 16 was not locked. "Better wait outside," said Lee as he entered. There was a short hall with, on the left, a door leading to the kitchen of the lower apartment, and the dumbwaiter door at the end. Lee pulled a string that lighted a bulb overhead.

He opened the dumbwaiter door, and stood there. Fanny glanced into the passage. She could see nothing. She guessed from his silence that he had made a discovery, and her heart rose in her throat.

"Is he there?" she whispered.

"Yes." He swung the door to. "Don't look."

Gooseflesh rose on Fanny's skin. She backed away. She had no desire to look. "Dead, Pop?"

"Very," said Lee.

"Oh, Pop. . . . How did he get there?"

"The dumbwaiter was run up to the top, and he was dropped down the shaft."

"A little woman could hardly have done that."

"I don't know," said Lee grimly. "A little woman can perform surprising feats when she is pushed to it." He latched the dumb-waiter door. "Nothing must be touched here until the police come. Go and telephone to Inspector Loasby while I keep watch. If he has left Headquarters, keep on phoning until you locate him. Ask him to come at once. Tell him it's a homicide case, and to bring a medical examiner, a photographer and a fingerprint expert. Ask him not to notify the press until he has seen me."

Fanny hurried away.

CHAPTER SIX
THE COUNTERSIGN

WITHIN A QUARTER OF AN HOUR she was back again. Lee was leaning against the frame of the service door, smoking a cigar and studying.

"Inspector Loasby had not left his office," she said. "He's on the way here. I called our office, and learned that Mr. Oberry had been trying to get you. So I gave him a ring. He had located the taxi driver who picked up René Doria last night. Doria ordered him to drive to the corner of Third Avenue and 46th Street. That's right here, of course. Doria got out and started walking east on 46th. The taxi driver said further that he suspected they were being tailed by another cab. After he had dropped Doria he saw a man across the road who might have been following Doria. It was dark and he could not describe this man except that he was a tall, slim fellow. The driver felt that it was none of his business and drove away."

"Only one man?" said Lee. "Doria ought to have been able to handle any one man."

"Mr. Oberry further reported he had established by several witnesses that Mrs. Vosper attended the St. Nicholas ball last night. Shortly before twelve o'clock she was paged for a telephone call, and apparently she left, because she was not seen again."

"Thanks, my dear. You may go home now. I'll have the assistance of the whole police department from now on."

"Are you sending me away?" she said reproachfully. "Police or no, you need me to take notes for you; to run errands; to phone."

"We may not get any dinner."

"The heck with dinner!"

"Very well. I'll be glad to have you with me."

Inspector Loasby in plain clothes, confident and soldierly, entered the garden accompanied by several assistants and detectives. A short distance behind followed another group, and Lee's face turned grim—newspaper reporters, including the red-haired Tom Cottar of the *Herald Tribune*.

Loasby, observing Lee's expression, said deprecatingly, "I'm sorry, Lee. They watch me like cats. I can't prevent them from tailing me."

Lee suspected that the handsome Inspector had to keep in with the press in order to make sure that he received his own due publicity.

Lee shrugged. "Well, don't say I didn't warn you. Inspector. There's T.N.T. in this case. The dead man is René Doria."

Loasby's ruddy face paled. "Oh, my God, Lee! This will blow off the roof of the town!"

Tom Cottar shouldered up. "Hello, Blondy," he said to Fanny. "Nice to see you again!" And to Lee: "Mr. Mappin! Here's a stroke of luck."

Lee said, "Keep my name out of it, Tom."

"We know your modesty," said Tom, grinning. "But you ask the impossible. Whatever it may be, the fact that you're in it quadruples its news value."

Inspector Loasby looked a little sour.

"Who's dead?" asked Tom cheerfully.

"René Doria," said Lee.

Tom Cottar stared at Lee open-mouthed and cried, "Good kind Heaven! There never was such a story! And I'm here to get it. For the lova Mike, Mr. Mappin, answer a couple of questions so I can send a flash to my paper. Killed, how?"

"Apparently by a bullet through the head."

"Got the gun?"

"It was with the body."

"Self-inflicted?"

"Impossible."

"How did you get into it before the police?"

"Doria has been missing since last night, and I was asked to investigate."

"By whom?"

"I decline to answer."

"What was Doria doing here?"

"Nothing has been established, but apparently he rented Number 16 here under another name."

"*What!* The famous love nest! This case has everything! Do you know who did it?"

"Not another word," said Lee. "Anything further must come from the Inspector."

Loasby was inclined to bluster a little. "Give me a chance, boys! I haven't even looked at the body yet. I'll have nothing to say until I've made a complete examination of the premises. And, by God, if you plague me, I swear I'll draw a cordon around the house and keep you all out."

"We'll play ball, Inspector," said Tom cajolingly. "We won't get in your way." He ran to telephone to his paper. The others had already disappeared.

Lee led Inspector Loasby into the service passage and opened the dumbwaiter door. Side by side the two men looked at the hideously contorted nude body in the bottom of the shaft. Doria had dropped head first and would have broken his neck if he hadn't been dead already. He had been wearing a gaudy dressing gown of crimson brocade, which had been yanked off and wound around his head, no doubt to soak up the blood. Entangled with the gown was an antique brocaded scarf used for the same purpose. The handle of an automatic protruded from under his shoulder. That had been thrown down the shaft before him. One of his red morocco slippers had come off above, and had been dropped after him. It lay on his naked breast.

"My God!" murmured Loasby. "What an end for the hero of the night clubs!"

The body was photographed. Meanwhile Lee had sent Fanny to break the news to Peggy Brocklin. Afterward he said, "I suggest

we carry the body back to the rooms upstairs. We will need to re-
fer to it when we are examining the scene of the killing."

"Can we get in?"

"I have a key."

Loasby looked at him oddly. "Damn it, Lee, you always seem to
have the inside track!"

Lee offered him his snuff box.

Loasby posted a man at each entrance to keep out all but those
who could prove they had business in Lancaster Court. The body
was difficult to handle because it had been lying at the bottom of
the shaft for 12 hours or more, and had stiffened in its sprawling,
upside-down position. Even in this condition Doria's physique was
impressive.

The body was carried upstairs and laid on the divan in the living-room, and the gun brought along, with care not to let it be
touched by hands. While awaiting the medical examiner, Lee and
the inspector made a preliminary examination. Meanwhile the fingerprint experts busied themselves with the gun and the various
articles in the kitchen. When the head was unwrapped, the two
saw that it had bled scarcely at all. "This scarf lay across the
piano," Lee informed the Inspector. "It was jerked off in haste."

René's shapely nose was flattened, as if from a blow. "I suppose he got that in his fall down the shaft," suggested Loasby.

"Hardly," said Lee. "He fell on his head."

On the other side of the head from the wound, the skin was
broken, and when Loasby felt of it, the bullet came out in his hand.

"Strange it didn't go right through," suggested Lee. "A gun like
that shoots with great force."

In the back of Doria's head they found a rounded break as from
a blow or fall. Judging from the matted condition of the hair, this
wound had bled more than the bullet hole. Loasby called Lee's attention to the old-fashioned steel fender in front of the Victorian
grate. It had a low steel rail finished off at intervals with knobs.
He said to Lee, "If you have established that he was killed in this
room, I take it that when he was shot he fell backward and struck
his head on one of those knobs."

"The wound is not on the middle line of his skull," Lee pointed out, "but a little toward the top. His head must have been drawn far back to hit just there."

"A man's body jerks into extraordinary positions in the spasm of death," said Loasby.

Borrowing Lee's magnifying glass, he dropped to his knees to examine the fender. It was a quaint old piece, semi-circular in form, with a steel floor inclined toward the fire, for the purpose of catching any coals that might hop out of the grate.

"Yes," said Loasby. "You can see it has been washed recently. There are still a couple of black hairs clinging to one of the knobs."

Lee took the glass and inspected the fender for himself. "It has lately been moved out from the grate and shoved back again."

"That was so he could wash beneath it."

"There's a curious little dent in the steel floor." said Lee. "How do you suppose that got there?"

"It's an antique," said Loasby. "More than 100 years old. Who can say what may have dropped on it during that time? A big piece of coal, perhaps."

"Possibly," said Lee.

The man whom Loasby had left to guard the door below reported that the assembled newspapermen had appointed a committee of three, for whom Tom Cottar was spokesman. Tom wanted to know if they might come upstairs now.

"Not yet," said Loasby.

In going through the rooms the Inspector had given heed to the state of the mirror room above, and had examined René's clothes in the closet. Lee had shown him the second gardenia he had picked up, and the odd little disk of black glass. Loasby did not appear to attach much importance to this article.

Lee said, "I'll keep it if you have no objection." Lee showed him the circle and the four dots on the clean desk blotter. "This may not be of any importance," he said, "but I suggest that you take it and say nothing about it for the present. There's another clean blotter beneath it, so its removal will not be noticed."

"I'll do that," said Loasby.

The fingerprint men now reported that the prints on the glass of water served to Mrs. Vosper were identical with those on the kitchen utensils, and in many other places about the apartment.

"So Mrs. Vosper was his lady friend last night," said Loasby. "My God! How many more big names are going to be drawn into this?"

"We are just beginning," said Lee.

The prints on the gun, however, had been left by a man's fingers. Apparently only one person had handled the gun. His fingerprints did not show up anywhere else. The gun had been fired once only. No prints were found anywhere in the apartment except those of Mrs. Vosper and the dead man. Nothing could be read from the handles of the doors—they had been grasped too many times.

"At any rate, a man shot him," said Loasby.

Lee took a pinch of snuff. "Why?" he asked.

"The gun proves it."

"Frankly, I don't see how he could have done the job without leaving prints somewhere else."

Loasby stuck to his point. "Some man shot him. The bullet took a level course through his head. Therefore, it was fired by a man as tall or taller than René."

"Sure, if he was standing up when he was shot."

Loasby stared. "What's on your mind?"

Lee shook his head. "Not prepared to say. We've got a lot of work to do yet."

The detective guarding the lower door came back to say René's servant was applying for admission.

"Let him come up," said Loasby.

The waxy face of the correct English servant was the color of ashes. He cast a terrified glance at the nude body on the divan, and hastily looked away.

"So you knew of this place," said Lee.

"No, sir, Mr. Mappin," gasped Baddely. "Not until a newspaper reporter told me what happened. He wanted my story, but I didn't tell him anything."

"What newspaper?" asked Lee.

"I was so shocked I didn't think to ask, sir."

"Has Mr. Dona any relatives who should be notified?"

"If he has, I don't know who they are, sir."

"His closest friend was Mr. Vynson, I have been told."

"He had so many friends, sir."

"Well, I don't see any necessity of notifying them. They will learn it from the newspapers."

"Should I—make the arrangements, sir?" the servant stammered, "in the absence of relatives?"

"It is too soon for that," said Lee dryly. "I wish you'd go to Mr. Doria's bedroom and fetch me the gardenia from the lapel of his evening clothes. I want to show it to the Inspector."

"Yes, sir; certainly, sir."

Lee noted that Baddely went direct to the mirror room. He presently returned with the faded flower which was put away with the other exhibits. Baddely then backed away to the front of the room and made himself inconspicuous. Lee did not fail to mark how sharply he watched everything that went on, and listened.

Loasby now saw fit to admit the reporters. Tom Cottar and his two mates entered the living-room quick with questions. Lee left Loasby to deal with them, while he went into the kitchen for a further study, especially of the dumbwaiter door.

In the kitchen was a wooden chair which upon being unhooked and turned over became a small stepladder for reaching the topmost shelves. Upon turning it into a ladder, Lee perceived a little smudge on a step which might have been blood. The linoleum on the floor gave indications that the little ladder had been shoved to the door of the dumbwaiter, and Lee guessed that the murderer had used it to assist him in working the body over the sill of the dumbwaiter.

He called Loasby in to show it to him. "With the help of a ladder, the woman could have done it."

"You seem to be determined to hang it on Mrs. Vosper," said Loasby.

"Not at all," said Lee equably. "I am keeping all the possibilities in mind. A man of even average strength could have hoisted the body over the sill without the aid of the ladder."

"How about the male fingerprints on the gun?"

"She could have thrown the gun down the shaft without touching, it with her bare hand."

A detective whom Loasby had assigned to question the tenants of the lower maisonnette now came up to report. The tenants were a Mr. and Mrs. Nostrand, a young couple who had no children. Nostrand was an officer in one of the minor insurance companies. They had retired shortly before twelve o'clock the night before, and had immediately fallen asleep. Sometime later, they could not say how long, they were both awakened by a noise. They supposed it came from outside, and went to sleep again. Once again they were awakened simultaneously, and lay for a while discussing what it could have been: but hearing nothing more, finally fell asleep.

"The first noise would be the shot and the fall," said Loasby, "and the second, the thump of the body at the foot of the dumb-waiter shaft."

"It could be," said Lee, "but it is not established. What are you going to do about Mrs. Vosper?"

Loasby rubbed his chin, "I suppose she'll have to be arrested. It's not a job I relish."

"There's no need of haste in arresting her. A woman like that could scarcely make a getaway."

"She might do away with herself."

"If she killed the man, it's the best thing."

Loasby looked scandalized. "No, sir! She mustn't be allowed to cheat justice. No matter how high placed she may be, an example must be made of her."

Lee sucked in his cheek. "Matter of opinion, Inspector. If you wish it, I'll go talk to the woman again. With what we have learned now, perhaps I can get the truth out of her."

"I wish you would, Lee. Shall I send a man with you?"

"No, please," said Lee. "I'll get along better alone. I'll phone you from the house if it appears that she ought to be taken into custody."

They returned to the living-room. Tom Cottar and the other reporters were grouped around the desk beside the window. "Look here, Inspector and Mr. Mappin!" sang Tom. "Here's something funny."

They went to him. He was pointing to some pencil marks on the fresh green blotter—a rough circle with four dots inside it. Both Lee and the Inspector looked a little queer.

"What the devil!" muttered the latter, scowling. "Would you mind retiring for a moment, gentlemen?" asked Lee politely. "I want to discuss this with the Inspector." The reporters, bursting with curiosity, backed away.

"What do you make of it?" asked Loasby.

"You put the first blotter away?"

"Sure, with the other exhibits."

"Nobody could have seen it?"

"Nobody but my own men."

"Notice that these marks were not made by the same hand," said Lee. "That first circle was drawn with one sweep by a hand accustomed to the pencil. This one is painstakingly and crookedly drawn."

"Tom Cottar might have done it himself," muttered Loasby. "He trains with all these people."

"That's an idea," said Lee dryly. "We must bear it in mind. Also Baddely has been in the room."

"But what does it signify?" asked the Inspector.

"I don't know. Maybe nothing. We must wait until something turns up to throw more light."

"You suspect the servant of being implicated?"

"Not necessarily. But I think he knows more than he is willing to tell. I couldn't get anything out of him. I suggest that you hand him over to a hardboiled examiner who will press him hard."

"I'll question him myself," said Loasby.

The newspapermen came pushing back with their questions. Lee left them to the Inspector. Fanny had returned by this time, and he took her with him to the Vosper house.

In the cab Fanny said, "When I told Peggy Brocklin what had happened, she went into hysterics. The whole house was in an up-roar."

"Did you see her father?" asked Lee.

"Yes, he was there with the smelling salts."

"What sort of an impression did you get?"

"In all that excitement he scarcely registered. The typical husband of a rich wife—everybody's yes-man. Soft, luxury-loving, with a reedy voice and a kind of spurious elegance about him."

"And the aunt, Mrs. Thorne?"

"The official mamma, and overdoes the part."

"How about the nephew, Eliot Brocklin?"

"He wasn't there. They phoned for him. A curious thing, Pop—it wasn't grief for the loss of her lover that upset Peggy, but fear of the publicity."

"Very likely."

A few minutes later they were ringing the bell of the Vosper mansion for the second time. When the door was opened, Lee handed the servant a card on which he had written: *Very important.*

They were shown to Mrs. Vosper's boudoir. She was pacing back and forth in her restless manner, wearing a pale blue negligee that did not become her, and had apparently been interrupted at her dressing table, because her sallow cheeks bore no make-up. She waved them to seats, and sat down herself on the edge of a chair, ready to spring up again.

"René Doria is dead," said Lee gravely. "The body has been found."

All the color drained out of her yellowish skin and her lips tightened, but the expression of her hard black eyes remained unchanged.

Fanny jumped up. "Can I get you anything?"

Mrs. Vosper smiled superciliously. "I'm not the fainting kind."

There was a silence.

Mrs. Vosper was the first to speak. "I suppose you think I take the news very strangely. Something like this was bound to happen. I'm not surprised. I would explain if I was sure of not being quoted."

"You are safe with us," said Lee.

"I wasn't in love with him," she said with an inexpressibly bitter smile etched around her lips. "It was infatuation. The news of his death breaks the spell. I am free again. Can you understand that?"

"Certainly," said Lee. "Another woman has referred to him in almost the same terms."

"What woman?" she demanded.

"She knew him long ago," said Lee. "Your feelings are perfectly understandable," he went on. "But apparently you overlook the danger you are in."

"Danger?"

"You were the last or almost the last person to see him alive."

"I told you I hadn't seen him for a week."

"Sorry, but we know now that you had supper with him last night."

"That's a lie!"

"Mr. Doria made two phone calls from a pay station at quarter to twelve. One was to his servant Baddely; the other—well, you were called to the phone at the Waldorf at that hour, and you left the hotel immediately afterward."

Mrs. Vosper was not shaken. "Very ingenious, Mr. Mappin, but it's not proof."

"Your fingerprints have been found on the utensils and dishes used for supper, and in many other places about the apartment."

It was curious to see how Mrs. Vosper's clawlike hands crept within the folds of her dress to hide themselves. "How do you know they're mine?"

"You left your prints on the glass from which you drank water."

Still showing that dreadful smile, she muttered huskily, "You're clever, Mr. Mappin! Have you come to arrest me?"

"I have no authority to make arrests. The Inspector of Police was considering that course, but I persuaded him to wait a while."

"Why?"

"To give you a chance to clear yourself."

Mrs. Vosper, with a face as hard as stone, said, "I'm glad he's dead, but I didn't kill him."

"If that is true, you have nothing to lose and everything to gain by telling exactly what happened."

She laughed harshly. "No woman of my position was ever so publicly exposed. How the dear public will roll in it!"

She fell silent, and Lee waited.

Suddenly she resumed, "It's true René called me up at the Waldorf last night, and a few minutes later I met him at the apartment on 46th Street. He got there first. We cooked and ate supper. While we were cleaning up there was a ring at the bell. A special ring—one long and three short. That was a countersign that René had given to two or three friends. Every now and then, to protect himself, he would change the countersign. We waited and the ring was repeated. René said that he had better answer it. So he went down and I slipped up to the bedroom. He brought a man upstairs. I listened with the door open a crack, but I couldn't hear what they said. Just a rumble of voices. They went into the living-room, closing the door after them, and I got out of the place as quick as I could.

"Why didn't you wait to see if Doria could get rid of the man?"

"Too dangerous. The fact that Rene had been obliged to let him in frightened me. It seemed to me that he had closed the living-room door on purpose to let me get out."

"Did you use the elevator?"

"No, it makes a noise. I stole down the stairs."

"Did the voices sound excited?"

She considered before answering. "No. They weren't raised. But the voice of the man who came was under a heavy strain. It frightened me."

"Would you recognize that voice?"

"I doubt it."

"Was it a high-pitched voice?"

"Neither high nor low."

"Was it your husband's voice, Mrs. Vosper?"

She was not at all put out by the question. "No, I should have recognized even a rumble of his voice."

"Was your husband jealous of Doria?"

She shrugged. "Don't ask me! My husband and I have had very little communication lately."

Lee took a new line. "Naturally you were angry when you heard of Doria's engagement to Miss Brocklin."

"I didn't know anything about it until I read the paper this morning. René never told me."

"You were angry when you spoke of it before."

"Sure, I was. And I'm angry now. After the engagement had been published in the late editions which I didn't see, he had the effrontery to ask me for my emeralds to get him out of a jam!" She jumped up with clenching fists, and they had a glimpse of the passions that were tearing her. "Oh, God! I could have killed him for that if I had known!"

"Had you no inkling of how matters stood between him and Miss Brocklin?"

"Sure. I knew he was after her, but I never thought she'd he fool enough to marry him."

"Where did you go when you left the apartment?"

She sneered. "You think you're pretty smart, don't you? I'm not afraid to answer you. I went to a drug store on 42d Street and called René up. He has a private phone in the apartment."

"I saw it."

Mrs. Vosper pressed a handkerchief to her lips. "I couldn't get any answer. I was worried. I walked through 46th Street and looked up at the windows. They were dark. I called up again from another place, but he didn't answer. So I came home."

"What time did you get home?"

"One-thirty."

For half an hour longer Lee led her back and forth over her story, but without tripping her up in any important particular. So good was the woman's control, it was impossible to tell if she was lying. She affected not to give a damn whether she was believed or not. When Lee rose to go she asked:

"Do you believe what I've told you?"

"I have an open mind," replied Lee blandly. "You must remember you have already told me two stories which were not true."

"I'll stick to this one," she said, turning her back.

To the pleasant-faced manservant who opened the front door for them, Lee said, "Humphreys, do you know what my profession is?"

"Yes, Mr. Mappin. I have read your cases."

"Do you concede my right to ask questions?"

"Yes, sir."

"Where did Mr. Vosper spend last evening?"

"At his club, sir. The Knickerbocker."

"What time did he get home?"

"Do you mean the first or the second time, sir?"

"The first time."

"About twelve o'clock, sir."

"And he went out again?"

"Yes, sir. I thought he had gone to his room, but he came downstairs and asked me where Mrs. Vosper was. At the St. Nicholas ball, I said, and he went out again. He returned about 1:45."

"Alone?"

"Yes, sir. Mrs. Vosper had come in just a few minutes before."

"Humphreys, this is important. When he came in the second time did he ask if his wife had returned?"

"No, sir He went upstairs without saying anything. If I may say so, he was out of temper."

"Did you notice if he was wearing gloves?"

"My master always wears gloves out-of-doors, sir."

Lee gave the man a tip. "Thank you very much."

"Mr. Mappin," the servant asked anxiously, "if it's not presuming, what is the reason for asking me these questions?"

The door was standing open, and from down the street they could hear newsboys crying an extra.

"Read the papers, Humphreys," said Lee.

Lee ordered the taxi driver to take them to his apartment. "Just for a bite of dinner," he said to Fanny. "Jermyn will take care of us. Our day's work is not over yet."

"What do you think, Pop?" Fanny asked.

"I don't think. I haven't enough to go on yet. Either one of them had time enough to do it."

"But if Mr. Vosper was indifferent to his wife, would he shoot her lover?"

"It often happens, if the husband's *self*-love is wounded."

His first act on getting home was to call up Stan Oberry. He asked him to establish whether Beekman Vosper had gone to the Waldorf shortly after midnight, and what had become of him afterward.

Later in the evening Oberry reported that Beekman Vosper was well known around the Waldorf. He had entered about 12:80. He had been drinking but was not drunk. ("Stopped for a couple of stiff ones on the way down," commented Lee.) After mixing with the dancers, Mr. Vosper came out and asked the major-domo if he had seen Mrs. Vosper. Upon being told that she had left some time before, he went away. A few minutes later he was recognized by the carriage starter at the tower entrance to the hotel. This man called one of the hotel taxis for him. The driver of the taxi stated that he carried Mr. Vosper to the corner of Third Avenue and 46th Street, where he got out and started walking east.

"We're getting warm, Pop," said Fanny.

Lee smiled.

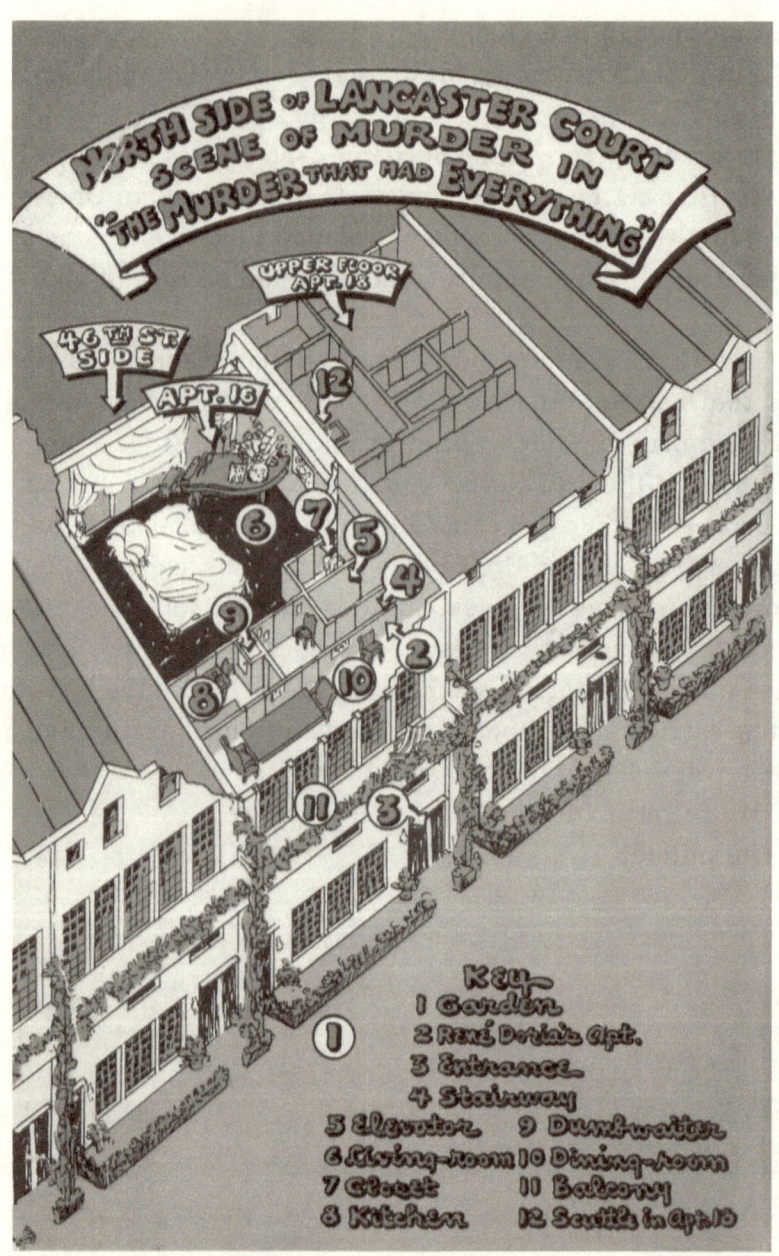

CHAPTER SEVEN
THE PLAYBOY AND THE COLUMNIST

INSPECTOR LOASBY TURNED UP at Lee's apartment to learn the result of his interview with Mrs. Vosper. It was not a subject they could discuss over the telephone. Loasby's feelings toward Lee were mixed. He genuinely liked him and was grateful because Lee, while keeping himself in the background, never missed an opportunity of lauding the police. At the same time Loasby had an uneasy jealousy of Lee. Loasby was an able officer, yet Lee, without intending to, often had the effect of making him look like an overgrown schoolboy. Finally, Loasby hated to admit it, but he needed Lee's help.

Lee said, "I really have no further standing in the case. Inspector. I was hired to find René Doria, and I found him. That lets me out."

"I hope you're not going to drop out, Lee."

Fanny looked down her nose because she knew that power under heaven could divert Lee now.

"Well, if you'll permit me to work with you—"

He gave Loasby the substance of his interview with Mrs. Vosper, and the Inspector agreed that they had better give themselves another 24 hours before proceeding to arrest. Loasby had been engaged in routine police work, and he had nothing of first-rate importance to offer. His examination of Baddely had proved futile. The servant protested he knew nothing about his master's private life, and that he had never heard of the 46th Street apartment until he was told of it by a newspaper reporter, and the Inspector could not shake him.

He had elicited that Baddely's savings were out of all proportion to his wages. Baddely explained it by saying that whenever Mr. Doria was flush he was in the habit of making him a present. This did not sound likely, since Peggy Brocklin had told Lee there was no love lost between master and man.

"I'll go after him again tomorrow," said Loasby.

He left, and after they had eaten, Lee and Fanny spent a couple of hours studying René Doria's scrapbooks. The gossip columns gave them a pretty complete account of his meteoric social career and his love affairs. René's rise had been consistent; for each lady with whom his name was connected was more prominent socially than the last one, or richer, or both. But nothing threw any light on his murder.

Fanny said, "It's a waste of time, Pop."

Lee leaned back and took a pinch of snuff. "Oh, I wouldn't say that, my dear. It is not often that we have a chance to inform ourselves so completely about the victim. Usually his past is hidden in a fog."

"What do you get out of this?"

"I am struck afresh by René's genius for publicity. All these little escapades, unimportant in themselves but always good for a paragraph to the commentators. He was bound to become famous— yet they all say he was stupid."

"What does that suggest to you?"

"I'd rather have you dope it out for yourself."

"Beau Gramercy doesn't seem to have had much use for him, and he's the most important society reporter of them all."

"It doesn't matter whether the paragrapher approves of him, so long as he gives him plenty of space."

At eleven o'clock Lee sent Fanny home to "put on her best bib and tucker" and an hour later they drove to El Zingara, the night club the scrapbooks had informed them had been René Doria's favorite port of call after midnight.

Pavel Czerny, the proprietor of El Zingara, had chosen to establish his resort in an old tenement house on a sordid street far over on the east side. It caught on from the start. Pavel had done nothing to refurbish the exterior, and men enjoyed taking a girl there for the first time to see her shrink from entering such a den, and later to hear her gasp at the luxury of the interior. This was a big night at El Zingara. Lee did not ordinarily attend such hot spots, and a bowing captain of waiters barred the way and explained with deep regret that every table was taken.

Lee produced a card. "Please have that taken to the proprietor," he said. "We'll wait."

Czerny himself, once a busboy in Budapest and now, in his way, a leader of New-York society, came hastening to the door. It was his business to recognize the value of names. As one gentleman with another, he shook hands with Lee and assured him that a place could always be found for him.

Fanny's eyes shone at the scene. A long, low room of no great extent, beautifully decorated with birds against a dawn sky, and tall palms rising and spreading graceful cellophane fronds under the ceiling, it was packed so close that the chairs were touching and it was a marvel how the waiters could get around. A blue haze of tobacco smoke hung over all. Most of the supper parties were engaged in earnest talk with their heads drawn close together. Some had newspapers. By this time the accounts of the murder were pretty full; however, Mrs. Vosper's name had not yet been printed.

They picked out faces here and there that they had seen in René's scrapbooks. Fanny drew Lee's attention to a young man with a bold, dark face, who was making love to an exquisitely beautiful girl. His face had the completely shameless expression that some women find irresistible.

"Jack Vynson," whispered Fanny.

"We must talk to him," said Lee.

Further along with a large party sat a man of 50 who had the look of a youth who had started to age before quite maturing. He played up to his type by dressing and acting in the manner of a young man. He was pretty drunk. This was Beekman Vosper. He had the futile air of a man who, having inherited wealth, has never worked in his life.

"Strange he should want to be seen here tonight," murmured Fanny.

"It's smart to make out that you are superior to the common feelings of mankind," said Lee.

They saw the red-headed Tom Cottar at one table; Delphine Harley, blond and vivacious, at another. And from table to table strolled the odd, distinctive figure of Beau Gramercy. Here he was in his element. Loud cries of welcome greeted him. Beau Gramercy was like a little king in El Zingara, for he possessed the power to make or break all aspirants to social notoriety. He was almost the only man in the place who was not wearing tails. Even at night he stuck to the double-breasted jacket reaching halfway down his thighs to give him height, only now it had silk revers. He was Beau Gramercy and he wore what he pleased.

In the middle of the room with her back against the wall sat his rival—Miss Vida Cadbury, with a man's bulging shirt-bosom showing above the table and a gardenia in her lapel. She never circulated about the room; people had to come to her, and her table was always surrounded. Fanny noted that some of the most desirable young men present were in attendance. Vida, catching sight of Lee, hailed him from across the room with an almost anxious eagerness, but Lee, with an airy salute, passed on.

The tables were already encroaching on the dancing floor, small at the best, but still another little table was rolled up and made ready for Lee and Fanny. When the music started, they saw Tom Cottar winging his way toward them between the tables.

"Mercy, he's ugly!" said Fanny.

Lee looked at her anxiously. "That's what a woman always says when she's impressed by a man."

Fanny blushed. "Oh, he's attractive in a way. But not a man you would take seriously."

"I hope not," said Lee.

"I expect he's going to ask me to dance," said Fanny self-consciously. "Do you wish me to?"

"Why, of course! We must act as if we had come here for fun."

Tom led Fanny out on the pocket-handkerchief of a dancing floor. It was packed so close the couples could only stand still and sway a little to the rhythm of the music. The music was divine.

"How lucky I am to run into you three times in one day," murmured Tom, looking down into Fanny's eyes. "Lord! what a pretty thing you are!"

"Oh, yes?" said Fanny.

"It gave me a shock to find you in that den on 413th Street. You're too sweet for that sort of work."

"What are you trying to do, charm me? Because if you are, it's only kind to tell you that you're taking the wrong line."

"Don't tell me you've got sense, too," said Tom. "That would be too much. That wouldn't be fair."

They swayed a while in silence. Tom was nice to hang on to, his chest stuck out so reassuringly.

"What's the latest news?" asked Tom.

"So that was what you were leading up to?"

"No, but everybody is talking about the Doria case."

"I'd like to forget it for an hour."

"Answer one question and I'll forget it with you. Is it true that Mrs. Vosper had supper in René's den last night? It's a matter of common gossip, but with a woman as prominent as that, none of us dares print it without making sure. Inspector Loasby is generally talkative enough, but on this subject he is mum."

"I never talk to the press," Fanny dryly. "It would cost me my job."

"Just one word," pleaded Tom. "I won't quote you. It's terrifically important to me, darling."

"Look at Pop's—I mean Mr. Mappin's—expression," murmured Fanny. "He is watching to see if I give in."

"Pop couldn't be hard on you. He's as crazy about you as I am."

"Oh, Pop and I understand each other."

"Some woman had supper with René last night. I saw the dishes in the kitchen. If it was Mrs. Vosper it can't be hidden long. What happened when you went to the Vospers' this evening?"

"When we went there?" echoed Fanny, making her eyes big.

"Sure, you needn't look so innocent. Pop was overheard giving the address to the taxi driver."

"You're supposed to be a clever fellow. Look me in the eye." He did so. "Do you really think you can wheedle me into letting Pop down?"

"No, damn it!" he grumbled. "You've got too much sense. I said it wasn't fair." He drew her closer to him. "Well, anyhow, I have the satisfaction of hugging you."

"I like it," said Fanny.

"Let's keep it up for hours and hours."

Fanny glanced toward Lee. Beau Gramercy was approaching his table. Fanny's eyes asked: *Do you want me?* And Lee's glance replied: *Go ahead and enjoy yourself.* Fanny leaned her temple against Tom's jaw and murmured, "All right, Red, until further notice."

A hundred pairs of eyes followed Beau Gramercy from table to table. It was odd to see how the little man with the butterfly manners was feared. There was nothing of the butterfly in his powerful eye. When he sat down with Lee people whispered, "Who is that man? Pavel had a table shoved up in front of everybody for him."

Those in the know answered, "That's Amos Lee Mappin, the celebrated writer on crime. He's working on the Doria case." Both Lee and the Beau were aware of how closely they were being observed.

Beau cried for everybody's benefit, "Well, Lee, you old sinner! What are you doing in this haunt of vice?"

"Studying sociology. I'm writing a book."

Without altering the professional grin, Beau Gramercy lowered his voice. "You didn't come here just for fun, Lee. Can I help?"

"Perhaps you can."

"How is the big case opening up?"

"Slowly."

"Does suspicion point to anybody yet?"

"Unfortunately it's pointing in several directions."

"Good God! Who? I'm safe."

Lee shook his head. "I'm not going to harpoon any reputations until the evidence is complete."

"Definitely, was it Mrs. V in the place last night?"

"I won't tell you, Houson. All official communications must come from the police."

"I'm not interested in the official news. Sidelights are my dish. You and I ought to make a deal, Lee."

"Well, I'm always open for a deal."

"I know the scandalous history of everybody connected with this case, and of everybody who may be drawn into it. All that is at your service."

"If—?" put in Lee, smiling.

"If you'll furnish me with a paragraph a day for my column. Exclusive. Not news, but little human touches to bring it to life. I'll suppress all names unless I have your permission o publish."

"How is this to begin with? At supper in René's apartment last night, two people consumed eight eggs, a pound of sausages, and an indefinite amount of toast. I found the cellophane wrappers and the egg shells."

"Marvelous!" said Beau Gramercy. "Eggs are so deliciously suggestive!"

"What have you got for me?"

"Something important if true. Two weeks ago I received a letter at the office from a woman signing herself Rose Bosi. It had been posted at the G.P.O. on Eighth Avenue, and gave no address. This was the day after René's name had first been linked with that of Peggy Brocklin in the press. The woman stated she was the legal wife of the man who called himself René Doria, and she wanted me to publish the fact in my column in the interests of justice."

"Well, I'll be damned!" said Lee. "What did you do with the letter?"

"Well, we're all bombarded with letters from cranks, you know. I couldn't put it in the paper without verification. I have no funds to conduct an elaborate investigation, and so I did nothing."

"But the Brocklins ought to have been told about it. They have plenty of money to investigate."

"That's what I thought. I sent the letter to the girl's father with a covering note to say there might be nothing in it, but I thought he ought to be informed."

"Did you hear from him?"

"Just a brief note thanking me."

"And it did no good," said Lee grimly.

"You can't stop an enamored woman."

"Do you know Jack Vynson?" asked Lee.

The Beau made a face of distaste. "As I know everybody. I'm obliged to. Vynson's a brute."

"So I surmised. But introduce me to him."

"Sure." Beau Gramercy glanced down the room. "His girl is dancing with another man and he's gone to the bar. Your girl is well occupied. Let's stroll to the bar. It will be less conspicuous than bringing Vynson all the way to your table."

The bar extended across the front of the room. Stags were lined up three and four deep in front of it. The short Lee and the still shorter Beau Gramercy were at a serious disadvantage, but the latter seized a chair and, standing upon it, shouted an order for two Haig and Haig highballs to his friend, the bartender.

When they received their drinks, they stood away a little, and maneuvered close to the tall Jack Vynson who was talking idly to a couple of men. Suddenly Beau Gramercy appeared to discover him. "Oh, Jack!" he said, "I want you to meet a friend of mine, Amos Lee Mappin—Jack Vynson."

Notwithstanding his casualness, Vynson instantly took alarm, and his hard face became harder still. "H'are you," he said to Lee with an offhand nod. He was turning away again, but Lee detained him.

"Let's move away a step or two where we can hear ourselves talk. I want a word with you."

They retreated a little way from the bar. "What is it?" said Vynson, affecting a hard surprise. He was a big fellow, and there was an ugly glint in his black eyes. He was accustomed to quelling men with a glance. Lee, however, was quite undisturbed. He had dealt with Vynson's kind before.

"I take it you read the papers," he said in his mild way.

"When I've nothing better to do."

"Then you know that I've been projected into the Doria case."

"Well, what's that got to do with me?"

"As René's closest friend—"

"Who told you I was his closest friend?'

"I heard it from several quarters."

"Well, if you hear it again I'd be obliged if you'd deny it."

"You have been going about with him so many years—"

"Sure. As I go about with a hundred other men. Technically, I'm friends with them, but we don't give a damn for each other. In this world"—he waved his hand to indicate the well-dressed crowd—"there are no friends. It's every man for himself." He laughed loudly. "Isn't it so, Beau?"

Beau Gramercy tittered. "Sad but true, I'm afraid."

"We can't talk here," said Lee. "Won't you come to my apartment?"

"When?"

"Tonight. Whenever you would be going home."

Vynson laughed again. "Sorry. I have a date. If I have any luck I won't be home until tomorrow."

"Tomorrow, then."

"No," said Vynson bluntly. "I know nothing about Doria, so I can't tell you anything. Ask some of the women who've known him and you'll get an earful."

"I would respect your confidence," said Lee.

"So you say, but what assurance have I? No. I'm not coming to see you tomorrow or any other time. I know nothing about this dirty business and I'm damned well not going to be dragged into it." Turning his back, he moved away.

"I told you he was a brute," murmured Beau.

"Well, he's honest," said Lee pleasantly.

"What did you expect to get out of him?"

"Just wanted to do a little exploring. There are ways of making him talk should it become necessary. What's his domestic situation?"

"Well, he married the Fitch heiress eight years ago. She soon found him out. He deceives her openly, but she's a Catholic and will not divorce him. She makes him an allowance and lets him go his own way."

"What was his origin?"

"I can't tell you. He just seemed to appear out of nowhere."

"Another René Doria!"

CHAPTER EIGHT
THE HUSBAND

As THEY STOOD sipping their highballs, they saw Beekman Vosper making his way with a slightly uncertain gait toward the entrance. He had taken a sudden distaste to his hilarious companions. He had a drunken man's expression of complete absorption.

Lee took a sudden resolution. "Do something for me, will you, Houson? Tell Miss Parran I've been called away on business, and ask Tom Cottar to take her home." He thrust a bill into the other man's hand. "For the wine I ordered."

"Sure," said Beau Gramercy. He looked at the disappearing Vosper. "Are you going with him?"

Lee nodded.

"Well, good luck!"

Lee followed Vosper out. In the foyer he assumed an appearance of drunkenness to match the other man's. As they stood side by side at the coatroom door, Vosper muttered, "This is a lousy joint!"

"Put it there, friend!" said Lee with drunken solemnity. They shook hands.

On the sidewalk Lee said, "Going home?"

"Home? Hell, no! Home's the last place I want to go. My home's a hell on earth with a she-devil running it! Want to go to a joint where I'm not known. The fouler the better. And drink myself blind!"

"I'm afraid of those places," said Lee. "The liquor's poisonous. Come to my place and we can drink in peace."

"No! Don't want to go any man's place. A joint down the Village. The driver knows 'em."

Nevertheless Lee gave his own address to the driver. Vosper paid no attention, but fell back in the corner of the cab muttering, "Fed up. Life's a filthy mess! Tell me, is there anybody in this rotten world who gets any satisfaction out of life? I got too much money. When you can do anything you want, you never want to do anything."

Lee's home was only a few blocks from El Zingara. When they drew up before the door, Vosper said, "What place is this?"

"My place."

"Hell!" he grumbled. "I said I wanted to go to a joint." However, he followed Lee in.

Lee studied him: tall, slender, elegant, gray—a likable fellow, a gray-haired boy, unstable as water.

Jermyn had gone to bed, but he had laid a fire in the living-room, and left the coffee ready on a small table. Also in a refrigerator concealed behind a wall panel, there was beer, cheese, caviar, anything Lee might fancy for a snack. He lit the fire and switched on the coffee. Vosper dropped in a chair.

"Nice place you got," he mumbled.

"Take off your overcoat," said Lee.

Vosper shook his head. "Not going to stay. Going to the Village. Damn it! I like the Village, because it's dirty! What's your name?"

"Amos Lee Mappin."

"I seem to have heard that name somewhere. I'm Beekman Vosper."

"I know," said Lee. "You were pointed out to me."

"What did they say about me?" snarled Vosper. "Did they tell you I had horns?"

"No," said Lee smiling, "real estate."

"Well, I have!" he cried violently. "And all the town knows it! Every husband wears horns whether he knows it or not. Those women have got nothing else to do!"

When the water boiled, Lee let it percolate twice. Vosper was still sitting opposite him wearing hat, topcoat and gloves. "Take

off your things," Lee said again. "For God's sake, be comfortable!"
Vosper shook his head. "Well, take off your gloves anyhow." He
finally condescended to peel off his white kid gloves. He had sin-
ewy, well-shaped hands. Lee drew a cup of the strong brew and
offered it to him.

"What you trying to do?" Vosper demanded. "Sober me up?

"Sure," said Lee, smiling.

"Don't want to be sober! Don't ever want to be sober again!" His
voice broke. "God! I can't face it. You said you'd give me a drink."

"Afterward," said Lee. "If you drink the coffee first, the liquor
will have twice the kick. That's my method."

"And a hell of a state your stomach would be in," grumbled
Vosper. Nevertheless he took the cup, and began to sip the coffee.
And when it was finished, he leaned forward and drew a second
cup without waiting to be asked. Lee talked on idly to lull his sus-
picions. Meanwhile he studied his guest. Probably an only child,
he thought: spoiled rotten in the beginning and so grew up neurotic and aimless. Such a man has no control; liable to fly off at
any tangent. The fire blazed up generously, and Vosper was finally
obliged to put down his cup and take off the topcoat. Lee had the
curious experience of seeing a man come gradually sober before
his eyes.

"Mappin," Vosper said suspiciously, "you're the great detective."

Lee shrugged deprecatingly. "I dislike that word intensely. I
write books on crime."

"And now you're investigating the death of René Doria. Tell
me, does anybody really give a damn what happened to that cur?"

"No," said Lee. "It's only to satisfy an abstraction called Justice."

"Would it be just to punish a man for shooting such a dog?"

"Lord!" said Lee, "there's no answer to that, and you know it.
However, we have to play the game according to the rules."

Vosper abused the dead René with the foulest language. Lee
wondered where the man had learned those words. Surely as a boy
he had never played in the streets. He let Vosper run on because
obviously it eased him, "God!" cried Vosper, "to kill that swine
slowly, to mutilate him, would not pay for the wrong he's done me!

Whoever rubbed him out is my friend! Or course, you know all about it. Everybody must know."

"Yes, I know," said Lee soberly.

With a sudden *volte-face* Vosper cried, "How the hell do you know? It hasn't been in the papers."

"That is because Inspector Loasby and I have succeeded in keeping it out."

Vosper scowled at him. "How did you find out that my family was mixed up in this?"

"I've been investigating the case. Many things have come to light."

"Who did it?" Vosper demanded hoarsely.

"I don't know."

With another abrupt change of mood, Vosper asked, "What did you fetch me here for?"

"I wanted to talk to you about the case."

"Why didn't you say so like a man?"

"You were in no fit state to talk."

"Think you can make a monkey of me!" muttered Vosper. Then with sudden violence: "By God! I don't have to talk to you about my private affairs!"

"Certainly, you don't have to."

"What made you suppose I'd talk?"

"Well, I thought it would be easier for you to talk to me than to the police."

Vosper's jaw dropped. "The police! What the hell have the police got to do with me?"

Lee spread out his hands. "You had the strongest motive for killing Doria."

"I could name a dozen husbands with the same motive."

"Yes, but it was your wife—why shouldn't I say it? You know it—it was your wife who was with Doria last night."

"I didn't know it," Vosper said with a sly look.

"I'm not going to beat about the bush with you," said Lee. "Shortly before one o'clock last night you were seen walking east in 46th Street. It was about this time that Doria was killed."

Vosper stared. "Who told you that?"

"There's no magic in it. You left a wide trail. The doorman at the Waldorf knew you, and the taxi driver told us where he put you down."

Vosper grinned stiffly. "Well, I'm damned! And so you think I smoked René Doria?"

"You could have done it."

"And you want a statement?"

"If you're willing."

"Shouldn't I talk to my lawyer first?"

"That's up to you."

Vosper considered for a moment. "No! The hell with lawyers. I can run my own show. Just give me a moment or two to dope things out."

"Surely. Would you like a drink?"

"No. The coffee has cleared my head. I need a clear head now."

Lee poured himself a highball while Vosper, resting elbows on knees and chin in palm, stared into the fire. *A boy's attitude*, Lee thought, *and he's all of five years older than me*. It was odd to see how, the moment Vosper discovered he was in danger, he became calm. Turning his head, he asked casually:

"Find any of my fingerprints around the dump?"

"You were wearing gloves," said Lee.

Vosper laughed briefly. "True! I was!"

After a silence: "You have talked to my wife?"

"Yes."

"What did she tell you?"

"I can't repeat that."

"Well, anyhow she didn't clear me, or you wouldn't be after me now."

Vosper gazed at the fire and Lee waited.

Finally Vosper got up with a brisk air. "Okay, I'll come clean, it was me that killed René Doria."

"So," said Lee.

Vosper looked at him full of annoyance. "Is that all you've got to say? One would think men confessed murder to you every night of your life."

Lee ignored it. "How did you learn the countersign that brought René Doria down to the door?"

"I won't tell you. It involves another woman."

"How did you persuade René to let you in?"

"With a gun," said Vosper, grinning. "I made him go back upstairs. I wasn't going to shoot him there in the court and be caught red-handed. I told him a few things. That was to give my wife time to get out. I shot him in the living-room. He fell over and cracked his skull on the fender. I dumped him down the elevator shaft. Took my time about cleaning up. Anything else you want to know?"

"It scarcely matters," said Lee, "You'll have to tell a detailed story to Inspector Loasby." Lee pressed the bell for Jermyn, knowing that however soundly he slept, it would bring him.

Vosper's vanity was wounded because Lee refused to get excited. "Not much interested, are you?" he sneered "Such a commonplace murder! Jealous husband shoots his wife's lover! But there's more in it than that. I'll tell you why I did it—"

"It can be used against you," Lee warned.

"I'm not afraid. No jury is going to send me to the chair. The hell with juries and newspapers. This is something for you to know—the famous writer on crime! It isn't just a case of common jealousy. All the feeling I had for my wife died years ago. Look, I've been pretty useless. I was brought up too soft. Never had any incentive. Of course, when I was young I didn't know what was the matter with me. I kidded myself. I found plenty of others as useless as myself, we kidded each other along. We set out to be the complete cynics, see? We outdid each other in mocking all decent feelings. Well, that was all right in a crowd, but when I was alone and sober, oh, God!" Vosper beat his fists against his breast. "Empty! I couldn't bear it! More than once I've been on the point of putting a bullet through my own head!

"And then Doria came along and my wife fell for him. I felt sorry for her—that is, I could have felt sorry if I had let myself. Doria couldn't make a woman happy. He maddened them; he degraded them in their own eyes. My wife was a proud woman and she had to swallow her pride when she went with him. But never mind her, this is my story. My friends kidded me about the affair and I made out it was a hell of a joke. The modern husband, see? I went out of my way to act friendly toward Doria though I hated the sonofa-bitch."

"Topsy-turveydom!" murmured Lee.

"And then the thought of killing him came to me. It was like a soothing balm! And so I killed him, and I'm glad of it. It was the first positive action of my life. It was something real! So what do you think of that, Mr. Writer?"

"It is something new in my experience," said Lee.

"Worth a story, eh?"

"Oh, very much so."

Vesper's hurt vanity was soothed again. He lit a cigarette with an air.

Jermyn entered, wearing a dressing gown and looking startled.

"Jermyn," said Lee, "I wish you'd get Inspector Loasby on the phone. You know his private number. Let them ring until some-body answers."

Vosper looked frightened. "So you're going to turn me over?"

"What else could you expect?" said Lee.

Vosper swaggered again. "Well, I'll see it through. Nobody can say now that I didn't play a man's part." He poured himself a stiff drink.

CHAPTER NINE
THE WIFE

THE STORY OF BEEKMAN VOSPER'S CONFESSION and arrest broke too late for the morning papers, but the afternoon papers brought out extras with scareheads four inches high.

Fanny Parran arrived at the office at the usual time and soon afterward Lee turned up. After skimming over his mail, he dictated to Fanny a memorandum of what Vosper had told him. When it was written he said, "Let's go up to the 46th Street house."

"Why, Pop!" said Fanny. "Isn't the case closed?"

Lee smiled inscrutably. "There's many a loose end."

"For instance?"

"How many visitors did René Doria have night before last?"

"What difference does it make now?"

"Was René killed by a blow or a bullet? The medical examiner refuses to commit himself."

"Mr. Vosper said he shot him."

"Who got the hundred $1000 bills? Oh, call up Headquarters, will you? Start the machinery to arrest anybody who may try to pass one of those bills."

Fanny obeyed and put on her things to accompany Lee. She kept her mouth shut, for Pop didn't like to be questioned. Lee had himself driven first to the Vosper house. "There is a question I must put to Humphreys, the butler," he explained.

Luckily the Vospers were childless. A whole ring of reporters and press photographers was gathered outside the handsome entrance, and Lee and Fanny had to submit to having their pictures taken.

"What's new, Mr. Mappin?" asked the reporters.

Lee made the invariable reply: "Nothing to say, boys. All information must come from the police."

They entered the foyer. "Humphreys," said Lee, "is Mr. Vosper accustomed to wearing a flower in his buttonhole when he goes out in the evening?"

"Yes, sir. Invariably."

"When he came in from the club night before last, Tuesday night, did you see the flower?"

"Yes, sir."

"And when he came home an hour later was it still there?"

"Yes, sir."

"Hm!" said Lee. "Are you positive?"

"Oh, yes, sir. Mr. Vosper was in a temper as I told you. When I took his topcoat from him he snatched the flower out of his buttonhole and threw it on the floor. I couldn't be mistaken, sir, because I picked it up and dropped it in the trash basket."

"What kind of flower?"

"A pale yellow carnation, sir. That's what Mr. Vosper favors."

Lee looked at Fanny. "Well, I'm damned! Thank you very much, Humphreys; that's all."

In the taxi, Fanny could no longer hold herself in. "Pop, what does it mean?"

"Vosper's story is full of holes. I could see that last night, but I had to turn him over to the police."

"What holes?"

"You took his story down—dope it out."

"Pop, if you say that again, I'll scream."

"Well, I want to sharpen your wits. Vosper told me that after he shot Doria he took plenty of time to clean up. And certainly somebody did clean the place up, carefully. Yet Humphreys told us yesterday that Vosper came home night before last only a few minutes later than his wife."

"Then you don't think he did it at all?"

Lee shrugged and spread out his hands.

"What led him to confess—to shield his wife?"

"Is that likely?" asked Lee.

"No!" said Fanny, almost crying with vexation.

Lee patted her hand. "Patience, my love. After all, it's not 24 hours since we entered the case."

Another crowd was around the entrance to Lancaster Court. The police were keeping them out. When Lee and Fanny entered the garden, they found a plainclothes man at the door of Number 16. Against one of the pillars of the covered way, stood a pretty young woman weeping quietly and desperately. She seemed to be in her early twenties and was smartly dressed, with the planned effect of a clever working girl. Her clothes were not expensive. Tears had worked havoc with her make-up. The big brown eyes suggested an Italian heritage.

"Who is she?" Lee asked the detective.

"Ahh! she fainted in the street and they let her sit in the office till she felt better. When nobody was looking she sneaked into the garden. But she was quiet so I didn't run her out. She says she's René's wife. She's sure nutty!"

Fanny looked at the girl. Another of René's women! What a contrast to the imperious rich girl and the sophisticated Mrs. Vosper!

"Well," said Lee. He approached the girl. "Good morning, Mrs. Bosi."

She stared. "How you know my name, Mister? I never seen you before."

"I was just taking a chance," said Lee blandly. "Wanted to see if you recognized that name. Let's go in where we can talk quietly."

"Is he in there?" she asked breathlessly.

"No."

"Where is he? I got a right to see him!" She wept.

"The police have taken the body away. I assume it's in the morgue."

"Pete don't have to lie in the morgue," she said indignantly. "He's got plenty money."

"Of course, said Lee. "As soon as the investigations are completed, they will release the body."

"Are they cutting him up?" she gasped in horror.

"Of course not," he lied. "Come in. This is my secretary, Miss Parran."

"Of course if you say so it's all right, Mr. Mappin," grumbled the detective at the door.

Upstairs Rose Bosi looked around the living-room with bitterly twisted lips. "So this is what it's like! Is it true what I read, that he brought women here?"

"What does it matter now?" said Lee. "No more women for him!"

She dropped on the divan and wept afresh.

"Pull yourself together," said Lee in friendly fashion. "Would you like a drink?"

She shook her head.

"Tell me about yourself."

She looked at him suspiciously. Though she knew exactly what to put on, she was not otherwise very sure of herself. Lee was a new type to her. "How did you know my name?" she demanded.

"A newspaperman that I know, the one who writes under the name of Beau Gramercy, told me he had had a letter from a woman who signed herself Rose Bosi, who claimed to be René Doria's wife."

"I *am* his wife, and his real name was Pete Bosi."

"You mean that was the name he married you under. God knows what his real name was!"

"Why didn't the man print my letter?"

"He wouldn't dare do that without some proof. You gave him no address."

"Well, I didn't want to show no proof then. I just wanted to throw a scare into Pete."

"You can prove, then, that you are his wife?"

"Sure! I have a certificate, and the marriage is registered at the Los Angeles City Hall."

"Any witnesses?"

"Two clerks at the marriage bureau."

"Not so good!" said Lee.

"Are you against me?" she demanded.

"On the contrary," said Lee, "I'm for you! But now he is dead, it might be difficult to prove that Pete Bosi and René Doria were one and the same."

"He come to see me here in New York. He come twice. And both times I had a witness."

"That's better! During these interviews did he acknowledge you as his wife?"

She was more at her ease now, "Sure! He claimed he had divorced me."

"Hm!" said Lee.

"I don't know much law, but it takes two to get a divorce, and I never heard about it. He said it was a Mexican divorce, and he never was in Mexico."

"Well, it can be looked into."

"I know the divorce is a fake, because Pete tried to buy me off."

"In the presence of a witness?"

"Sure. Slim was listening outside the door. He heard everything."

"Who is Slim?"

Rose looked somewhat self-conscious. "Slim Markoe. He's a fellow I met on the bus coming from L.A. We got to be good friends."

"You told him all about your husband?"

"Sure. He's got a room in the same house as me,"

"Now your legal husband is dead," suggested Lee innocently, "I take it you're going to marry Slim."

She bridled angrily. "And if I do—?"

"I merely wanted to establish the nature of the relationship," Lee said hastily.

Fanny was fascinated with Rose, so different from anyone she had ever known—alternately weeping and defiant, hard and soft, cunning and simple.

"Let's get this straightened out," said Lee. "When did the marriage take place?"

"What I want to know is," Rose demanded suspiciously, "after I tell you, what you going to do?"

"Your story's got to be investigated," said Lee, "to establish your right to inherit René's property. He was a pretty rich man, you know."

The streaming eyes glittered at this. "All right. It was eight years ago in Hollywood. I was 15 and Pete was 20. I worked as a counter girl in a lunchroom in Culver City and Pete hung around the movie lots, trying to get extra work. They said he was too dumb to act and he was only hired when he could take off his clothes, because of his handsome shape. So he was always broke and in off hours at the lunchroom when the boss was out, I'd give him a handout. It was mostly beans. I was crazy about him, and when he give me the old hooey about two could live as cheap as one, I went to City Hall with him and we were married. After that I had him to support mostly, but I was crazy about him. Pete was nice then—human, full of fun. He didn't run after women. Or if he did, I didn't know it. He's changed a lot."

"How long did it last?" asked Lee.

"Three months," she said with a bitter grin. "He run out on me without a word. I got a letter from him in New York, after. Said he was working, but didn't tell me what at. I got a couple of letters and then nothing more. My letters come back. For four years he was like dead to me, then he come back to L.A. to be a star in pictures. Called himself René Doria. He was as crazy about me as ever—took me to live with him again, only now he was in the money and we had a suite in a first-class hotel and a Lincoln car, and we went out every night." She hung her head and smoothed the velvet covering of the divan. "It was pretty swell, but I liked it better when we lived in a cheap room and I was working. When he had nothing, I was more sure of him, like."

"Did he tell you about his life in New York?"

"No. Only he seemed glad to be out of it—a free man again, and earning his own living."

"And then?"

"Right in the middle of the picture he was making, he hightailed it back to New York. He never wrote to me. Left me stranded in the hotel, and I had to sneak my clothes out. I went back to work.

I could read every day about the figure he was cutting in society, because Beau Gramercy's column is published in an L.A. paper, and on Sundays I went to the public library to look through the slick magazines if there was any pictures of him. I could see he was changed. Like he had a mask on. I read about the women he went with and how he hypnotized them. That made me laugh. Hypnotize my foot!

"Well, I kept thinking about it. I didn't believe any of these women could mean the same to him as I did. He couldn't be himself with them high society dames. And I thought maybe if he saw me he would come back to himself. So I saved my money, and last month I come to New York."

Lee took a pinch of snuff. "I believe your story;" he said. "It joins up with things I knew before."

Rose continued, "I wrote to Pete soon's I got here, but he didn't answer. I went to see him three, four times but I was never let in. So I got the idea he was purposely keeping out of my way, and I wrote that letter to Beau Gramercy."

"Slim Markoe suggested it?"

"Sure. And it wasn't printed. But one day Pete came to see me anyhow. Said he'd been down at Pinehurst. But that was a lie because I read in the paper what he was doing. He made out he was as crazy about me as ever. Said he'd never had any satisfaction since we was pals and kids together, and could let ourselves go. And me, I was still foolish about him. It was then he said he had divorced me like I told you, and was sorry for it, but he had to do it, he said, because he had a chance to marry the richest girl in America and if I would be good and keep quiet for a while, it would come out all right. Because them rich girls always divorced their husbands after a couple of years, he said, and he could fix it so she'd be glad to get rid of him maybe even sooner. But he'd make her fork over a thumping sum for her freedom, and then him and me could be married again, in a church this time if I wanted, and live on Easy Street for the rest of our lives.

"Well, I agreed to let the thing ride, but Slim told me I was a damn fool and that I ought to stand out for a good sum down to prove he was going to do the right thing by me in the end. I wrote to Pete and told him so. So Pete came again to my room and carried on again how wild he was about me." Rose's voice softened. "Maybe it was true. He didn't wear no mask with me. This time he told me he didn't have no money of his own, but just as soon as he could get it out of Peggy Brocklin, he'd bring it to me. And he wasn't talking about no measly five grand, or ten grand, or twenty grand, neither, he said, but a hundred grand flat. Maybe he was talking through his hat."

"No," interrupted Lee, "that's the strangest part of the story. He actually kept his word."

Tears threatened again. "I never got it!"

"He drew it out of the bank on Tuesday, presumably for you."

She wept—tears of chagrin. "Just my rotten luck! And all my money's gone!"

"I'll take care of that," said Lee. "For God's sake, pull yourself together until you get the story told. You can cry all you want then."

"Pete, he come to my place Tuesday evening," Rose went on between sniffs. "I suppose he had the money, because he was carrying a little satchel."

"A briefcase," put in Lee, "made of pigskin and new?"

Rose nodded miserably. "Yes, that's what they told me. The landlady, I mean, and Slim. And I was gone to the store. I wasn't out of the house half an hour, and Pete couldn't wait, he told the landlady. But would come back Wednesday morning—and Wednesday morning he was dead!"

"What time did he call at your place Tuesday?"

"Just before seven in the evening."

Lee turned to Fanny. "What time was dinner served at the Brocklins'?"

"Seven o'clock."

Lee put another question to Fanny. "Was René carrying the briefcase when he arrived at the Brocklins'?"

"Yes," said Fanny. "He left with it at 11:30."

Lee took a turn back and forth across the room. Coming to a pause in front of Rose he asked in his mild, disarming fashion, "What does Slim do?"

"He's looking for work—would take anything."

"You have been supporting him?"

Rose bridled. "I lent him money, if that's what you mean."

"No offense!" said Lee waving his hands. "I'm a man of the world, my child. And so's my secretary. Has Slim told you anything of his past?"

"Nothing particular. He's knocked around like most fellows. Hasn't been home for years."

"You said he saw René when he called at your place Tuesday?"

"Slim saw him, but he didn't speak to him. Naturally Slim didn't went to—"

"I understand. And Slim told you about Pete's visit when you got home?"

"No. It was the landlady told me first. Slim had gone out. He had to see a man about a job. While he was out he met a fellow he knew, and he didn't get home until late. I didn't see him until Wednesday morning. Then he told me."

"Where is Slim now?"

"Waiting for me in the street. When they wouldn't let us in," Rose went on. "Slim told me to throw a faint, and I did and they took me into the office, and when nobody was looking I slipped through the back door. But they wouldn't let Slim in."

"Slim has his wits about him," said Lee dryly.

"Sure, Slim's wise, all right," said Rose.

"Let's have him in." Lee looked meaningly at Fanny. He wanted Fanny to see that an officer was handy in case Slim was coy about the invitation.

However, Rose was sharp, too, and she had gone to a hard school. "Oh, my God!" she gasped suddenly, and they saw her go livid under her make-up. "You think—you think maybe Slim tailed Pete away from the house and stuck to him all night until he got him alone here, and killed him for the hundred grand! He could. He was out all night!"

"It's just a possibility, said Lee soothingly. "It's true, the money is gone. But don't distress yourself until we get confirmation. Did Slim have a gun?"

"Not as I know of. I don't see how he could have hid it from me." Rose was piteous now. "I liked Slim," she murmured. "Always such good company, and so friendly. But who can you trust in this world? A hundred grand is an awful temptation!" She jumped up, showing her teeth, "I'll fetch him!"

"Smooth out your face," warned Lee, "or he'll take fright from it."

"Don't you worry—I'll make my face behave."

"Go with her, Fanny," said Lee, "and speak to the detective at the door. Let him go out into the street first and keep an eye on you. Then if Slim makes a break to get away, he can be nabbed. Tell the detective it may be an important capture."

The two girls hastened out, and Lee strode up and down the living-room. After a quarter of an hour, he was called to the telephone.

It was Fanny. "We didn't get him, Pop. I fancy he was watching the entrance to the court, and he saw Rose first and did a sneak. Rose insisted on going direct to her room and I thought I had better stick to her. The detective came along, too. It's number — Second Avenue, care Wetzel. I'm telephoning from a store. Slim was not here, and if he has taken alarm, he'll never come back here. He has nothing of value in his room. Rose has already been through his things—there's no money. She is convinced now that Slim is guilty, because he had promised to wait for her in the street. What should I do next?"

"Tell Rose not to talk to anybody."

"That's too much to ask of her, Pop. She's already told the landlady."

"Has she got a photograph of Slim?"

"Yes. Snapshots."

"Bring 'em along. And get at least two detailed descriptions of the man—one from Rose and one from the landlady to check. Tell the detective to stay there on the chance Slim might show up. I'll square him with Headquarters. You come back here."

"Right, Pop."

Lee called up Loasby, and the Inspector was so much disturbed that he dashed right up with sirens blowing. He and Fanny arrived about the same time.

"Good God, Lee!" cried Loasby. "What's this you're telling me? We've got the killer of René Doria! He's lodged in the Tombs, and his confession's in the hands of the District Attorney!"

"I'm not saying Slim Markoe was the killer," said Lee calmly. "It is possible Markoe is only the robber. The money is gone, and it's not reasonable to suppose that Vosper took it."

"How could Markoe have got into this place? It's not possible that he knew the private ring."

"Fanny," said Lee, "do you remember when we looked at the empty apartment next door, the door was not locked. The renting agent turned the handle and walked in."

"Yes, Mr. Mappin."

"And when we got up to the top floor we noticed that the scuttle was unhooked? Suppose Markoe got in that way? It would be easy to prize up the scuttle of this apartment. The wood is old."

"But this scuttle has never been disturbed," objected Loasby.

"Well, let's go and look."

They hastened to the upper floor. Plump little Lee toddled up the ladder. He had drawn on his gloves so as not to leave any fingerprints and he put a hand under the scuttle. It lifted with little resistance. The screw eyes pulled out of the wood. Lee examined the screws and laughed briefly.

"Chewing gum! He filled the screw holes with chewing gum, and put the screws in again!"

"Well, I'm damned!" said Loasby. "So he *did* come in this way!"

"Somebody came this way," said Lee, "but we have no proof yet that it was Markoe."

"A man don't run away for nothing," said Loasby. "I'll send out a general alarm. We'll pay particular attention to the busses leaving town. The $1000 bills won't be any good to him, and he can't have much other money."

Fanny said, "Rose told me he hadn't any money this morning. She gave him a dollar. She said he would probably make for Chicago. She said he was accustomed to travel all over by hitch-hiking. People always picked him up because he was a good-looking young fellow with a pleasant smile."

"Good!" said the Inspector. "We'll put a watch on the roads."
He made for the telephone.

CHAPTER TEN
FATHER AND DAUGHTER

LEE WAS CALLED TO THE TELEPHONE. It was his servant Jermyn, who said that Mr. Houson Bell, otherwise Beau Gramercy, had been trying to reach him. Mr. Bell had a piece of information he wanted to pass along to Mr. Mappin. Lee called up the office of the Sphere, where Mr. Bell spent his mornings. In the very tones of his voice, Beau Gramercy expressed a complete sophistication and scorn for humanity.

"Ah, Lee! Where are you speaking from?"

"The apartment on 46th Street."

"The love nest, eh? I guessed as much. Lee, if I came up there, might I view it? My public is enormously interested, and I might pick up a picturesque detail or two the newsmen have missed. Besides, I have something for you. It may not be of the slightest importance, but anyhow you ought to see it."

"Come ahead," said Lee.

While they were waiting for him, Vida Cadbury was most unexpectedly brought upstairs. She was wearing another immaculate mannish suit but her usual expression of sly humor was disturbed. "Oh. Lee, I'm so thankful to find you here!" she breathed. She dabbed an inadequate handkerchief to her broad face. "I'm so dreadfully upset!"

"What's the matter?" asked Lee. "A glass of water?"

She shook her head. "Its such a relief to be able to drop the mask for a moment! In my world, you know, one can never show one's feelings! Never! I was so attached to the poor boy!"

105

"I'm glad to know he had one friend," said Lee.

"Of course I've been reading the papers," she went on, "but something is being held back. I thought perhaps you would tell me the truth. I can't believe Beekman Vosper did it. That weakling! Haven't you reason to suspect somebody else, Lee? You can tell me. I'm as deep as a well. I damned well have to be!"

Lee slowly shook his head.

"But isn't there some unexplained evidence? Haven't you found clues that don't fit Vosper?"

"I know no more than you do, Vida. But I'm glad you came. Maybe you can help me. You knew René better than anybody. Have you information that points away from Vosper?"

She shook her head.

"Then why are you so distressed?"

"I couldn't stand by and see him railroaded."

"He will never burn for this crime," said Lee.

"How can you be so sure?" she demanded.

"His story doesn't hold water."

"Then who did it?" she cried.

"I can only pass your question back—who?"

"I know nothing!" A bell sounded in the kitchen and Vida started nervously. "What's that?"

"We're expecting Beau Gramercy."

The little fat woman sprang up in terror. "Oh, my God! He mustn't find me here!"

"Why not?" said Lee.

She searched wildly for a reason. "Because—he—he would run a spiteful paragraph about me—my morbid curiosity. How can I get out?"

"Go through the kitchen and wait in the dining-room. When he is brought in here I'll close the door, and you can slip out."

She flew.

"She's acting very strangely," said Fanny.

"Aren't we all?" said Lee.

Beau Gramercy entered, sniffed delicately. "What's that perfume? Ah! Chanel's Seventeen! Do you use it?" he asked Fanny.

Fanny used no scent during office hours. "Yes," she said, moving away from him. "You have a remarkable nose!"

"Seventeen is usually called the fat woman's perfume," said the Beau. "I don't know why."

Even at eleven in the morning he was perfectly turned out. It was said he went home four times a day to change his clothes, and was never at home any other time. It was doubted if he slept. The highly individual style of his attire never altered: the long, double-breasted jackets; the small Homburg hats with narrow, curly brims. He was one of the last men in New York to carry a stick. He favored a stout ebony stick topped with a gold knob, but today's stick had a boar's tusk for a handle. Cloth-topped, buttoned shoes built up inside to provide an additional inch or two of height gave him an odd prancing walk.

"Ah, Lee, my clear fellow! Still on the job? I thought you had solved the case."

"There are still ramifications to be explored."

"What's the latest?"

"Well, it will be on the streets in an hour—there's no reason why I shouldn't tell you. An alleged wife of René Doria has turned up. She has a boy friend, and it looks as if the boy friend had made off with the $100,000 René had drawn to insure the wife's silence."

"Merciful Heavens!" cried Beau Gramercy. "The newspaper reporters will strangle and the presses break down if you feed them double sensations. Let it out a little at a time, for God's sake."

"So I would, if I had my way," said Lee, "but everybody seems to be afflicted with a flux of talk."

He conducted Beau Gramercy through the rooms himself. Lee liked to be with Beau Gramercy; he was so tiny it made Lee feel like Gulliver.

"I suppose the place has been all cleaned up since yesterday morning," said Beau Gramercy.

"No," said Lee. "Things have been moved around a bit; not much."

In the dining-room Beau Gramercy made notes of the wines and liquors in René's closet. "This will give a fillip to the public's

imagination." His chief interest was in the room of mirrors upstairs. "Was the bed tumbled?" he asked slyly.

"No."

"Too bad. I hoped for the worst." He pointed out two strong
hooks that had been let into the ceiling.

"What were they for?" asked Lee.

"What could they be for but a swing?"

"Of course! The seat with the ropes wound round it is on the
shelf of the cupboard yonder. I'm so simple I couldn't figure what
it was!"

"A marvelous item!" said the Beau, making a note.

Back in the living-room after their tour, Lee asked, "What have
you got for me?"

"Another letter came in the mail this morning, this one anonymous. Anonymous letters are perfectly worthless, and I despise
'em. Still I thought you ought to see it."

"Certainly. Let's have a look."

"One question, first. Are you satisfied that Beekman Vosper is
the murderer?"

Lee parried it. "Are you?"

"No," said Beau Gramercy. "I have studied his confession and
it looks to me like a piece of bravado. The impulse of a weakling
who wanted to pose before the public as a real man."

"I have that possibility in view," said Lee.

Beau Gramercy handed over the letter. It was printed with a
pencil on a sheet of sleazy white paper with torn edges. The letters
were awkwardly formed and the lines of writing traveled up and
down. It had been folded up small and slipped in a cheap white
envelope. The address was written with a pencil in longhand slop-
ing in every direction:

> Dear Beau Gramercy:
> It may interest you to know that the police are on an
> entirely wrong track in detaining Mr. Beckman
> Vosper for the murder of René Doria. It was not he
> did it, but a man very close to Miss Peggy Brocklin.

You will be safe in printing this, because I know the
facts and they are certain to come out in the end.
One who wants to see justice done.

"What do you think of it?" asked Beau Gramercy.

"What do you?" asked Lee.

The Beau shrugged in his continental fashion. "If there's anything in it—notice that I say '*if*'—it suggests the work of a servant
in the Brocklin household. Mark how he speaks of 'Mister' Vosper
and 'Miss' Brocklin. And the postmark is the branch nearest to the
Brocklin house."

"The pretense that this was written by an ignorant person is
overdone," remarked Lee. "The familiar form of salutation, 'Dear
Beau Gramercy,' and the entire phraseology indicates that the
writer was educated."

"Of course it does. But among the regiment of servants and
hangers-on in the Brocklin household there are many educated
people. Do you consider it worth investigating?"

"Surely," said Lee. "I despise anonymous letters as you do, but
in dealing with crime you can't ignore them. I suppose one out of
every three crimes is solved by an anonymous letter or a telephone
tip."

"Is it all right if I run it in my column? I wouldn't treat it seriously, of course, but merely offer it as a sample of what comes in a
columnist's mail."

Lee shook his head. "Give me 24 hours—48 hours, first. If there
should be something in it we don't want to broadcast it. It will be
just as good for the column two days hence if nobody else gets it."

"Very well, you're the doctor. "What have you got for me now?"

Lee smiled. "Aren't the hooks in the ceiling enough?"

"I found those for myself," said the Beau. "Remember our agree-
ment. Haven't you opened up some odd lines that the newsmen
haven't got hold of yet, or stumbled on peculiar clues?"

"I can't give you any clues," said Lee. "That's up to the police.
But there's no lack of human interest."

"For instance?"

"In the old days when René was a movie extra he lived princi-pally on beans."

Beau Gramercy made a face of distaste. "Beans! Horrible! Beans are no good—they don't fit in with the popular conception of the luxurious René Doria."

"That's the best I can do today," said Lee.

Beau Gramercy departed; Lee consulted with Loasby. The In-spector agreed that Lee was the best one to handle the Brocklin angle of the case. An inquiry at Headquarters established that Dex-ter Brocklin was licensed to carry a gun. Eliot Brocklin was not.

Later, Lee and Fanny set out for the Brocklin palace. A small crowd was still hanging about. It was Lee's first visit to the house. He cocked an eye at the gorgeous hall with its carved pilasters, tapestries and the great bank of flowers and murmured, "Set for a super-super-special." They were shown up to the small sitting-room on the second floor where Fanny had been received on her first visit. Miss Brocklin was there, and with her a big young man whom she introduced as Eliot Brocklin, her cousin.

Peggy was her pretty, fragile, artificial self; she was wearing deepest black and making play with a handkerchief, but her eyes were tearless—they glittered. She disliked Lee because he brought no devotion to her shrine, and Lee fairly reveled in it.

"Ah, how do you do," she said. "I suppose you've come about your fee."

Lee's eyes sparkled behind his glasses. (Fanny thought. *He'll add $10,000 for that!*) "Not exactly," he said pleasantly. "My sec-retary will address you later."

Eliot Brocklin was a tall, strongly built, ordinary-looking fel-low, beautifully dressed but not at home in his fine clothes. He had not the slick air associated with café society and was none the worse for it, but Fanny saw that Peggy was a little ashamed of her cousin. His hands were too big; his ears stuck out and his glance was simple. In rough farming clothes with his shirt open at the throat, he would have been better dressed. At the same time Lee and Fanny had the feeling that they had interrupted an amorous scene. The young man was flushed and self-conscious. (Fanny thought, *He's trying to catch her on the rebound.*)

"What did you want to see me about, then?" asked Peggy rudely.

"If I might speak to you a moment alone?"

"My cousin has my entire confidence. Go ahead."

"I had better open the subject in private," suggested Lee politely.

"You can speak in front of him or not at all."

Lee bowed. "Very well. One of the papers received an anonymous letter which has been turned over to me." He drew the letter from his pocket and read it to her. Fanny, slyly watching Eliot Brocklin, saw the young man turn greenish. After all, he was one of the two men who were closest to Peggy Brocklin. Peggy's first reaction was a dry laugh.

"How perfectly ridiculous!" she exclaimed. "Do you take that stuff seriously?"

"Not necessarily, but it has to be investigated."

Peggy put her handkerchief to her eyes. "René is gone!' she wailed, "and the man who killed him has confessed! Why can't the papers leave me alone?"

"I am not connected with the press," Lee pointed out dryly. "Inspector Loasby thought it would be better for me to come to see you than a representative of the police."

Peggy flew off at a new tangent. Jumping up, she paced the room. "I can't bear it!" she sobbed. "After losing René it is too dreadful to have to hear these horrible lies about him day after day! It is nothing but envy and jealousy. I know how fine he was! The newspapers respect nobody. I shall leave this horrible country and never come back!"

Lee took a pinch of snuff. "Excuse me," he said blandly, "but this is nonsense."

It was effective. Peggy whirled around. "How dare you!" she gasped. "In all my life I have never been spoken to like this!"

"It would perhaps have been better for you if you had," said Lee.

She stared at him in voiceless rage. "Oh! Oh!" She turned to Eliot. "Are you going to stand for this?"

The young man rose, exquisitely uncomfortable. "Look here," he blustered, "you can't talk to Miss Brocklin like that!"

"I'm old enough to be her father," said Lee, "and I'm saying it for her own good. After René Doria has been shown up for what he was, for her to be talking in this manner is silly."

Eliot cast a frightened glance at the speechless Peggy. "You don't know what you're talking about! René was a fine fellow!"

"You say that?" said Lee quietly. "He cut you out, didn't he?"

Eliot swallowed hard. "I gave her up," he stammered, "because—René was the better man."

Lee shook his head sadly.

Peggy found her voice. "What do you want of me?" she demanded. "What did you come here for?"

"To ask your permission to question the servants."

"I refuse! Leave the house!" She ran to the wall and pressed the button for a servant.

Lee bowed. "Then the servants will be subpoenaed." He and Fanny left the room.

"Go with them and see that they get out!" Peggy cried shrilly to Eliot.

He followed them, closing the door after him. "Look," he stammered, lowering his voice. "I didn't mean what I said in there. Nobody knows better than me what a skunk René Doria was. But with Peggy feeling the way she does, what could I do?"

"Deal with her like a man," said Lee. "She doesn't feel anything for Doria; she's only trying to save her face."

"You don't know Peggy," he said in fright. "She's never been crossed since she was a child. When she's opposed she gets in a terrible state."

"A little brutality is the best way to deal with such states," said Lee dryly. "That was René Doria's way, and you see how she fell for it."

"I couldn't!" murmured the young man.

"Then God help you if you marry her!"

They had reached the head of the stairs. At the same moment a servant reached the bottom and Lee signaled to him to remain where he was. He said to Eliot. "What is your work, Mr. Brocklin?"

The young man could not stand against Lee's directness. "I—I am not employed at present."

"Are you living in this house?"

"I'm staying here for the present—just to see Peggy through."

"This dinner on Tuesday night at which your cousin announced her engagement, I take it that was a nasty shock to you."

Eliot nodded miserably. "Yes, sir. After her father told her of Doria's previous marriage and the questionable divorce, none of us thought she would; not until after we'd made an investigation anyhow."

"How did Mr. Brocklin learn about the apartment on 46th Street and how to get in it?"

Eliot grew even paler than before, "Oh, God, Mr. Mappin, he couldn't have known that. Or if he did, he never told me!"

"What did you do on Tuesday night after the party broke up?" Lee asked bluntly.

The young man hesitated painfully.

"Answer!" said Lee. "Everything's got to come out now."

"I went out," he said very low.

"Where?"

"I couldn't tell you that, sir. I just walked the streets. I felt awful."

"Did your walk take you to East 46th Street?"

"No, sir. I never heard about that place until I read it in the newspapers."

"Did you meet or talk to anybody during your walk who knew you?"

"No, sir."

"What time did you get home?"

"I guess it was after two."

"Did a servant let you in?"

"No, I have a key."

"Well, it's too bad you can't furnish an alibi."

The young man began to sweat. "Mr. Mappin, you don't think that I—that I had any hand in it! I'm not the killer type, Mr. Mappin!"

"I don't think you are," said Lee dryly. "But you never can tell! What about Miss Brocklin's father? He must have been badly cut up, too, on Tuesday night. What were his movements?"

"I don't know—I didn't see him after dinner."

The door of the small sitting-room opened abruptly and Peggy stood there. "Eliot, what are you telling him?" she demanded stridently.

"Nothing," he mumbled.

"I told you to see him out of the house. Come here!"

He obeyed with a hangdog air. Lee and Fanny exchanged a glance, and proceeded down the stairs. The servant waiting at the foot was one of the sleek robots that move stiffly about the homes of the rich. To him Lee said, "What is the butler's name?"

The man hesitated, but Lee's quiet glance was not to be disputed. "Mr. Wilton, sir."

"And Mr. Dexter Brocklin's man?"

"Mr. Cockey."

"Is Cockey in the house?

"I'll see, sir."

The footman hurried away, glad of the excuse to go for help with which to meet this situation.

While they waited Fanny said ruefully, "We are likely to get chucked out, Pop."

Lee took a pinch of snuff. "I am quite enjoying myself. A little opposition is so stimulating!"

The footman returned accompanied by both of the upper servants. Wilton, the butler, as the chief of so immense an establishment, was a personage: a tall, handsome man whose manner exhibited a perfect blend of deference and command. There was no nonsense about Wilton. The valet, Cockey, on the other hand, was a meager little man, elderly and brisk. He wore his hair long and curled at the ends.

The butler bowed. "What is your pleasure, sir?"

"I am Amos Lee Mappin," said Lee. "I am associated with the police in the investigation of the Doria case, and I would like to ask you and Cockey a few questions." He glanced at the young foot-man. "Where can we go where we may be private?"

"To my office, if you will be so good. This way, sir."

He opened a door to the right and they entered a small office opening directly off the hall.

"You will excuse me, sir," said Wilton, but I took it that the case was closed."

"A case is not closed so long as one circumstance remains un-explained." Lee and Fanny seated themselves. "Sit down, men. You are not on duty with me."

They obeyed.

"Referring to last Tuesday night," said Lee. "What were Mr. Dexter Brocklin's movements?"

The two men exchanged a startled glance. Wilton coughed and drew a hand over his long face to gain time. "But excuse me, sir, wouldn't it—wouldn't it be very irregular for me to answer such a question without consulting my master?"

"Very irregular!" echoed the valet.

"Your duty to the law comes first, Wilton."

"Of course, sir," he murmured in distress. He recovered him-self, and spread out his hands. "After all, we have nothing to hide here. There was nothing special about Tuesday night, sir. My mas-ter went upstairs at the usual time and I did not see him again."

"At the usual time," put in Cockey.

"Cockey was in attendance upstairs," the butler continued, "and he can give you particulars."

The valet took up the tale. "Yes, sir. Mr. Brocklin came upstairs at twelve o'clock or a little before, and I prepared him for bed."

"Did he go to bed?"

"Yes, sir. I saw him in bed."

"Could he not have got up later and have gone out without your knowing it?"

"It is not possible, sir."

"Where do you sleep?"

"In a room adjoining the dressing-room, sir. And the door is always open. Mr. Brocklin wishes to have me within call during the night."

"Hm!" said Lee, considering. A wary note had come into the voices of both servants, and there could be little doubt that they were lying. "Did Mr. Brocklin get a phone call after dinner?" he asked.

"No, sir," they answered together—a little too quickly.

"Calls from outside the house are received here, I take it," said Lee, indicating a small switchboard.

"Yes, sir," said Wilton. "I take them if I am in my office; otherwise a bell rings in the servants' hall. If a late call came in for Mr. Brocklin, it would be switched up to the dressing-room and Cockey would take it."

"Cockey," said Lee, "think before you answer. Are you prepared to swear that Mr. Brocklin received no telephone call after dinner on Tuesday night?"

"Yes, sir! Indeed I am!" answered the valet, making his voice very positive—but there was a quaver in it. *So there was a telephone call*, thought Lee. He let it go for the moment.

"Wilton," he said, "did you notice if the gentlemen at the dinner were wearing boutonnières?"

"Yes, sir. Every gentleman had a gardenia. Miss Brocklin ordered them special because it was an engagement dinner. It was a surprise."

"I believe you," said Lee dryly. "Did you handle the flowers?"

"No, sir. Miss Brocklin kept them by her. She pinned one on each gentleman's coat."

"Who was the florist?"

"I couldn't say for certain, sir. She usually patronizes Schling."

A bell rang and both men rose hastily. "I'll take it," said Wilton. "It may be the master.'

He left the room, but immediately returned and beckoned to Cockey to come. Lee, curious to find out what this maneuver signified, followed them into the hall. Through the grill at the entrance he could see a chauffeur standing outside. A footman was approaching from the rear of the house, the front door was opened, and all three servants passed out. Lee went forward to look through the door.

A superb, convertible town car was drawn up and the crowd was pressing up. The top was up and Lee could not see who was inside. But when Wilton went to open the door Dexter Brocklin's agitated face came forward. He would not get out until his four servants were at hand to guard him from the crowd. Lee observed that Wilton took time to whisper to his master before opening the door all the way. Flanked by his servants, Brocklin scurried up the steps and through the open door.

He was not an old man, but he appeared to have gone soft. Ordinarily a pleasant-looking idler dressed in a beautiful, fawn-colored suit too young for his years, he was now in a bad state of nerves. His encounters with detectives, reporters, photographers and the populace during the past few days had given him a hunted expression. When he got inside he wiped his face and was for passing by, but Lee interrupted him with dry politeness.

"One moment, Mr. Brocklin, if you please."

"Who is this gentleman?" Brocklin plaintively asked of his servants.

"Mr. Mappin, sir," murmured Wilton,

"What does he want of me?"

There was an embarrassed silence.

"I represent the police," said Lee.

Brocklin flinched away as if Lee had revealed a set of fangs. "May I have a few words with you in private?" asked Lee. Brocklin merely stared at him. He looked so desperately frightened that Lee added, "Let Wilton be present. He's a dependable man."

Peggy Brocklin came running down the stairs. "Dad," she cried shrilly, "I sent that man out of the house half an hour ago, and he didn't go! He's been trying to pump the servants! Put him out!" She came up to the group in the hall. "Well, what are you standing around for?" she demanded of the servants. "Aren't you men enough to put this man and woman out?"

"If you please, Miss, he comes from the police," Wilton answered in a hoarse whisper.

She burst into a hard, dry sobbing. "Oh, this is outrageous! Aren't we safe from intrusion in our own house? What have we got to do with the police?"

An older woman, fat and very showily dressed, appeared from somewhere and instantly burst out crying, too. "Oh, my pet!" she wailed, trying to put her arms around the girl. Peggy thrust her away. "Let me alone, can't you!" She turned on Lee again. "Are you going to get out of my house?"

Lee looked quietly from one to another and none dared move.

Peggy burst into loud weeping like the tantrum of a child. "I *will* have him put out!" However, she was beaten and she knew it. She turned toward the stairs.

"Go with her!" stammered her father to his sister.

Peggy flew upstairs and her aunt, holding up her skirts, ran after her with remarkable speed, considering her weight. The maid-servants scampered after the aunt. Something absurd in the scene caused Lee and Fanny to exchange a glance and bite their lips.

"Shall we go into the butler's office?" suggested Lee to Dexter Brocklin.

Brocklin nodded with a distracted air and followed him. "Come, Wilton," he said to the butler. He paused at the door saying, "I want my man Cockey, too."

Lee smiled dryly. "That's quite all right with me, Mr. Brocklin. My secretary and I are not going to attack you."

The five persons entered a little office and the door was closed. They all stood. Mr. Brocklin endeavored to summon his dignity. "Now, I'd be glad to hear the reason for this intrusion, Mr. Mappin."

"I shall come direct to the point, sir. The police have received an anonymous tip implicating you in the murder of René Doria."

The elegant Mr. Brocklin stared at Lee like a clown. His jaw dropped slackly. "Me? Another man has confessed to the crime!"

In the background Wilton and Cockey permitted themselves to laugh discreetly at the utter absurdity of such a charge.

"Quite so," said Lee. "But in so grave a case the police are obliged to follow up every clue."

"An anonymous tip!" said Brocklin indignantly. "Obviously somebody is trying to injure me."

"Very likely," said Lee soothingly. "You can easily dispose of it, I'm sure."

"What have my servants told you about Tuesday night?" demanded Brocklin in ill-concealed terror.

"That you were in bed before midnight, as usual."

A look of relief broke in the other's flabby face. "Well then," he said, "what more proof do you want?"

"I'm sorry," said Lee, "but it's hardly sufficient. Loyal servants are disposed to lie to save their master."

Brocklin became freshly excited. "So you're accusing them of lying now!"

"There is no need to distress yourself, Mr. Brocklin," said Lee blandly. "It will be the simplest matter in the world for you to disprove the charge."

"How?" he asked suspiciously.

"Let me have a look at your gun."

Brocklin stared at him in affright and all the color slowly drained out of his face. "I—I have no gun."

"Now, Mr. Brocklin," said Lee reproachfully, "the police records show that you took out a license to carry a gun many years ago, and have been most particular to keep it renewed."

"Well, a man in my position,' he stuttered excitedly, "the victim of so much unwelcome publicity, I'm a target for all the cranks."

"I'm not questioning your right to carry a gun, sir. I only want to examine it."

Brocklin lowered his eyes. "It's not in my possession at present."

"All! Where is it?"

The man had a hunted look now. "I—I lent it to a friend," he said, swallowing hard. "He was about to travel and wanted it—for protection."

Fanny could scarcely bear to look, he was giving himself away so completely.

"What's your friend's name?"

Brocklin wiped his face with his handkerchief and in so doing gained 10 seconds time. "I won't tell you."

"Why?"

"My friend—didn't have time to take out a license. I'm not going to get him into trouble!"

"But that would only be a little trouble for him, whereas a very grave trouble faces you."

"I don't care!" cried Brocklin hysterically—and how like his daughter he sounded then! "I'm not going to get a friend into trouble."

Lee stroked his chin and considered. "Well, let the gun go for the moment. There is another way in which you can quite easily explode this charge."

"How?"

"Give me your fingerprints. There is ink and paper on the desk here. We can make shift with that."

Brocklin's eyes darted from side to side like those of a trapped animal. "My fingerprints!" he gasped. "A man in my position! You have the effrontery—treating me like a common criminal!"

"This is not official," said Lee soothingly. "No record will be kept. They will never pass out of my hands, and if they do not co-incide with certain unidentified prints found in Doria's apartment, I will destroy them immediately."

Brocklin thrust his plump hands behind him like a schoolboy when the master produces a strap. "No! No!" he cried shrilly. "I will not submit to such a humiliation!"

Lee shrugged. "I'm sorry!"

"Who are you, anyhow?" Brocklin went on. "What right have you to speak for the police?"

"You will find that out only too soon," said Lee regretfully. "Naturally, since you refuse to co-operate, the investigation must be carried on. In the meantime I will bid you good afternoon."

Lee and Fanny presently found themselves out on the sidewalk. "Well, anyhow, we left under our own power," said Lee.

He hailed a cab from Fifth Avenue, and ordered the driver to draw up across the street from the Brocklin door. Fanny he sent to the Madison Avenue corner to telephone Inspector Loasby that Dexter Brocklin was frightened enough to try to make a getaway, and that he had better put a watch on the house. Lee seated himself in the waiting taxicab where he could keep an eye on the door.

Very soon the big town car returned and drew up before the Brocklin entrance. Lee crossed the road and mixed with the crowd hanging about on the sidewalk. When he saw Brocklin approaching the door from the inside, flanked by his servants, Lee went up the steps.

Brocklin started back at the sight of him, and looked for his servants. "What are you doing here?"

"I must ask you to return to the house, Mr. Brocklin," Lee said in a tone too low to reach the ears of listeners below.

"How dare you!" gasped Brocklin. "Stand aside, sir!"

From his waistcoat pocket Lee produced a police whistle, and showed it to Brocklin cupped in his hand. "There's a patrolman on the corner," he said mildly. "Unless you obey I shall be obliged to summon him. Believe me, I should hate to give these loafers such a treat!"

Brocklin gave him a look of helpless hatred, and went back into the house. Lee, coming down the steps, said blandly to the chauffeur, "You needn't wait."

Fanny returned from the telephone booth and a few minutes later two plainclothes men arrived from Headquarters to relieve Lee's vigil. They were acquainted with Dexter Brocklin by sight, and they had their instructions.

On the way downtown Lee stopped at Schling's flower shop. When he identified himself, the clerks were very willing to give him information. The man was found who had taken Miss Peggy Brocklin's order for five gardenias on Tuesday afternoon to be arranged as boutonnières for gentlemen. Certainly, each had been wrapped in tinfoil in the usual manner, he said, and proceeded to show Lee how each flower with its attendant leaves had been bound first with thread, and how the tinfoil was pinched so that it could not come off except with a sharp pull.

"Thank you very much," said Lee. "I would be obliged if you would say nothing about my inquiry."

"Yes, sir—I mean, no, sir. Certainly not, sir."

Lee and Fanny then proceeded to Lancaster Court. Inspector Loasby was all agog at the new turn in the case. "Good God! what next? Lee, do you think it possible that Vosper and Brocklin could have pulled this off together?"

"It doesn't seem to make sense," said Lee. "Have you tried to trace the sale of the gun we found here?"

"I have, but there's nothing doing. That type of revolver was brought out 20 years ago. In those days records of sales were not kept as carefully as they are now. Judging from the condition of the gun, it has been kept put away ever since. It would not surprise me to learn that it had never been fired but the once, since the day it was bought."

"Very likely."

"Lord! if we had Brocklin's fingerprints it would settle everything! What can I do? I can't take a man of Brocklin's caliber into custody just on suspicion. It would bust the town wide open!"

"I can't see that another bust or two would make much difference," said Lee dryly. "But I'm not recommending that you arrest him. We have nothing against him except that he's panicky. But don't give him a chance to slip off to Mexico. Meanwhile, you can shadow his two servants also. If you are able to corner them outside the house and apply a little heat, you may get something valuable."

"I'll do that, Lee."

"This still does not tell me what became of the hundred grand," said Lee thoughtfully.

CHAPTER ELEVEN
THE GIGOLO

ON THURSDAY NIGHT the body of René Doria was relinquished by the police. By this time Rose Bosi's story had been published, and she was generally recognized as René's heir, When the size of his fortune became known, Rose found plenty of friends. The largest undertaking establishments were bidding for the privilege of conducting René's funeral, for the sake of publicity. Rose chose Chapman's Funeral Parlors.

Chapman's got more than they bargained for. On Friday morning it was estimated that more than 10,000 people were attracted to the scene in the hope of getting a glimpse of the body. So great was the crush that the immense plate-glass windows of the funeral parlors were forced in, and many women trampled in the confusion. The police reserves of four precincts were called out to handle the crowd. Meanwhile the body was hastily carried out through a rear entrance and dispatched to the cemetery without any mourners.

In the afternoon Lee and Fanny were in the office on Madison Avenue trying to catch up with correspondence when a detective on duty at Lancaster Court telephoned to say that Mrs. Rose Bosi had come there looking for Mr. Mappin. Lee instructed the man to send her to his office.

She arrived a few minutes later. Since morning she had changed her funeral trappings and now looked smart in a burnt-orange outfit. Rose's clothes would not bear too close an examination, but the general effect was always striking. Lee brought her into his

private office where Fanny was taking dictation, and the latter got
up to retire.

"You don't have to go out," said Rose. "You're my friend. I want
you to hear this, too." It was evident from the way the black eyes
were snapping that she was the bearer of what she considered to
be important information.

Lee passed both girls cigarettes. "What's new, Rose?"

Opening a crumpled paper package, she produced a man's white
shirt with soft collar and cuffs, somewhat soiled. "I found this in
Slim's dirty clothes," she said. "Look!" She spread a cuff out flat
on Lee's desk and they could distinguish some scribbled pencil
marks on it. After a little study they made it out to be an address:
1420 Blackstone Parkway.

"What do you take it to be, Rose?" asked Lee.

"Some dame's address," she said with extreme bitterness.
"Slim's business in life was picking up girls. Always hoping he'd
catch a girl with money."

"Hm!" said Lee, producing the snapshots of Slim and studying
them.

"He wasn't much of a looker," said Rose, "but they fell for his
grin. Where is Blackstone Parkway?"

"There may be more than one," said Lee, "but the famous avenue
of that name is in Chicago."

"That's what I thought. Because he knows Chicago, see? And if it
was any other place, he'd write the name of the place, wouldn't he?"

"That seems reasonable," said Lee.

"Is it a ritzy street?" asked Rose.

"Eminently so! Some of our most effulgent meat packers have
squatted there."

"Well, Slim would know that. And if he picked up a girl and she
fell for him and gave that as her address, he would know she had
money. I guessed he would make for Chicago because he knows
the ropes there. Well, if he was up against it, he'd look up this girl
the first thing."

"Up against it?" questioned Fanny. "If he has that money?"

"If he don't dare change the hundred grand, it's no more use to him than a roll of toilet paper."

"Would Slim have the nerve to present himself at a Blackstone Parkway mansion?"

"Sure. Slim has nerve enough to go anywhere if he was dressed right. I staked him to a good suit myself when we come to New York, and he had it on."

"Are you suggesting that I ought to fluff out to Chicago on this tip?" asked Lee.

"Wouldn't do no good for me to go," said Rose. "He might see me first."

"If he reads the papers my face must be almost as familiar to him as yours. But here's Fanny. Her photograph hasn't been published."

"Is Slim so important now?" put in Fanny.

"Important!" cried Rose, staring. "He's got my hundred grand! I'll give you ten percent if you recover it," she slyly suggested to Lee.

Lee made believe to consider the proposition.

"Slim couldn't have shot René," suggested Fanny.

"Why not?" asked Lee with his deceitful mildness.

"He had no gun."

"Suppose René had a gun," suggested Lee. "True, he had no license, but a young man who lived so dangerously would be pretty sure to have one anyhow. And suppose Slim was man enough to take it from him?"

"René was shot with a bullet fired from the gun found lying under his body."

"Sure. How does that destroy my hypothesis?"

"You produce a new hypothesis every hour, Pop!"

"But of course! That's my job."

"We know that the fingerprints left under the scuttle of Number 18 Lancaster Court and those on the gun were not made by the same hand. How do you reconcile that with your new hypothesis?"

"I don't. However, fingerprints are never conclusive. A glove can always be pulled on or off."

"And if it was not Dexter Brocklin's missing gun that you found under the body," persisted Fanny, "what is he in such a sweat of terror about?"

"Ask me another," said Lee calmly. "We have still a lot of work to do on the case. One thing I know. Whoever shot René Doria, the crime will never be completely solved until we find the hundred grand. And so I'm inclined to act on Rose's tip. Have you dates for tonight and tomorrow night?"

"Nothing that I can't get out of," said Fanny.

"I suppose you won't take me," said Rose, knowing in advance that she would be denied.

Lee shook his head. "If he happened to see you with us, the jig would be up. Telephone to Grand Central," he went on to Fanny, "and reserve two bedrooms on the Century this evening. You can send up a messenger for the tickets. Then call up Headquarters and ask Loasby to supply me with the necessary credentials for the Chicago police, and also a warrant for Slim's arrest."

Upon arriving in Chicago next morning, Lee and Fanny sent their bags to the Palmer House and drove direct to police head-quarters. Lee, who made it a practice to keep in touch with the leading police executives—they were his principal source of copy—was already acquainted with the Commissioner; and upon describing his errand to Chicago, he received prompt co-operation. The police prepared to reproduce the snapshots of Slim, and to print a circular to be distributed to the force. A watch was put on all railway stations and bus terminals.

It was no trouble for the police to dig up the information that the house at 1420 Blackstone Parkway was the residence of Mortimer Torrey, president of the Great Lakes National Bank. Mr. Torrey was a widower with four children. The two oldest were married; a younger girl and boy lived at home. Miss Rachel Torrey, 20 years old, was a debutante of two seasons; the boy, Mortimer, Jr., 18, was a sophomore at Yale. Fanny, who meanwhile had been skimming over the recent society news in a file of the Chicago *Tribune*, added the information that Miss Rachel Torrey had just returned from a visit to New York. A photograph of Miss Torrey appeared with the item.

Slim was known to the Chicago police and his photograph and fingerprints were on file. He had been arrested three times for obtaining money from women under various pretexts but had escaped conviction owing to the failure of the victims to follow up their charges. It gave Lee satisfaction to discover that his fingerprints were identical with those photographed on the scuttle of 18 Lancaster Court. "Now we can bring a real charge against him," he said, "and it will stand up."

The Police Commissioner offered to supply Lee and Fanny with a plainclothes man to go about with them, but Lee declined. "An old codger like me might naturally be moseying around town with a pretty daughter," he explained, "but the addition of one of your efficient operatives to our party might attract attention. I'll keep in touch with you by phone."

Lee and Fanny drove out Blackstone Parkway and took a look at number 1420. The mansion, standing in extensive grounds, was about 20 years old, built of yellow stucco in the Spanish Mission style fashionable at that time, and exquisitely unsuitable to the climate of Chicago. An expensive family car stood waiting at a side entrance.

Lee said to Fanny, "I'll leave it to you to approach the girl."

Fanny said, "if you approve, I'll watch the house and, if possible, the girl, before I try to make contact with her. If Slim has already approached her she will be wary, and in the meantime I may learn something that will give me a good lead."

"All right," said Lee, "but how can you watch the house without attracting attention?"

"Why, Pop, you talk as if I had learned nothing from you. The stream of traffic in the street will give me cover. I'll just ride up and down in front of the house in a taxicab."

"Okay," said Lee. "The waiting car suggests that somebody in the house is going out now, so you stay in this cab and let me out at the next corner. At one o'clock, if you're still on duty here, you can pick me up at the same corner and I'll have the makings of a lunch for you."

At one o'clock Fanny picked up Lee as arranged, and while munching the sandwiches he had brought, told her story:

"Soon after you left me Miss Torrey got in her car and was driven downtown. A pretty, dark girl—you know the type, Pop, sophisticated yet childishly ignorant. Needs a spanking. She went into a fashionable beauty shop and I followed. Being late for her appointment, she had to wait for a few minutes, and the chance seemed too good to pass up. So I sat down beside her and played the bright little moron. But she was snooty, and I couldn't get a thing out of her. However, I'm pretty sure that Slim has not yet approached her."

"If she wouldn't tell you anything, how did you work that out?"

"Because she was bored and discontented."

"Set a woman to catch a woman!" murmured Lee.

"I couldn't get anything done in the place without a previous appointment," Fanny went on, "so I left and watched for her outside. She stopped at a candy store and at a florist's and then came home. And she's in there now unless there's a subterranean exit."

"Good work," said Lee.

He left her, feeling satisfied that his business was in good hands, and spent the next few hours pleasantly browsing among second-hand bookshops. Lee's hobby was the collecting of books pertaining to crime, and his library in that respect was said to be unequaled on either side of the ocean. At intervals he called up his hotel, but found no message waiting. At five he returned to the hotel for a restorative cup of tea, and while he was drinking it in his room and looking over his purchases, the telephone rang.

It was Fanny. "That you, Pop?" Her voice was cool. "I have our man."

"The hell you say! Where?"

"Cocktail lounge of the Hotel Mannering. The girl is with him. I've been on their tail all afternoon but couldn't get them placed long enough to phone you. I reckon they're good for an hour here.

They won't let a lone woman in the lounge, so I'm sitting in the waiting-room just outside the entrance. If you want to nab the guy you'd better bring an officer."

"Be there in 10 minutes," said Lee.

Phoning Headquarters, he asked for a plainclothes man. They met at the door of the hotel, having bettered the 10 minutes a little, and in the anteroom to the lounge Fanny arose with a beaming smile from among the women waiting for their men. Lee introduced the personable and well-dressed young detective that Headquarters had supplied.

"Aren't you nice!" said Fanny. "What a pity we're here on business!"

Entering the lounge, they were shown to a table adjoining the dancing floor. A blue haze of smoke filled the air, and over the disturbing hum of many voices, the fiddles sang, the saxophones moaned and the drums beat softly.

Fanny said to Lee, "They are directly in front of you, Pop, about 30 feet away. Little table alongside the wall, shaded candle on it. She is wearing a doll's hat that seems to be sliding down in front."

So this was the much-wanted Slim Markoe! Lee saw a pleasant-looking young fellow with tawny hair, quite as well turned out as the other men in the place. He was wearing an expensive brown suit, soft white collar and orange tie—the kind of lad who looks 23 until after he has passed 30; only his experienced, mirthful eyes betrayed his real age. He was slim to the point of leanness, but there was muscle in his long limbs, and every movement was instinct with grace. He was not handsome—his features were somewhat miscellaneous, and there were deep lines between nostrils and lips, suggesting a high degree of sensuality. He was no less attractive to women for that—not with those good-humored eyes and that engaging grin. Lee could not see the girl's face because she had her back to him; Slim's masterful air suggested that he had obtained a complete ascendancy over her.

"Where did he get his fine clothes?" asked Lee.

"She bought them for him," said Fanny. "Shortly after two o'clock the Torrey car came dashing back to the house. I suppose

Slim had phoned the girl. She was so impatient she waited for the car on the sidewalk. She was no longer bored. She dismissed her car at Marshall Field's and as soon as it had gone, she came out of the store again and met Slim around the corner. He looked fairly neat, had been shaved and got his hair cut, but his clothes had been slept in for a couple of nights, so she called a taxi and took him for a round of the most expensive men's shops to buy that outfit."

"Times have changed!" said Lee, shaking his head. "No girl ever bought me a suit of clothes when I was young!"

"We have a name for that sort of lad," said the young detective.

"He dances divinely!" put in Fanny with a sigh.

"What became of his old clothes?" said Lee. "That's important."

"They took their packages to a small hotel on the South side where Slim engaged a room. The girl waited in the taxi while Slim went upstairs and changed. The old clothes were left there. Then they drove to this hotel."

"We don't want to make a scene here," said Lee. "I'll go over and speak to them. If I get him started for the door you follow and take him in charge outside. I'll look after the girl. Wait for me in a taxi at the door."

"Shall I put the cuffs on him?" asked the detective.

"Not unless he tries to make a break."

Lee toddled over to the other table as if he had suddenly discovered friends. "Why, how do you do!" he said. "So nice to see you again!"

"Guess again, friend," said Slim coolly. "I never saw you in my life."

Miss Torrey looked bored.

Lee lowered his voice. "My name is Amos Lee Mappin. I am sorry to break up your party, but this young man must come with me."

Slim started violently. "What the hell!"

"Quiet!" murmured Lee. "Let's not start anything here for the young lady's sake. If you doubt my authority, there is a member of the Chicago police force at the table I have just left, who has a warrant in his pocket and will show you his shield if you insist."

Slim hesitated, snarling. He glanced over at the detective, who had somewhat the air of a dog straining at the leash, and decided to obey. He got up without a glance at the girl, and marched out of the lounge. The detective and Fanny followed him. Lee slid into the chair he had vacated. It was all done so quietly that nobody's attention was attracted.

The girl had lost her haughty and sophisticated air. Her head was down. "Where are they taking him?" she stammered.

Lee's glance softened; she was so young—and so foolish! "To Police Headquarters for questioning," he said offhandedly. "It's not a hanging matter. But, oh, my dear, don't do it again! This young blackguard lives off women!"

"Let me get out of here!" she gasped.

"Take it easy! Have you paid the check?"

"No."

"Allow me to do it. Then I'll go with you and put you in a cab, and no harm done! But you've had a narrow escape!"

When he had sent the girl home, Lee joined his friends waiting in another taxi, and they started for Headquarters. The three men sat on the rear seat, the prisoner in the middle, and Fanny sat sideways on one of the small seats in front.

Slim asked nonchalantly, "What's the charge? My conscience is clear."

"You'll be told in good time," said Lee.

After that Slim, ignored his captors, gave himself up to the pleasure of looking at pretty Fanny. "Say," he said with his attractive impudence, "where you from?"

"Shut up!" rasped the detective.

"Oh, let him talk," said Lee mildly.

"Where you from?" repeated Slim.

"New York," said Fanny, dimpling.

"I knew it!" he cried. "There's a certain something about a New York girl you can't mistake! Say, what are you doing with these bulls?"

"I'm a bull myself," said Fanny, "or perhaps I should say a heifer!"

"Fanny!" said Lee reprovingly.

"I don't believe it," cried Slim. "You're far too good for such work. Say, you've got twice the class of that jane in the Mannering, and she's one of these here now debutantes. On the level, the bulls have got nothing on me. When I clear myself will you come out with me some time?"

"All right," said Fanny.

The young detective appeared to be ready to burst. "Mr. Mappin," he said in a strangled voice.

"Here we are!" said Lee.

While Slim waited outside the Commissioner's office, a detective was dispatched to the hotel where he had taken a room to search his effects. When Slim was brought before the Commissioner, he demanded to know what charge there was against him.

"Unlawful entry."

"Entry into what, for God's sake?"

"The apartment of René Doria on 46th Street, New York."

Slim was momentarily taken aback, but quickly recovered himself. "There's nothing to it! Never was inside the joint and you can't prove it."

"Then why were you in such a hurry to get out of New York?" asked Lee.

"Well. I'll tell you, Captain," said Slim with his derisive grin. "I been playing round with a dame called Rose Bosi, see? The one who claimed to be the wife of René Doria. It was all right as long as she had a husband, but when he was liquidated I thought I better get out while the getting was good. No wedding bells for me!"

"Even if she was worth half a million?" suggested Lee.

"Well, I admit that might alter the case."

"That's about what Rose stands to inherit."

"Now ain't that too bad?" drawled Slim. "Too late to try to patch it up with her now."

Slim steadfastly denied knowing anything about the $100,000. He asserted that he had had less than a dollar in his pocket on leaving New York. A fellow on the road had staked him to a couple of cheap meals, and had loaned him a dollar to get a haircut, shave and bath in Chicago. The $10 bill they found on him had been given him by Rachel Torrey to pay the check at the Mannering.

"Would I take money off a girl if I had any of my own?" he demanded virtuously.

"You knew it would be dangerous to try to change a $1000 bill."

"Not in Chicago," said Slim grinning. "I know just where to go. Of course, I'd have to take a heavy discount, but what would I care if I had 99 more?"

Questioning Slim was a tedious business. He told what sounded like a straight story of his movements since leaving New York.

"It was about 10:30 Thursday morning that I got the notion to beat it. I took a ferry over to Jersey, and stood on the curb thumbing West until a guy picked me up. I was in luck because he was going right through to Philly, and a fast driver at that. In the afternoon I got a couple of short hitches along Route 30, and then a guy took me to Harrisburg. Thursday night I slept in a barn. All day Friday I was hitching West until evening when I was picked up by a truck driving right through to Chicago. The guy was glad, when he found I was a driver myself, so I could spell him while he slept."

"Do you mean to tell me," put in Lee, "that he picked up a stranger on the road, and was willing to trust him to drive while he slept?"

"Sure! Why not? He watched me first until he could see I was an experienced driver. Everybody ain't as suspicious as the police, Captain. On the road a man learns to give and take."

"Go ahead."

"We made such good time we was able to lay off in Gary this morning for a good sleep. When I was on the truck, I didn't go in with the driver when he stopped for lunch and he asked me if I never ate, and when I told him I was flat, he set me up a couple of lunches. We got to Chicago at one o'clock and when I told him I had friends here he loaned me a dollar to fix myself up. I had a haircut, a shave and a bath in a barbershop. I telephoned the girl from the same place, and quarter of an hour later I met her."

Slim then described his movements with Rachel Torrey which Fanny could corroborate. He named the barbershop where the truck had dropped him, and also furnished the Chicago address of the driver with whom he had ridden all night. Cross-examination failed to develop any holes in his story, and when the detective returned to say that there was nothing in Slim's room but his old clothes, Lee was forced to believe that he never had had his hands on the $100,000. It was a serious disappointment.

As to his movements on the night of the murder, Slim told a rambling tale of drinking in various bars with men who were strange to him. This part of his story was almost certainly untrue, but Lee had no means of checking it.

"Are you willing to waive extradition and come back to New York with me?" Lee asked.

Slim considered it. "Why not?" he said. "You haven't got a thing on me. Is she going?" he added with a jerk of his head toward Fanny.

"Yes."

"When?"

"We'll take the night plane for New York."

"Okay by me," said Slim. "I've never ridden in one of those fancy airliners."

In the plane Lee applied himself to drawing Slim out as to his mode of life. It was not very difficult to do so. Slim said with good-humored cynicism:

"It's simple to make these young girls fall for you, Captain. They're always glad to stand you meals and drinks or an outfit like this so they can go around with you without attracting attention; and they'll hand out a ten or a twenty if you give them a good line. You see these rich girls are kept pretty close when they're kids, and as soon as they begin to go about they want to see life. It's exciting to them to be picked up by a tough like me, and to meet him on the sly and go places. But it don't get a guy anywhere. They're not going to damage their social position by marrying a tough. So I'm no better off than I was five years ago. I'm looking for a way to settle myself. My boyish charm won't last forever."

Later, dozing in the cabin, Lee was diverted by watching Slim's efforts to make a conquest of Fanny across the aisle. With his sly tongue, his merry eye, and his insinuating grin, there was something damnably attractive about the fellow. Slim changed his style, of course, according to the type he was dealing with. Lee suspected that he was telling Fanny the story of his ill-spent life and Fanny was enjoying it. However, Fanny was no debutante, and Lee fell asleep confident that this was one pretty head that would not be lost.

CHAPTER TWELVE
POSITIVE IDENTIFICATION

On Sunday morning in New York Slim Markoe passed successfully through the ordeal of the line-up at Police Headquarters. He had no police record in New York, and the Inspector, who quizzed him, was not able to bring out any further damaging facts. Later, however, the police produced the taxi driver who had put down René Doria at the 46th Street corner on the fatal Tuesday night, and this man positively identified Slim as the man he had seen following René through 46th Street. Slim was not allowed to learn the significance of this identification, and his confident smile remained unchanged.

In the afternoon Lee had the notion of confronting Slim with Rose, hoping that the truth might come out, and Rose was brought down to Headquarters. Rose faced the grinning Slim with blazing eyes, but the result was the exact contrary of what Lee wished for. Slim not only succeeded in convincing Rose that he had never cast covetous eyes on the hundred grand, he went on with his caressing voice to melt her completely, and to reawaken the passion she had felt for him in the beginning. The upshot was that Rose begged the police with streaming eyes to release Slim.

When she had gone, Lee said to Loasby with a shake of his head, "I would not have believed it unless I had seen it myself—this average, sprawling kid, this grinning loafer, this long-legged bum, has a devilish power over women. How do you account for it?"

"Don't ask me," said Loasby. "I can't explain it, never having been able to charm the sex myself."

Slim, having come through with flying colors, now began to demand his release, and to talk vaguely and threateningly of *habeas corpus*. Lee said to Loasby:

"Let's tell him what we have on him now, and see if that won't break him down."

When Slim was brought into the Inspector's office for the third time that day, he said without waiting for the officer to speak, "Well, are you going to let me out now? This is a free country and you have absolutely nothing against me!"

"I'm going to tell you what we have against you," said Loasby, "and you can judge for yourself. We know that on Tuesday evening you followed René Doria from the Second Avenue house to the Brocklin mansion, and later that night from the Brocklin mansion to his hide-out on 46th."

"How do you know it?"

"A taxi driver has positively identified you as the man he saw following René through 46th Street."

Slim began to be impressed and the grin faded.

"We know further," Loasby continued, "that in some way you discovered that the door of 18 Lancaster Court was not locked. You went in there. It is an unoccupied apartment. You discovered the scuttle in the roof and went up that way. You wrenched up the scuttle of Number 16, René's apartment, and entered. To cover your tracks you filled the screw holes with chewing gum and put back the screws so that the scuttle looked intact."

Slim had grown pale. "This is all guesswork!" he cried. "You have no proof that it was me!"

"You left a perfect set of fingerprints on the scuttle of 18."

"Why should I want to shove off René Doria?"

"For the hundred grand. A very handsome stake."

Slim looked around him. He was breathing hard. "Can I sit down?" he asked.

"Sure. Take your time. What we want to know is, what happened after you got into René's flat? So come clean!"

Slim took a long breath. Soon the irrepressible grin came back, "Okay, Inspector. But it's not what you think, It wasn't me smoked

René Doria, nor did I lay hands on his money. René had plenty of
other visitors on Tuesday night and I saw them. I'm in the position
to help you solve this case."

"Well, shoot!" said Loasby.

"Wait a minute! What are you going to do for me? There's this
charge hanging over my head. I did break in, but I didn't get
anything and I didn't do no harm. Will you drop it if I tell all I
know?"

"I can't bargain with you. It would destroy the value of your
evidence in court. The police always do what they can for those
who help them."

Slim abruptly started his story. "René Doria had been to Mrs.
Wetzel's flat on Second Avenue twice before Tuesday. I watched
him and listened to all he said, but he didn't know about me, of
course. If he thought Rose had another boy friend, he would never
have come across. Believe it or not, he was still crazy about Rose.
She had something that none of his swell dames could give him.

"On Tuesday evening about seven he come again. He was
carrying a little satchel that I supposed had the hundred grand in
it that he promised Rose. Rose had gone out to the store. The
landlady tried to get him to wait, but he wouldn't. Said he'd come
back Wednesday. My God! I hated to see that money go back down
the stairs, but what could I do? It was so damn foolish for anybody
to carry a hundred grand through that tough neighborhood in a
satchel! I didn't know what might happen. So I followed him just
to protect him if anybody tried to snatch it."

Lee and Loasby grinned, and Slim grinned back in perfect good
humor.

"I followed him to the Brocklin house just as you said," Slim
continued, "and I waited four hours outside there for him to come
out, and didn't have no dinner. I didn't have sense enough to realize
it was a party and he'd be there all that time. I was afraid he'd give
me the slip. He finally appeared about 11:30, still carrying the
satchel, and I followed him to a drug store on 59th where he
telephoned, and afterward in another cab to the corner of 46th and
Third. From there he walked to the flat, with me following on the

other side of the street. He went through into the garden, and I took a squint around the corner of the passage and saw him let himself in at the door of Number 16 with a key.

"I took it was his own place since he had the key to it, a hide-out because I knew he didn't live there regularly. The windows were dark until he went up and turned on lights. Well, if he was going to make a night of it, I was all the more worried about that cash. I thought he might get drunk or lose it or something, or give it to another woman. It was on Rose's account I was worried. I made up my mind the money would be safer in my hands, and I began to plan how I could get hold of it. For Rose."

"Very commendable." murmured Lee.

"In the garden there was a bush in front of René's door, and I squatted behind it. It seemed to me it would be no great job to climb up the outside of the house by the balconies and the vines, if only the windows wasn't all locked when I got up there. Before I could try, a woman come into the court walking fast, and damned if she didn't let herself in at the door of 16 with a key."

"Could you identify her?" asked Loasby eagerly.

"I guess so. It was dark, but she passed within 15 feet of me. A little woman, quick and nervous."

"Go on."

"Well, the woman's coming sort of crabbed my game. I decided I couldn't do anything until they settled down. I knew that would take quite a while, so I went over to Third Avenue where I got myself a good feed. I also bought a little pocket flashlight to use later. I was gone 40 minutes or so. The lights were still on in René's windows. I hadn't much more than settled myself behind my bush again when René had another visitor. This was a tall, slim guy, but not young; a swell guy in a topper and white gloves."

Lee and Loasby exchanged a glance.

"Well, this guy didn't seem to know just what he was after," Slim continued. "He walks up and down; he goes out into the garden to look up at René's windows, and I had to press right into my bush to keep out of his sight. Then he walks some more, lighting one cigarette after another and throwing them away as soon as lighted. Finally he took up his stand in the doorway of 18, waiting and watching. He didn't realize it, but his white muffler and gloves was showing up in the dark. Me, I was getting pretty discouraged, but I thought I'd see it through.

"Pretty soon another guy comes into the court. This was a classy guy, too. He had on a black soft hat, and when his overcoat blew open I could see his big white shirt front and a flower in his buttonhole. He was pretty heavy-built but not fat; I couldn't tell you his age but he walked heavy, not like a young fellow. Yeah, I would know him again. This one knew what he wanted. He went direct to the door of 16 and pushed the button. There was no answer at first and he pushed it again. After a bit the door opens and I see René in his bathrobe. There was a few words I couldn't hear, then the guy went in and the door closed. I couldn't figure this out at all, because generally when a fellow has a girl with him, he ain't so glad to see his friends. The slim guy in the next doorway pressed back and never made a move.

"In a little while, maybe 10 minutes, the door opens again and out comes the little woman in a hell of a hurry. She closes the door real soft and hot-foots it for the street. She was the slim guy's mark, it seemed it was her he was waiting for. He follows her out and I don't see either of them again.

"After he left the doorway of 18, I crossed over to it because it was closer. I didn't have nothing white on to show me up in the dark. I put my hand behind me and tried the door handle, I couldn't tell you why, and the door opened. I flashed my light inside and seen that it was a vacant apartment, and it come to me that it would be a lot safer to cross over from balcony to balcony instead of trying to climb up outside. So I figured to try it, but I couldn't do nothing until that other guy left, so I waited some more. And after a while he come out."

"One minute," interrupted Lee. "How long was this man in René's apartment?"

"I couldn't tell you exactly, Captain. Maybe it wasn't as long as it seemed to me, waiting there. Something under a half hour."

"Did you notice anything peculiar about him when he left?"

"Can't say as I did, Captain. He didn't want to be seen because he stuck his head out of the door to take a look before he showed himself. He wasn't drunk because he walked perfectly straight. He held his head down as if he was thinking things over."

"Go on."

"Well, when he went, that left René alone in his flat, but I didn't know what he would do so I waited to see. He might sleep there the rest of the night, or he might take it in his head to go home to his regular flat. His windows was still lighted up."

Loasby put in dryly, "If he had come out still carrying the satchel that quiet court would have been an ideal place to try a snatch, eh?" He glanced at Slim's long legs. "You're a pretty good runner, I take it."

"You do me wrong, Inspector," protested Slim, but his derisive grin belied his words.

"Well, go ahead."

"I waited what seemed like a hell of a time," said Slim, "but René never come out, never turned out his lights. So I figured that he'd been drinking and had gone to sleep and left the lights on, and I decided to go up and have a look.

"From the garden I had seen that the windows of his flat which opened on the balcony were both closed. I didn't have no glass-cutter, and if they were locked it would have made too much noise to break the glass, so I went up to the top of the house to have a look at the scuttle. These old-type houses with flat roofs always have a scuttle. I unhooked it and went over the roof to the scuttle of 16. I prized it up without making no noise to speak of. The wood was old and soft and the screws drew right out."

"What did you prize it up with?" asked Loasby.

"Coming back from Third Avenue I had passed an old house with an iron rail to the steps. I seen that one of the bars under the rail was loose and I worked it out and took it. I went down the ladder into René's apartment. It was dark then. René had gone home, I thought. Every room was empty. The bed had not been disturbed. But when I opened the door of the bedroom closet and seen his clothes hanging there it gave me a nasty turn. His overcoat, his tail-coat, his topper, his patent leather shoes, just what I had seen him wearing. If the bathrobe had been there I would have thought he kept other clothes in the place, but the bathrobe was gone.

"The satchel lay on the floor of the closet and it was empty. God! All that trouble for nothing. I was scared as hell, too. I smelled murder in it. I fixed the scuttle the way you know, and beat it. If I'd had my right senses I'd have gone into 18 again to hook that scuttle on the inside and you would never have known anything. But I only thought of getting out of the place. I never thought I could be traced back to it. That's my story."

"Which may or may not be true," said Loasby.

Slim shrugged. "You can't disprove it."

"What did you do with the iron bar?"

"Dropped it down the first sewer opening I come to—at the corner of 46th and Second."

"You say the place smelled of murder," put in Lee softly. "What do you mean by that?"

"It was just a way of speaking, Captain. I didn't smell nothing out of the way." Slim's grin was suddenly wiped out. "But maybe I did without knowing it—fresh blood!"

"You read the papers, I suppose. Did you mark anything different in the description of the apartment as it was found next morning?"

"No, Captain. It was just as I had seen it; the dirty dishes in the kitchen and all."

Both Loasby and Lee cross-examined Slim at some length without shaking his story. Finally Slim was taken out of the room.

"Damn!" said Loasby. "Then there's nothing in Beckman Vosper's confession! That's going to make us look foolish."

Lee took a pinch of snuff. "It will make Vosper look much more foolish than us—if Slim's story is true."

"How can we check it?"

"I suggest we confront him with the various persons he says he saw that night. Mrs. Vosper, to start with. We couldn't get her to come to Headquarters unless we dragged her, but if you'll send Slim to my office under guard, I'll get her there."

"Okay."

"After that we'll take him to the Tombs and after that—well, you know where!"

"That's not going to be easy," growled Loasby.

Lee drove uptown to the Vosper house. Since Beckman Vosper had made his confession and his wife's association with the case was public knowledge, Mrs. Vosper had gone into strict seclusion. Lee, however, was counting on feminine curiosity to bring her downstairs, and it did. Since everything was known as far as she was concerned, her line now was to brazen it out. With a face as hard as flint, she wasted no time in polite phrases. "What do you want of me?"

Lee was open with her. "A new witness in the Doria case has turned up. If his story is true, it will clear your husband of all complicity in the murder."

Mrs. Vosper sneered. "I could clear him myself."

"Quite," said Lee. "But a wife's testimony does not carry much weight with a jury. To try Mr. Vosper would be farcical, and I want to stop it. But before I can do so, I must test the truth of this man's story."

"What is his story?" she asked.

"He had learned that Doria was carrying a big sum of money, and he was following him about, looking for a chance to rob him. He claims that he saw you come to Lancaster Court and leave again; that Mr. Vosper followed you there, and followed you away when you left."

Mrs. Vosper twisted her bracelet. "What can I do about it?" she asked indifferently.

"Come to my office with me. He'll be there. If he recognizes you as the woman he saw, it will prove he was there."

"And there will be a new sensation for the newspapers," she said bitterly. "With photographs."

"In my office, there will be no reporters, no photographers, and no police—except the guard who brings the witness. I have kept my word with you so far," Lee reminded her.

"All right," she said with bitter irony, "I want to do my duty as a citizen. I'll go with you."

Fifteen minutes later they entered Lee's office. Slim was sitting there under the eye of a Headquarters detective, making himself at home. Having straddled a chair, he was leaning his arms on the back, carrying on a brisk flirtation with Fanny and Judy. Both girls, Lee noticed, while they affected to treat him with scorn, were bending warm glances on him. When Mrs. Vosper entered, Slim transferred the mocking challenge of his grin to her simply because she was a woman. All were fish who came to Slim's net. To Lee's astonishment, Mrs. Vosper looked away.

The two girls, who had been tipped off in advance, greeted Mrs. Vosper as "Mrs. Jackson." Lee led her into his private room and seated her in such a position that Slim could still see her through the open door. She was uneasy under his gaze.

"Who is he?" she murmured.

"A loafer, a hitchhiker, a bum," answered Lee with more than a little bitterness.

"I mean his name."

"We know him as Slim Markoe."

"Do you think," she asked with glittering eyes, "he killed René?"

"Frankly, I don't know. It is quite possible."

"How amazing!" she murmured. As if against her will, her eyes were dragged around to Slim again. Slim enveloped her with his mocking grin.

After a moment or two Lee let Mrs. Vosper out through the side door into the corridor. He returned to the front room affecting to ignore Slim. Slim had not been told why he had been brought there. He spoke up.

"Mr. Mappin, I don't know if it is of any particular interest to you, but that little woman is the same one who visited René Doria on Tuesday night."

"How can you be sure?" said Lee. "It was dark."

"I'm ready to swear to it," insisted Slim. "The nervous way she twists her shoulders, the quick turn of the head. She's no ordinary woman."

"Let's go back to Headquarters," said Lee.

The District Attorney had been requested to have Beekman Vosper brought to Inspector Loasby's office, and soon after Lee and Slim got there, he arrived, accompanied by a guard and one of the Assistant District Attorneys, who was curious to learn what new evidence the police had turned up. Before Vosper was confronted with Slim, two or three men were picked up around Headquarters who resembled the prisoner in a general way, and the whole party came into Loasby's office together. Unlike most men, the tall, elegant Beekman Vosper displayed an almost childish anxiety to ingratiate himself with the plainclothes men who surrounded him—guards, police, reporters, and so on. The sight of Slim, however, made him anxious because he could not guess what this new witness portended.

"Slim," said Inspector Loasby. "Have you ever seen any of these men before?"

Slim looked them over. After a moment he pointed to Vosper. "That is the man I saw in Lancaster Court last Tuesday night."

A look of plain fright came into Vosper's face. Loasby made Slim turn his back while he shuffled the men around. When he was invited to pick him out again, Slim went direct to Vosper. "This is the guy."

The extras left the room.

Loasby addressed Slim, "Are you prepared to swear that this man never entered René Doria's apartment on Tuesday night?"

"Absolutely, Inspector. He come into the court alone. He hid himself in a doorway until the woman come out of René's apartment, and then he followed her away from the place."

"He lies!" faltered Vosper, with a white face. "I can't imagine what his object is in lying!"

"Neither can I," said Loasby dryly. He nodded to the guard and Slim was taken outside. "What's the use of keeping up this pretense, Mr. Vosper?" Loasby went on harshly. "We know you followed your wife home. You couldn't have killed the man and cleaned up the place and got home 10 or 15 minutes after she did."

Vosper dropped in a chair and covered his face with his hands. "Oh, God! What will the newspapers say?"

"What shall we do with him?" asked the perplexed Assistant District Attorney.

"Turn him loose," said Lee.

"We can't do that!"

Loasby rose. Scowling and peremptory, the handsome Inspector typified the offended majesty of the law. "Tell the truth, Mr. Vosper! This farce has gone too far! What *did* you do on Tuesday night?"

Vosper was completely broken. "I'll tell," he stammered. Loasby signed to his clerk to take down his statement. "I lied when I said I killed René Doria. A kind of hysterical impulse impelled me to say I did. I wanted to justify myself for living. I was never inside his apartment. I had been having my wife followed for some time. I knew she went to the 46th Street place to meet Doria, and on Tuesday night when I heard she had left the Waldorf suddenly, I guessed that was where she had gone, and I followed her. I wanted evidence that would give me a divorce without having to pay alimony. I was sick of having her spend my money while she deceived me to my face. I raised her up from nothing when I married her. When I saw her come out of René's place at that hour I was satisfied I had her. That's all."

Nobody in the room spoke while this brief statement was being typed. After signing the statement, Vosper was led away.

"Hadn't we better keep him in custody for a while longer?" asked the young Assistant D.A. anxiously. "If you could produce the real murderer the release of Vosper would pass unnoticed, and the authorities would not be placed in such a—such a—" he paused for the right word.

"Such a ridiculous light," put in Lee with an innocent air.

"I was thinking of the public," said the young man with dignity. "It has a very bad effect on the public when the authorities are shown to be not infallible."

Lee shrugged. "That's up to you and the Inspector."

"It doesn't matter," said Loasby confidently. "I expect to have the real murderer within an hour."

Lee took a pinch of snuff audibly.

When the young man had left, Lee glanced at his watch. "Five-thirty," he said. "I take it you mean to follow the matter right through."

Alone with Lee, the Inspector looked a good deal less sure of himself. "Damn! I don't like this. How do you suggest I ought to proceed?"

Lee, not without malice, affected to be surprised. "Why you're an Inspector of Police! And no citizen in the eyes of the law is above any other!"

"Of course!" said Loasby hastily. "You'll come with me?"

"I wouldn't miss it!" murmured Lee.

Inspector Loasby, Lee, Slim Markoe and three detectives drove uptown to the Brocklin mansion in a police car. Slim had the air of a young fellow on a holiday. He kept the detectives laughing with his wisecracks. When they arrived in front of the big house, he was left sitting in the car under guard while the others went up the steps. The young footman who opened the door tried in futile fashion to bar ingress, but the Inspector pushed in, saying:

"I want to see Mr. Brocklin."

"He's—he's not at home, sir," stammered the footman.

"Don't lie to me," said Loasby sternly, "or you'll find yourself on the wrong side of a barred door. The house has been watched for the past 72 hours, and Mr. Brocklin has not left it."

Wilton, the butler, came hurrying forward. "Please pardon the man, Inspector. He is only following instructions. The truth is, my master is too ill to see anybody."

"Kindly tell Mr. Brocklin," said Loasby dryly, "that if he is unable to come downstairs, we will go up to his bedroom."

Wilton went away softly and the others waited. The scared young footman watched them from the rear of the hall, and the faces of maids peeped around the stairs.

In a little while Dexter Brocklin, wearing a dressing gown of blue and orange brocade, appeared on the wide stairway leaning heavily on the arm of Wilton. Lee noted that he was fully dressed beneath the gaudy robe. He looked sick enough, but Lee guessed that it was the sickness of fear. His daughter and his sister followed

him—Peggy stony and tight-lipped, Mrs. Thorne wringing her hands
and ceaselessly protesting.

"He can scarcely stand! It's cruel to make him come downstairs
in such a state! My poor brother! As if he hadn't suffered enough
already!" And so on.

"Be quiet!" said Peggy savagely under her breath. "You're
making a fool of yourself!"

Brocklin, with a ghastly attempt to appear humorous and at
ease, said, "Inspector, I'd be glad to know the reason for this
descent in force on an inoffensive family."

Loasby replied, "Mr. Brocklin, I have to ask you to assist me in
the performance of my duty. I could have had you brought down
to Headquarters, but it seemed more considerate to come here."

"How ominous that sounds. How can I assist you?"

"I want you to put on the topcoat and the hat you are accustomed to wear out-of-doors in the evening."

Brocklin stared at him blankly.

Without giving him time to protest, Loasby went on to Wilton,
"Please fetch Mr. Brocklin's hat and coat."

The butler hesitated. "Mr. Brocklin has many hats and coats,
Inspector."

"Please show me where they are kept."

Wilton looked at his master. Brocklin blustered feebly, but he
had not the strength of will to resist Loasby's official manner.
Wilton led Loasby to a coatroom opening off the hall. When they
returned the Inspector was carrying a plain black coat of medium
weight and a black velour hat.

"Put these on, if you please," he said to Brocklin.

"Really, sir!" stammered Brocklin, and the women broke out
indignantly, "What does this mean? In our own house? I never
heard of such a thing!" And so on.

Nevertheless Brocklin had to obey.

"Now if you will be good enough to step outside."

A look of childish terror came over Brocklin's flabby face. He
clung to Wilton. "I will not! Where are you taking me? What does
this mean?"

Loasby said, "I have a witness outside who claims he saw a man answering to your description in Lancaster Court after midnight on Tuesday. If you were in your bed you have nothing to fear, Mr. Brocklin."

Brocklin, with a look of ghastly fear, accompanied Loasby and the two detectives to the door. His knees gave a little with every step. Lee remained standing in the hall. Brocklin and his conductors went outside and stood on the top step for a moment or two. The crowd standing around the foot of the steps gaped at the group wonderingly. In the car below Slim leaned forward and studied Brocklin. The two detectives then led Brocklin back into the house and Loasby went down the steps to consult with Slim.

Inside the house Mrs. Thorne was still vociferously expressing her indignation. The two detectives quailed under the lash of her tongue and looked anxiously behind them for their boss. Loasby presently followed them in. He said,

"A positive identification has been made. My witness is prepared to swear that he saw Mr. Brocklin entering René Doria's apartment late Tuesday night. He remained there for half an hour or more."

Brocklin looked at him piteously. "No! No!" he stammered. "It is all a mistake—appearances are against me! I did not—oh, God! This is awful!" He turned to his daughter. "Peggy, I beg you not to—" His voice failed him. He slumped, and Wilton caught him in his arms. Mrs. Thorne screamed.

CHAPTER THIRTEEN
SLIPPERY SLIM

ON SUNDAY EVENING Mr. Dexter Brocklin, a figure in social life second only to his daughter, was lodged in the Tombs Prison like any common malefactor, and the printing presses were roaring afresh. The most expensive legal talent was instantly engaged on his behalf, and acting under their advice, Mr. Brocklin refused to make any statement whatsoever. The police did not care to bring pressure to bear on a man of Mr. Brocklin's position, and no effort was made to obtain a confession.

His servants, the butler Wilton, and the valet Cockey, were not so fortunate. Loasby, fearing that they might be spirited out of his jurisdiction, immediately took them into custody as material witnesses, and after several strenuous hours at Headquarters he obtained their stories. They were not mishandled—such methods have gone out of fashion, but hard-faced questioners brought up in relays are no less effective. Wilton and Cockey broke down, and the stories they told corroborated that of Slim.

A phone call for Mr. Brocklin had been received about midnight on Tuesday. Wilton took it in his office downstairs and switched it up to Cockey in the dressing-room. Both servants said that it sounded like a disguised voice; it might have been a woman speaking huskily or a man trying to speak like a woman. Cockey told the unknown that Mr. Brocklin had gone to bed, and was about to hang up when the person said he had a message about Mr. Doria. Cockey knew, of course, of his master's anger at the engagement of his daughter. It was René Doria's habit to be insolent and over-bearing with servants, and they all hated him and sympathized with their master. Consequently Cockey decided he had better give Mr. Brocklin the message.

Mr. Brocklin went to the phone. The message was brief. Cockey had not heard it, but Wilton was forced to confess that he had listened in at the switchboard downstairs. The voice had said:

"Here's an interesting piece of information for you, Mr. Brocklin. I suppose you've heard of René Doria's love nest. Wouldn't you like to know the address? It is in Lancaster Court, and the number of his apartment is 16. The place is so arranged that you can go direct to his door without meeting any hall men or elevator boys. He is entertaining a lady there at this moment. He went directly from your house to meet her. I thought perhaps you would like to catch him in the act. Your stubborn daughter could hardly refuse to see the truth then. Listen! When you get to the door ring one long and three short. That's his private code and he will let you in." The voice repeated the address and hung up.

Mr. Brocklin immediately dressed and left the house. When he had gone the two servants compared notes and discovered he had taken his revolver with him. After they had spent an hour of anxiety, Mr. Brocklin returned, "looking like a ghost," they said. He said nothing to either of them. Cockey, searching through his clothes, discovered he had not brought the gun back with him. Throughout the night Cockey heard him tossing and groaning in his bed.

Meanwhile, at Headquarters Mr. Brocklin had been fingerprinted, and Inspector Loasby's triumph was complete when it was shown that the prints were identical with those upon the gun found under René's body. Cockey, the valet, had already admitted this was his master's gun.

Late Sunday night Loasby dropped into Lee's apartment to tell him all this.

"By God! what a load off my mind!" cried Loasby when he finally rose to go. "I'll sleep tonight. I haven't had a good night's rest since Tuesday."

Lee merely looked down his nose.

"Haven't you anything to say?" demanded Loasby. "Aren't you satisfied that the case is closed?"

"I don't want to spoil your night's rest," said Lee.

"You couldn't do that. We have a perfect case against Brocklin. The phone call Tuesday night, the testimony of the servants, the gun, Slim Markoe's testimony, Mrs. Vosper's story—it all fits."

"Too perfect," murmured Lee.

"Why, Brocklin as good as admitted it."

"I was thinking of that. Somehow that cry, 'Appearances are against me!' doesn't sound like a guilty man."

"They'll say anything when they're cornered."

"Sure, sure. But I don't feel satisfied that our work is done. Who called the enraged father to the phone on Tuesday night? There's the real criminal!"

"I agree," said Loasby, "but as police we can't go behind the hand that pulled the trigger."

"And where's the hundred grand? Certainly Brocklin wouldn't have taken it."

"Probably Slim Markoe has it cached away."

"Possibly, but nothing shows that he has."

"Well, the disappearance of the hundred grand is a serious matter, but the murder is the main thing, and I, I mean we, have proved that. Good night."

"Good night." said Lee. "Pleasant dreams."

Lee settled down to his book again, but it presently appeared that he was not yet through with the case for the night. He was called to the telephone, and he heard the crisp voice of Beau Gramercy on the wire.

"That you, Lee? I've just been reading the latest news of the Doria case. What a story! Like one of those Chinese puzzles. Every time you open a box there's another box inside."

"Quite," said Lee. "But you've got to come to the last box in the end."

"Poor old Dexter Brocklin!" (Brocklin was at least 20 years younger than the speaker.) "I think it's a shame! However, no jury will convict him."

"I'm not so sure about that. If he took his gun and went out after the man, it is certainly willful murder."

"If his lawyer is smart enough to get some fathers on the jury he'll be all right. If your daughter had been bewitched by a scoundrel like Doria, wouldn't you want to go out and shoot him, Lee?"

"I can't say," said Lee. "I haven't any daughter."

"Look, Lee." (Lee understood from his tone that the Beau had now come to his real purpose in calling.) "Who is this mysterious new witness that the police have dug up?"

"I can't tell you that, Houson. For obvious reasons they have to keep him under cover."

"All right. The paper said Dexter Brocklin would be arraigned in a magistrate's court in the morning. Which court is it?"

"First district, ten o'clock."

"There'll be an awful mob applying for admission. Will you take me in with you, Lee?"

Lee smiled into the receiver. "It will be just a matter of form, Houson. He will waive examination and no evidence will be presented."

"I know, but I want to paint a little word picture of him in the dock for my column."

"Very well," said Lee good-naturedly. "Will you pick me up here at 9:45?"

"Right! See you in the morning, and thanks."

As Beau Gramercy had foreseen, the magistrate's court was crowded to the doors, and a mob unable to gain admission waited in the street. Lee and Beau Gramercy entered through a private door and were shown to seats in the front row. The little columnist, bright-eyed as a bird, was taking everything in. "The first time I've been in such a place. How it smells!" He put a scented handkerchief to his nose. Presently he called Lee's attention to the fact that the majority of spectators were women.

"Partisans of René's," said Lee. "They have come to see him avenged."

"Extraordinary!" murmured the Beau. "The influence René had over women who had never even laid eyes on him!"

"They read the newspapers," said Lee.

"Don't look right away," whispered the little man; "in the fourth row behind us against the wall across the room—Vida Cadbury, as I'm a sinner!"

Lee had already spotted Miss Cadbury, but after a moment he affected to look with surprise. Vida this morning was wearing the ordinary dress of a woman, which sat on her very oddly. She had on a comic pill-box hat with a veil hanging down in front.

"What on earth brings her here?" said the Beau.

"Morbid curiosity, I suppose."

"Why the disguise?"

"Oh, her face is pretty well known, and naturally she doesn't want to be recognized."

When Dexter Brocklin was led in a curious little sound escaped from the women spectators, and Lee frowned. It gratified the women to believe that Brocklin had slain their idol, and they were prepared to sacrifice him. The man had a wild and haggard expression; he looked as if he had lost 10 pounds overnight. He no longer cared for his personal appearance.

"The picture of guilt!" murmured Beau Gramercy.

The proceedings did not last five minutes. Brocklin, through his expensive lawyer, waived examination, and no evidence was presented. Since the charge was murder in the first degree, he was inadmissible to bail, and was returned to the Tombs to await trial.

"Well, that's all," said Lee.

The long-legged Slim Markoe was led in from the prisoners' pen. His blue eyes were liquid with mirth, and the incorrigible grin was etched around his lips. A stir went through the spectators. It was like the entrance of a favorite actor on the stage.

"By God, that's a remarkable young fellow!" murmured Beau Gramercy.

"Why?" said Lee.

"Did you notice how the women sat up? See how their eyes are fastened on him. He has it, too."

"Has what?" asked Lee ill-temperedly.

"What René had. This lad has it to an even greater degree. He's not even good-looking, but he gets them going with a glance."

Lee said nothing. He looked over his shoulder. Like all the other women Vida Cadbury was leaning forward staring at Slim.

These proceedings were likewise brief. No hint was dropped as to any connection with the preceding case. The charge was read: unlawful entry, and a representative of the D.A.'s office held a whispered colloquy with the magistrate. "I will fix bail at $15,000," said the latter. Slim laughed. No bondsman being forthcoming, he was led back through the prisoner's door.

Murmured Beau Gramercy, "The D.A. must want this lad badly."

Lee shrugged. They left the courtroom together.

That same afternoon Lee made it his business to call at the Brocklin house. He asked for the butler, Wilton, and through Wilton he got hold of Cockey.

Lee said, "I have a question to ask Cockey which may prove to have an important bearing on the case." The men sensed friendliness in Lee and were eager to help him.

"When Mr. Brocklin came upstairs to bed on Tuesday night was he still wearing the gardenia which had been presented as a favor before dinner?"

"Yes, sir," said Cockey. "It was still in his buttonhole."

"What became of it then?"

"When I took off his evening coat I removed it. It was still quite fresh and I stuck it in a glass of water. The maids like to get them, you know, sir."

"Good! Then when Mr. Brocklin dressed again and went out, he had no flower in his buttonhole?"

"No, sir."

"Could you swear to that?"

"Absolutely, sir."

"Very good indeed!" said Lee.

On the following morning Inspector Loasby called Lee on the phone in no very good temper. "Lee," he said, "Slim Markoe has found a bondsman."

"The hell you say!" said Lee.

"He's not only got a bondsman, but the most expensive criminal lawyer in town—Harry Harris."

"Well, I'll be damned!"

"He's to be brought up in the first district court at eleven o'clock. I thought you'd like to know about it."

"Sure, I'll be there."

Only the customary back-benchers were in the stuffy courtroom. The smiling Slim was brought in again. An Assistant District Attorney made an earnest plea that the prisoner should not be released under any circumstances unless in the custody of the District Attorney, whereupon the famous Harry Harris, as smooth as cream, arose and made an impassioned speech. So great was Harris's prestige that the magistrate was intimidated. He said:

"Since the District Attorney himself named $15,000 yesterday as proper bail in this case, I don't see how I can refuse it now, or raise it further."

A bondsman stepped forward, and a few minutes later Slim was free. The mystery thrown around the case gave the spectators an inkling that it was important, and there was a general exodus from the courtroom to get a closer look at Slim outside.

Lee and Harris ran into each other in the corridor. "How are you, Mr. Mappin!" cried the lawyer effusively. "You and I appear to be on different sides in this case, but I'm delighted to have the opportunity of telling you how much I admire your work. I possess every one of your books!"

"Why, thanks," said Lee. "I know I'll find a worthy antagonist in you. I expect you'll get the man off, too, though your mere presence in the case is strong presumptive evidence of his guilt."

Harris assumed an expression of gravity. "You wrong him, Mr. Mappin. He never touched that money. I satisfied myself of that before I took his case."

"Then who secured the bail bondsman," asked Lee dryly, "and who's going to pay you?"

"Slim Markoe hasn't a penny," said Harris, "but he is not without friends."

Lee had a brief talk with Loasby on the subject. "One of three things has happened," said the Inspector, counting on his fingers; "(a) Slim did get the hundred thousand and has succeeded in cashing part of it; (b) Dexter Brocklin's lawyers got him out and mean to prevent him from testifying against their client; (c) some woman has fallen for Slim."

Lee said blandly, "Fifteen thousand beside Harry Harris's fee seems like a high price for a gigolo when they're so common. You're keeping him under observation?"

"Sure," said Loasby. "My best men are on it."

All day reporters were camping in Harry Harris's office seeking to learn the whereabouts of Slim Markoe. Harris smoothly put them off.

"You see, boys, the District Attorney has pledged my client not to talk about his case. Therefore, it is easier all around for him just to keep under cover until his trial comes up."

Before the day was out, it was openly stated in the press that Slim Markoe was the dark horse in the Brocklin case. Nobody denied it.

This was Tuesday. On Wednesday the chagrined Loasby was forced to admit to Lee that Slim had given his trackers the slip, and he hadn't been able to pick him up again. Lee put Stan Oberry on the job. Several more days passed and Oberry could report no success. Slim's lawyer was taking the line that he could put his hand on his client at any moment his appearance might be required.

On Sunday afternoon, somewhat to Lee's surprise, Harry Harris called at his apartment. "I have long wanted to pay my respects to you, Mr. Mappin. I have learned so much from a study of the cases you have written up, that I feel I owe at least half my success at the bar to you."

Lee, not at all deceived, waited smiling for the real object of the visit to appear. In an easy chair before the fireplace in Lee's vast living-room, with cigar and highball, Harris finally said offhandedly:

"There's a little personal problem I would like to put up to you, Mr. Mappin, if I thought that you would indulge me so far as to keep my confidence."

"Well," said Lee, "I long ago learned the virtue of keeping my mouth shut. I ought to warn you, however, that if it concerns Slim Markoe, my first duty is to the police."

"Oh, sure, it's not the police I mind. You can tell Loasby if you want, but I hope you won't, because Loasby can't seem to keep a thing from the newspaper boys. They're the ones I'm afraid of. This Doria case has kicked up such a stink already, I think it's bad for the public. Particularly the drivel they are writing about Slim Markoe."

"If there's something you want to tell me, I promise unreservedly not to give it to the press, and I promise not to tell Loasby unless the interests of justice demand it."

"It's none of Loasby's business as yet," said Harris, and hesitated. "Do you know where Slim Markoe is?" he asked abruptly.

"Good God, no!" said Lee. "Don't you?"

Harris scowled into the fire. "No."

"Well, of course," said Lee to draw him, "he's got a perfect right to take a little trip if he wants."

"It's not so simple as that. When the money was put up, there was a certain understanding."

"Ha! a woman!" said Lee.

"And I get blamed for it!"

"What can she expect?" said Lee. "Gratitude? From a man like Slim? He has an inordinate appetite for women. That's the secret of his attraction for them."

"And what can I do? After all, he's my client and if I was to institute a search for him, it would stir up a stink in the press that would prejudice his case in advance."

"I see your difficulty. Suppose you leave it to me. I don't often do the actual sleuthing, but—"

"I was hoping you would say that, Mr. Mappin. If anybody can find him you can. And not a word to the police for the present?"

"Not a word!"

When Harris got up to go they shook hands.

Lee said, "We may be on opposite sides of this case, but we're united in this, eh? Slim Markoe is a first-class—" His lips moved soundlessly.

"You said it!" cried Harris, pumping his arm up and down. "All decent men despise a man of that type!"

"Would you say despise?" said Lee with dry bitterness. "Some might call it envy."

After Harris had left, Lee sat studying the fire. He was thinking, *One thing is fairly certain—I don't believe Slim has given him the slip. If he had, I would be the last one Harris would tell. And who is putting up for Slim? Harris was too quick to jump at my suggestion that it was an enamored woman. Yet a man so subtle as Harris sometimes finds that his best disguise is to tell the truth. I must keep both possibilities in view.*

Next morning at the office, Lee said to Fanny casually, "Do you still see Slim Markoe?"

A deep blush overspread Fanny's face and ran under her hair. But her eyes did not falter from Lee's. "I hear from him," she said.

"Where is he?"

"I don't know. He phones."

"Long distance?"

"No."

"Then he's still in town. I thought as much. Wants to take you out, I suppose. And you?"

"I have declined so far."

"So far? Meaning you will eventually accept?"

Fanny rested her elbow on the flap of Lee's desk, her chin in her palm. She looked sulky and maddeningly attractive. She said nothing.

Lee's temper began to rise. "How can you be so foolish! You know this man's history."

"It's not foolish," said Fanny with spirit. "It excites me to think of him, to see him. I can't help that. It's a biological urge."

"Biological fiddlesticks! Where's your good sense?"

"Good sense is something else again, Pop."

"Can't you see that it would be fatal to give in to this urge, as you call it?"

"Oh, I'm not going to give in all the way. Good God, how such a man could enslave you! But on the other hand, Pop, if I try to resist it altogether, it only gets stronger—it drives me wild. So I think the best way is to see him occasionally and listen to his foolish talk, and laugh at him."

In spite of himself Lee was impelled to grin at Fanny's quaint air of wisdom. He bit his lip to keep her from seeing it. "Many a foolish woman before you has persuaded herself in just the same way, only to come to later and find herself snared."

"I can't feel that I am in much danger," said Fanny. "Because I'm not kidding myself. You have taught me to face things. I'm not telling myself that Slim is a king among men. I know what he is. Nor do I suppose this feeling is great love sent from heaven. I know where it comes from. I can see that all women except female icicles are affected by him in the same way. But it's deliciously exciting, Pop, and you know you have told us we ought never to refuse the dish of life when it is offered."

"Damn!" said Lee. "It's not fair to turn my own words against me like that! I meant something entirely different. This dish is foul!"

When Lee lost his temper Fanny recovered her savoir-faire. "I'm not going to gobble it," she said with a wicked smile. "I'm just going to stick the tip of my finger in and taste it."

"I have nothing more to say," said Lee sourly.

However, after dictating another letter or two, he did find more to say. "I have a hunch that the key to the Doria case lies in Slim Markoe. It is essential that I keep him under observation. Will you help me?"

"I don't see how I can, Pop, she said in distress.

"Surely your first allegiance is to me."

"Of course it is! But it's this way: Slim won't take me out unless I first promise on my word of honor not to tip you off where he can be found. Up to now I have refused to promise." She looked wistful.

"But now you'd like to."

"I've already told you I would. But I wouldn't go unless you knew about it. You brought the matter up."

"Merciful heaven!" cried Lee. "Consider my position! I look on you as my—my daughter and you're asking my blessing on going out with a man we both know to be dangerous as hell!"

"Not particularly dangerous to me," said Fanny, "because I have his number."

"Permit me to have my own opinion about that."

"I'm not asking your *permission* to go out with Slim," she pointed out.

"I see," said Lee stiffly, "you're just telling me."

"You wouldn't want me to give my word and then break it?"

"Slim wouldn't think twice about breaking his."

"Pop! Am I to pattern my conduct on his?"

Lee had no answer to that, so he merely fussed among his papers.

"Aw, be reasonable, Pop," she pleaded. "I'm not betraying you—I simply can't help you at the price of breaking my word."

"This discussion is useless since you have informed me that I have no influence over you."

"I suppose I couldn't love you so much if you were not unreasonable sometimes," said Fanny with a sigh.

Lee kept a dignified silence. The rest of the morning he maintained his aloofness and was very unhappy because an inner voice told him he was in the wrong, and that Fanny was that rarest of creatures, a desirable woman who was capable of candor.

On the following morning he started out from home a half hour earlier so that he could stop off and see Stan Oberry without appearing late at his office.

Oberry conducted a small and very choice business of personal investigations directed from a single tiny room he shared with an owl-eyed secretary. He had a private wire to an office in another building where his operatives could receive their instructions. Thus they were never to be found in Stan's office, or seen entering and leaving. His force was a fluid one; he preferred to engage men and women like actors, to play a particular part, and let them go at the end of the engagement. There were a number of gifted amateurs on his list.

Stan himself was a big, ungainly fellow with a head too small for his bulk. He looked like a moron, and since it helped him in his business, always tried to look as moronic as possible. He was still in his thirties but looked considerably older. He had been an actor before he grew fat, and was a master of the arts of make-up and disguise. All consultations were carried on in the presence of the owl-eyed secretary, who was treated as if she were deaf, dumb, blind, and invisible. To clinch her loyalty, Stan had married her one day during the lunch hour, but that was not generally known.

"Stan," said Lee, dropping heavily in a chair. "I have a hell of a job to put up to you."

"That's what I'm here for, boss."

"I have reason to suspect my girl, Fanny Parran, is making a date with that so-and-so Slim Markoe, and I want you to put a watch on her."

"My God, boss, Fanny's an old hand at that business."

"I know it, and what's more, she probably suspects that I will have her watched, and will keep her eye peeled accordingly."

"It's impossible!" said Stan. "But I'll do my darnedest. I couldn't do it myself. Fanny knows me so well she could see through any disguise I might adopt. Where can I lay hands on a man smart enough to outwit Fanny?"

"Why not try a woman?"

Stan shook his head. "No. Women are smarter than men some ways, but a lone woman is too conspicuous after dark. And there are many places she wouldn't be let in without an escort."

"Well, a man and a woman, then."

"You've got something there, boss. Nobody ever notices a couple if they seem to be wrapped up in each other. I have just the couple in mind."

"Very well. Let her be picked up when she goes out to lunch, and again when she leaves for the day. And send the reports to my home, not the office."

CHAPTER FOURTEEN
OF BLACK GLASS

INSPECTOR LOASBY RECEIVED great press plaudits for his skill in solving the baffling Doria murder so promptly. Lee Mappin, according to his invariable custom, kept in the background. Following the arrest of Dexter Brocklin, several additional pieces of evidence were turned up—a pair of gloves found in the pocket of René Doria's dressing gown were identified as the property of Brocklin, and it was discovered that Brocklin had bought a box of shells for his revolver on the day of the murder. It was with one of these that René had been shot.

So great was the public interest that although nothing new was turned up, the newspapers continued to feature it day after day. If there was no new story to present, they re-told the old one. Dexter Brocklins guilt was taken for granted, and the press worked up a strong popular feeling against him. He was depicted as the jealous father who had wrecked his daughter's life by shooting her beloved fiancé, etc. René's sins were soft-pedaled.

Brocklin's clever lawyers, seeing the danger, got after Peggy Brocklin. The picture of a tragic, unwed widow that she was presenting to the public, they said—but in very diplomatic language—might result in sending her father to the chair. Since René was gone anyhow, would it not be more appealing for her to appear as a broken-hearted loyal daughter? Peggy rose to it without being aware of inconsistency, and appeared at the Tombs with a great armful of American Beauties. She came every afternoon subsequently, and touching accounts were given of the interviews between father and daughter.

Peggy, laden with roses, faced the cameras with an interesting, heartbroken expression. With a sob in her voice she said to the reporters:

"It's wicked to accuse my father of shooting René. He went to see René that night on my account. I sent him there. And when he came home he told me everything. They had a few words but no shot was fired. René was still alive when my father left him!" When the reporters undertook to question her further, she fled, crying: "I can't! It's too dreadful!"

Lee shook his head when he read this and looked at the photographs. "Unstable as water!"

Having given the public time to digest this, a couple of days later Brocklin's lawyers came out with a fuller statement of their case:

> Mr. Dexter Brocklin does not deny that he visited Rend Doria in the apartment on 46th Street late on the night he was killed. Mr. Brocklin was very averse to the marriage of his daughter to Doria until the validity of Doria's divorce could be established, and further, because of the reports of Doria's loose conduct. On the night, the very night the engagement was announced, he received a tip that Doria was actually entertaining a lady in Lancaster Court. Mr. Brocklin told his daughter what he had heard, and she promised him that if it proved to be true she would never see Doria again.
>
> Mr. Brocklin, as he conceived it to be his duty as a father, proceeded to Doria's apartment. He took his gun as self-protection. At the door of the apartment he realized that Doria would never let him in unless forced to; therefore, when Doria opened the door it was to find himself looking into the muzzle of Mr. Brocklin's gun. But Mr. Brocklin never had the slightest intention of shooting him. Mr. Brocklin forced Doria to lead the way upstairs. There were some angry words in the living-room; Doria was very

insolent and abusive, but Mr. Brocklin kept his head. Doria denied there was a woman in the place. Mr. Brocklin forced Doria to lead the way through the entire apartment, room by room. It is on two floors. He found no woman because, as is now known, she escaped while they were in the living-room. But he found plenty of evidence in the shape of dishes, glasses, etc., that two persons had just partaken of a meal there, and Doria, was in effect, caught *fla-grante delicto*.

On returning to the living-room, Mr. Brocklin inadvertently stepped in front of Doria, and immediately felt the muzzle of a gun pressed into the small of his back. Doria ordered him to throw his gun to the other end of the room. Doria, realizing that he had been discovered and ruined in the eyes of all decent people, covered Mr. Brocklin with the foulest of insults. Mr. Brocklin was very thankful to get out of the place alive.

A great deal has been made of the fact that Mr. Brocklin had bought a box of shells for his revolver that day. It was pure coincidence. The gun had been lying in his drawer loaded and unused for nearly 20 years. It occurred to Mr. Brocklin, who knows nothing about firearms, that the powder in the shells might very well have disintegrated in that time, and he resolved to buy new ones, that's all.

Inspector Loasby, naturally, was much excited when he read this statement, since it threatened his newly won laurels. He came to Lee s office waving it. "A tissue of lies!"

"Sure," said Lee. "Everybody lies to the newspapers. It's expected of them. The only way you can cover your tracks nowadays is to tell the truth."

"Brocklin's smart lawyers thought this up. He couldn't find a word to say for himself!"

"And yet," said Lee thoughtfully, "after you cut out the recognizable lies, that Peggy knew all about it and so on, the remainder has a curious plausibility. It comports with poor Brocklin's ineffectual character that he should have entered René's apartment like a lion and come out like a sheep!"

"What are you saying?" cried Loasby. "My case is watertight!"

"Maybe so," murmured Lee, "but to my mind, there's a fatal defect in your case, Inspector."

"Name it!"

"I find it hard to believe that a man, that Brocklin, that any man could be such a fool as to leave his gun with his fingerprints on it beside the body of the man he had just shot."

"Oh, he was flustered; they always do some fool thing like that."

"Not always. That's just an excuse to avoid facing a real difficulty."

"If it wasn't Brocklin shot him, who did? Maybe René shot himself because he'd been found out, and then threw himself down the dumbwaiter shaft."

"The suggestion is yours, not mine," said Lee dryly. "As to who did it, there is Slim Markoe, for instance. The first part of his story we know is true because it fits with what we have learned from other sources. But there is no proof that René had already been disposed of when Slim got into his apartment. Suppose Slim stole up behind him, cracked him over the head with his iron bar, and then, after covering his hand, shot him with Brocklin's gun just for camouflage."

"Slim had no gloves," said Loasby sullenly.

"There were gloves in the place, though. René had a pair, and Brocklin dropped a pair there."

Loasby's face lighted up. "A straight iron bar couldn't have made that shape of depression we found in René's head."

"True, you have me there. But Slim may have had another weapon. A blackjack could have left just such a dent. And Slim is able enough to have delivered the blow. But that theory won't work, either. It doesn't account for the telephone call that Brocklin got that night, nor the gardenia that we found under the divan."

"What a fellow you are!" grumbled Loasby. "Always building up theories only to knock them down."

Late that afternoon Lee was walking home up Fifth Avenue. He thought, *I know Dexter Brocklin was not wearing a gardenia when he went to René's apartment that night, and it's not reasonable to suppose that Slim Markoe was. Hence, there must have been another man there. It must have been the same night because the gardenia under the divan was fresh—fresher, in fact, than the one we found in René's buttonhole. This probably belonged to the man who telephoned Brocklin. But if Slim Markoe's story is true—and there is no reason why he should have lied as to this point—the man was already in René's place when René got there. In that case he couldn't have telephoned to Brocklin—he must have had an accomplice outside. This suggests a conspiracy to get René. They were trying to get poor old Brocklin to shoot him, and after that failed, they had to do the job themselves*

There is another possibility. Perhaps murder was not intended. Perhaps they only wanted to break up the marriage between René and Peggy. This suggests Eliot Brocklin. I must give more attention to him. He doesn't, however, seem to possess either the resolute or the crafty qualities necessary to pull off a job like this. And why, if the aim was only to break up the marriage, should René have been killed after Dexter Brocklin had left him? Eliot was wearing one of Schling's gardenias that night. The one I found under the divan, besides being fresher, was arranged in a different manner. I'm afraid Eliot must be ruled out as the unknown man in René's apartment.

But some man was there. He must have had a key to the apartment since there was no sign of the place having been forced. Why should René ever have given another man a key to his love nest? Perhaps the key belonged to a woman who formerly had the entrée there. And she procured a man to help her revenge herself on Rene. Her husband perhaps. Nobody who has been brought into the case so far corresponds to such a couple . . . it sounds pretty farfetched; it doesn't strike me as right. *I mustn't let my imagination run away with me. After all, Loasby has a strong case against Dexter*

Brocklin. He may be the murderer. And I mustn't forget Slim Markoe, either. Though it seems as if it must have been a man in the upper brackets of society, one who would naturally wear a gardenia. But anybody can buy a gardenia.

While Lee's mind was running on gardenias, he caught a side glance of a florist's window on the Avenue with a whole row of boutonnières—gardenias, rosebuds, carnations—held in a wire frame. Lee wondered idly what kept them fresh. He looked closer and saw that each flower was held in an almost invisible glass container—black glass! Feeling a little stab of excitement, he turned and entered the shop.

"I would like a boutonniere for this evening. A gardenia would be the most suitable. I suppose."

The girl brought one from the show window, removed it from its little glass, and was about to wrap its stem in lead foil.

"Wait a minute," said Lee. "Why not give me the container, too? That could stick right in my buttonhole and help to keep the flower fresh."

"Why, yes, sir. That's what these little glasses are for, black glass, you see, so they won't show against evening clothes. I am always surprised more gentlemen do not ask for them."

"How ingenious!" said Lee. "Let me look at it."

At the top the miniature vase had a disk or flange set at a sharp angle with the stem, to keep it from slipping through the buttonhole. It exactly corresponded with the little black disk that Lee was saving among the exhibits of the Doria case. He smiled with satisfaction.

"Do many men wear these?"

"Not so many as formerly, sir. The younger men regard them as a bit finicky or sissified, I fancy."

"Could you give me the names of some of your customers that use them?"

She shook her head. "In a location like this, we rarely know the names of our customers, sir. Most of our business comes through the show window—it is a strictly cash trade."

"Do other florists keep these holders?"

"Oh, yes, sir. I'm sure you'd find them in all the older estab-lishments."

"Well, thank you very much."

Lee continued his walk up the Avenue with a smoother brow. *I have made a real step forward,* he was thinking; *the first pieces of my jigsaw puzzle are fitting together.*

CHAPTER FIFTEEN
REPORT OF OPERATIVE R. B.

SHORTLY BEFORE ONE O'CLOCK yesterday I took a seat at
a table in the cocktail lounge of the hotel at the corner of Madison and 88th. Through the window I
commanded a view of the converted house across the
street where Mr. Mappin has his offices. A few minutes later a certain party appeared coming down the
steps and I went out after her. She seemed suspicious of being tailed, but there are a lot of people on
the street at that hour, and she never spotted me.

She led me to a drug store on 34th Street. She
had to wait to get a telephone booth and I drank a
soda. She got a booth but the booths on either side
of her were occupied and I couldn't get near enough
to hear anything. Her conversation was brief. It was
a man she was talking to, judging from her smile,
and I guessed she was making a date because she
kept nodding her head.

Afterward she went to Schrafft's on Fifth Avenue
and had her lunch. I followed her in just to make
sure the wanted man wasn't there. I am familiar with
his appearance. Afterward I waited in the street.
Nobody joined her at Schrafft's, and when she had
finished eating she returned to the office, and I
dropped her, knowing she was safe for the rest of
the afternoon.

At 5:00 I was on watch again and I saw her come out. The streets were so full of office workers going home I couldn't keep too close to her because she was still watchful, and I lost her. But that didn't worry me because I was sure she would go home before going out in the evening. I got there before her. She had stopped at a florist's to buy a corsage.

At 6:25 she appeared at the door waiting for a cab. She was all dolled up in a black velvet evening dress and a white wrap with a big fur collar. It's an uncertain business trying to follow a taxi—everything depends on whether you've got a better driver than the car in front—so I crossed the street and fixed it so that I was passing immediately behind her at the moment she stepped in her cab, and I heard her say, "Colony Restaurant" to the driver.

The Colony is not at all showy. Nobody would ever notice the inconspicuous entrance unless they knew the reputation of the place. The wanted man was waiting there. I scarcely knew him at first, he looked so smart. His hair is cut short now and he wears it brushed back in a pompadour like a Frenchman. It makes a big difference in his appearance but when he grins, you would know him anywhere. He was all turned out in expensive evening clothes that fitted his slim figure like a glove.

When they went into the restaurant to eat I couldn't follow them because I was wearing a lounge suit, but there was no need because I knew they would be good for an hour there. I went and telephoned my office that I had the man placed, and my instructions were to keep him under observation all evening; my particular object was to find out where he was living. I then went home and ate and changed to a tail coat and told my wife to hold herself ready

in case I needed her later. Afterward I sat up to the
Colony bar until they should be ready to leave.

While I was sitting in the bar Slim came out and
went into the telephone booth. He never saw me before, so I was able to move up close and I heard him
telephone to the Mansfield Theater for two seats. After
that I was able to take my time. I let them leave the
Colony without paying any attention to them, and
after awhile I taxied to the Mansfield, and buying a
ticket stood up at the back of the auditorium.

After the show they drove to El Zingara, which
shows how smart this young guy is, for that is the
last place anybody would expect to find him. I decided not to telephone my wife because, as we are
unknown there, they might refuse to give us a table,
whereas there are always plenty of stags lined up at
the bar, and nobody questions a stag if he's dressed.
To my surprise Slim and the girl were shown to a
table right near the dance floor. Somebody known
to the management must have recommended Slim.

The place got so crowded I couldn't watch them
very good from the bar, so I took a saunter through
the room as if I was looking for friends, and as luck
would have it a dame gave me a come-on look. I went
up to her table and she greeted me like an old pal
and introduced me to her husband or her butter-and-
egg man or whatever he was. I was invited to sit down
and have a drink, and I was now quite close to Slim
and the girl. They had ordered supper and the girl,
without making any display about it, was showing
Slim how to hold his knife and fork. They appeared
to be having a swell time joshing each other. When
they got up to dance I asked my lady to dance and I
was then able to keep close to the other couple. The
dance floor was so crowded you couldn't move much

anyhow. Close as I was, I couldn't hear anything they said to each other. Slim is a natural when it comes to dancing, but his style was too free for El Zingara and Miss P. was teaching him how to do it more sophisticated, like the other young fellows there.

Later Slim left the girl and sauntered up front to the bar. So I excused myself from my friends and followed. He ran into a guy at the bar as if by accident and they had a drink. It looked to me as if they had real business together. This was a tall, dark-complected guy, who seemed to be at home in the place. He knew everybody. A handsome guy, but hard-looking, like a man who had been hitting up the pace for years past; about 35, but looked older. Very fine clothes and jewelry.

When they had drunk they went out in the lobby and I followed on the pretense that I wanted to get something out of my overcoat pocket in the coatroom. The two men stood by the entrance talking together low and earnest. I would say that Slim was receiving some kind of instructions. Something passed from the dark guy to Slim; probably cash, but I couldn't swear as to that. Then Slim went back to his girl, and the dark guy came to get his coat and hat. I killed time with a cigarette. When the dark guy left I said to the coatroom girl, "I seem to have seen that fellow some place. Who is he?" And she said, "Everybody knows him. It's Mr. Jack Vynson."

Slim and Miss P. left El Zingara shortly after two o'clock. They had a little argument on the sidewalk when the taxi drew up. Slim wanted to go with her and she wouldn't let him. She drove away alone and he was good and sore. He walked east to Madison Avenue and north on Madison to 63d Street, I following on the other side of the street. At number — East 63d he let himself in with a key. It's a fine old

brownstone front which is now rented out in rooms,
a good class place. A minute after he had gone in
the lights of the second floor front went on. R. B.

Stan Oberry and Lee Mappin studied this report together in
the former's office. Lee murmured thoughtfully, "Jack Vynson, eh?
There's another piece of my puzzle. But I don't know yet where he
goes in."

"For a bum, this Slim seems to feel pretty much at home in
high society," remarked Stan.

"Sure, damn him! He has a natural grace and aplomb."

"Look, Mr. Mappin," said Stan, "if this fellow can wear a
starched bosom as if he was born to it, why couldn't he have had
on evening clothes when he went to René's, and a gardenia in his
buttonhole? You know nothing about his movements that night
except what he told you himself. He has powerful friends. Somebody put him up to it— somebody sent him there to get René."

"It is possible," said Lee, "but somehow the edges don't come
together as if they belonged. Why should Slim put on evening
clothes when he went in over the roof?"

"He said he found that way in by accident. That particular statement may be true. Perhaps he had intended to ring the doorbell."

"René would never have opened the door."

"Maybe Mrs. Vosper told him the private ring. Maybe she hired
Slim to do the job for her. She had reason enough. Maybe she put
up his bail."

"Maybe," said Lee, "but there is nothing to suggest that Mrs.
Vosper was acquainted with Slim. And in that case, what became
of the hundred grand?"

Stan Oberry shook his head.

"In the meantime, you had better keep Vynson under observation until further notice," said Lee. "He's so well known it ought
not to be difficult. If he gets suspicious, drop him at once and pick
him up later. Change your men frequently."

"Very well, Mr. Mappin. What about Slim?"

"I'll look after Slim myself."

CHAPTER SIXTEEN
TEACHER AND PUPIL

LEAVING STAN OBERRY'S OFFICE, Lee proceeded to the shop of a theatrical wigmaker who had served him on former occasions. "I want a toupee," he said.

"Excellent!" said the proprietor. "It will be perfectly invisible, Mr. Mappin. You will look 10 years younger, sir." He stood off, appraising Lee's bald pate with a professional eye. "How much time can you give me to make it?"

"I want to take it with me," said Lee mildly.

"But, my dear sir! I only have stock stuff on hand."

"I don't want too good a fit. I want it to look like a toupee. It's for a kind of masquerade."

"Ah, well, in that case I think I can suit you." With his toupee in a little box Lee went on to a ready-made clothing store where he bought a suit that didn't fit him, an unbecoming derby hat, and a few cheap shirts and ties at which he shuddered inwardly. He carried the stuff home and put it on. Jermyn, accustomed to his vagaries, lent him a battered Gladstone bag for his extra things. Replacing his rimless glasses with a heavy-rimmed pair, Lee strode up and down in front of the mirror surveying the effect.

"What do you think of it?" he asked Jermyn. "I want to look like a businessman from, say, Canandaigua, N.Y. I am visiting the big city for the first time, and naturally I am a bit overawed."

"It is perfect, sir," said Jermyn solemnly. "Your best friend would pass you without a second glance."

"The next thing is to get out of the house without giving the hall men food for gossip," said Lee. "You had better come with me and bring another bag. I'll wear my own outside clothes and change in the taxi. You can bring the things back."

About eleven o'clock Mr. Brown of Canandaigua, N.Y., was walking through East 63d Street, glancing timidly up at the old brownstone fronts. In a parlor window was a neat little sign announcing Vacancies, and he went up the steps. The landlady herself opened the door, a grim woman dressed in a style of faded elegance—like her house.

"I am looking for a room, please," said Lee. "Have you any small ones?"

"Third floor front hall," she said uncompromisingly. "Seven dollars."

"I suppose you haven't any on the second floor. I find the stairs a little trying."

"Nine dollars," she said, ready to close the door.

"I would pay that if I could get on the second floor."

She opened the door a little wider. "There's a young man in it now," she said, "but he would be glad to move into the cheaper room. I would have to have a week's rent in advance before shifting him."

"All right," said Lee.

They went up to look at the room. The landlady was almost affable now. Lee noted with satisfaction that there was a communicating door with the main bedroom adjoining. It was locked, of course, but one can hear much better through a door.

"Is the next room occupied?" asked Lee.

"Certainly. That's my best room with private bath and all. A very select young gentleman occupies it; a young man of means."

"Does he give parties? I was thinking of my sleep."

"He doesn't give parties," she said. "He goes to them—in the very highest society. He doesn't get up until afternoon, and I wouldn't want him disturbed mornings. He's sleeping now."

"Oh, I'm a very quiet sort of man," said Lee.

The deal was concluded, and an hour later Lee was established in the room. He heard a loud yawn from the next room and somebody began moving about. Presently there was the sound of a running shower, and a man's voice singing snatches of a sentimental ballad. Lee scowled.

Slim evidently rang for a servant, for in due course she came along the hall, knocked and entered his room. It was evident from the sounds that she was bringing a breakfast tray. Slim joshed her in his customary audacious style—maids or debutantes were all one to him. There was the sound of a scuffle, but the maid escaped into the hall, giggling. Slim presumably sat down to eat.

He was still eating when somebody else came along the hall, knocked, and was bidden to enter. "Hello," said Slim casually, and another male voice answered similarly. The tone suggested that the two were thoroughly accustomed to each other, but that there was not much love lost between them.

After a silence the newcomer said, "God! What a sloppy way to eat!"

"Well, I'm all alone," grumbled Slim. "Can't I act natural?"

"Naturally," corrected the other. "You've got to practice while you're alone until it comes natural to eat like a civilized person. Show me!"

"Cheese! You take all the fun out of eating!"

Lee had an excellent memory for voices and he was now smiling in satisfaction. Slim's visitor was Jack Vynson.

Vynson said, "Don't curl your little finger when you lift your coffee cup. That's a dead giveaway. When you're alone in your room you ought to eat in front of the mirror and watch yourself."

"I was all right until I started thinking about myself," growled Slim. "Now I don't know where I'm at!"

"That's the self-conscious stage. It will pass if you keep on practicing. You put on a fairly good show last night. I was watching you."

Slim's voice warmed. "Oh, I can always forget myself when I'm with a woman."

"You can have all the women you want as long as you don't get entangled. Understand, the minute any woman gets a hold over you, you're through."

"No woman has ever got her hooks into me yet."

When Slim finished eating he brought the tray out into the hall and put it on the floor. As he returned to the room, Vynson asked, "Did the morning coat come from Brooks Brothers?"

"Yes."

"Put it on and let me see how it looks."

There was a silence while Slim presumably was obeying. Finally Vynson said, with grudging approval, "You can wear clothes, all right."

"It's my manly figyuh," said Slim airily.

Vynson grunted. "Show me how you walk into a room."

Another silence, and Vynson said, "My God! Your hands hang down like two calabashes on a vine. No! don't shove 'em in your pockets either!"

"What the hell must I do with my hands?" asked Slim. "Put 'em to my nose?"

"Don't try to be funny. When you enter a room try touching your left cuff with the fingers of your right hand."

Slim no doubt obeyed. "What a sissy gesture!"

"Keep your elbows down!" commanded Vynson. "If you'd practice that 25 times every morning it would get to be like second nature."

The lesson proceeded. Lee listened with a peculiar smile. *This sounds like a case where the longest way round is the shortest way home*, he was thinking. Once Slim started to say:

"Fanny and me was having a—"

"For God's sake!" Vynson barked at him. "Mind your grammar!"

"God damn it!" retorted Slim. "Can't you tell me a thing without cursing? I'm the leading man in this show, ain't I?"

"My God! *Ain't I!*"

"Well, what should I say?"

"Am I not."

"Well, am I not?" demanded Slim.

"Don't get the big head," warned Vynson with dark meaning. "It's fatal!"

"You come here every morning with a hangover and a sour temper," Slim went on. "We'd get on faster if we did it after you began to liquor up for the day."

"Do you think I enjoy it?" snarled Vynson.

"I don't give a damn whether you do or not. We're both acting under orders, and you'd better get on with it."

As this curious lesson continued, Lee noted that Vynson took care to modify his arrogance. Slim clearly was a person to be propitiated.

Finally it was over. Vynson got up and pushed his chair back. He lowered his voice, but Lee, by putting his head closer to the door, could still hear. He said, "Orders are you're not to take the little blonde out again. She's too close to Pop Mappin."

Lee's ears stretched and his smile broadened. Slim said, "She swore she wouldn't give me away."

"Can you trust a woman?" Vynson asked contemptuously.

"Sure! As long as I can keep her crazy about me."

"Did you think you could keep tab on what Pop Mappin was doing through her?"

"No. She's a square-shooter. Absolutely."

"Well, I'm only transmitting orders. You'll have to keep away from her. What do you care? I can introduce you to a hundred other blondes."

"Damn!" grumbled Slim. "I like that girl! She stings a man! Keeps you on your toes."

"Another one of your girls is giving Harris trouble," remarked Vynson indifferently.

"Who's that?"

"Rose Bosi. She comes around Harris's office all the time asking where you are. It puts Harris in a spot because he tells the D.A.'s office he can produce you at any time, and when he refuses information to Rose she curses him. If it got around that you really had made a sneak, and Harris couldn't produce you, there'd be plenty trouble."

"What do they want me to do? Go and see Rose? She's an or-nery little piece—I'm fed up with her."

"So your taste is improving," said Vynson sarcastically.

"Well, that's the idea, isn't it, to improve my taste?"

"They don't want you to see her. Write her a loving letter and date it Los Angeles. Tell her you made a sneak out there hoping she'd be going home, and that you're up against it. Tell her she's the only one you love, and to come quick, or anything you like. I'll undertake to get it posted in L.A."

"That's all right," said Slim, "it's easy to get rid of Rose, but how's this all going to work out? I can't figure it."

"You don't have to," said Vynson. "All you've got to do is to obey orders. There's a hell of a big stake and it needs weeks of careful preparation."

"But if I'm put on trial—"

"It rests with you whether you are."

"How?"

"Well, your trial won't come up until after Dexter Brocklin is tried, because you would make a more creditable witness for the prosecution if you hadn't been convicted yourself."

"All right, I can see that. But if I testify against Brocklin, how could I—?"

"You will not testify against Brocklin. You will be allowed to skip your bail before that—*if you make good!*"

"Make good with who?" asked Slim, and Lee held his breath while waiting for the answer.

"With *whom*," corrected Vynson.

"Well, with whom?"

"You want to know too much too soon," said Vynson. "Let it ride. You're living well, aren't you?"

"Oh, hell, yes," said Slim. "It's like a punk's dream. But I'd sooner be on my own."

"It will cost a lot of money to let you skip your bail, and natu-rally you've got to show you're worth it. If you play your cards right, within three months you'll have the wherewithal to run your own show for the rest of your life."

"Oh, boy!" said Slim. "Life would be perfect if I had money. I have everything else. But if I don't make good?"

"The law will be allowed to take its course."

"I might skip bail on my own account."

"Try and do it," said Vynson with a peculiar grimness. Slim was silent.

They made an appointment to meet at five in the apartment of a Mrs. Whittlesey on East 58th Street for cocktails. "She's not important," said Vynson, "but you can practice your parlor tricks."

He then left. Lee let him go, knowing that he would be picked up outside. After Vynson had gone, the sounds that reached Lee's ears suggested that Slim was getting ready to go out. Lee left the house ahead of him and, hailing the first taxi that came along, ordered the driver to stop at the next corner. Lee watched the house through the back window, and when he saw Slim come out and board a cab, he instructed his driver to follow it. Slim was now wearing fashionable riding togs.

Very little came of it. Lee had to sit in his cab for an hour while Slim took a lesson in speech from a well-known professor. Squirming with impatience and smoking innumerable cigarettes, he quickly decided that he had had enough sleuthing on his own account. Anyhow, the way things were shaping, Vynson was the important lead at the moment—Slim was only a pupil.

When he had taken his lesson in diction, Slim taxied to a fashionable riding stable in 58th Street, and came out of the place mounted on a horse and accompanied by a riding master. Lee couldn't very well follow him into the Park, and there was no object in doing so. Instead, he went to a telephone and, getting Stan Oberry on the wire, asked him to station a man in a cab outside the riding stable to wait for Slim's return.

Lee went back to the 68d Street house and asked for the landlady. With an appearance of great agitation he told her he had just received a message saying that his wife was very sick and he therefore had to return to Canandaigua immediately.

The landlady primmed her lips. "I'm sure I'm very sorry to hear it, but you can't expect me to return any rent after I have been put to the expense of shifting my other tenant to a cheaper room."

"I suppose not," said Lee regretfully.

He packed his bag and left. Shortly afterward a personable young man (on Stan Oberry's staff), walking through 63d Street, appeared to be attracted by the Vacancies sign. He made inquiry and engaged the room that Lee had vacated. This man had been chosen for the job because he could write shorthand and was therefore able to take down overheard conversations verbatim.

After returning home and changing to his usual clothes, Lee proceeded to the office. There was a lot of correspondence to attend to, and Fanny brought her notebook into the little private office. She was still pretty stiff with her employer, and Lee was exasperated with her, she was so *very* pretty, and so stubborn. However, he said nothing.

In the middle of the dictation Fanny was called to the phone, and Lee guessed from what he overheard that it was Tom Cottar, and that he was asking for a date. "I'm so sorry," said Fanny, "but I have a date tonight." After the usual telephone persiflage, she hung up.

When she came back to his desk Lee could no longer forbear plaguing her. "Have a good time last night?" he asked casually.

"Swell!" said Fanny, as casual as himself.

"At the Colony Restaurant, the Mansfield Theater and El Zingara," murmured Lee.

Fanny stared. "Pop, I knew you were churning with something this morning. I could feel it!"

"I play fair," said Lee.

"I didn't say you didn't. But you're a devil!"

"Afterward your escort was overheard to boast to another man that you were crazy about him."

Fanny flamed to her hair with anger—a good sign. "Why do you tell me that?" she demanded.

"I thought it would be salutary."

"He had no reason to say such a thing! There was a certain attraction, as I told you, but I never let him see it!"

"Of course not. It was just male vanity. What could you expect? However, I have no further cause for anxiety," Lee went on, "because he's not going to ask you out again."

"How do you know?"

"His master has ordered him to stay away from you. You're considered dangerous."

"His master?"

"I can't tell you any more at the moment. I just wanted to prepare you for the fact that he is going to break the next date." Lee's voice changed. "Good God, my dear, you were in dangerous company last night! If I had known how dangerous, I would have locked you up sooner than let you go!"

Fanny glanced swiftly in his face. His eyes were shining with earnestness—he was not trying to get back at her then. "I'm sorry, Pop," she murmured, lowering her head. "Please forget it."

Lee resumed his dictating. He paused in the middle of a letter and said, apropos of nothing, "If I'm any judge of human nature, Tom Cottar would make an exciting lover." Fanny only moved her shoulders pettishly, and repeated the last sentence he had dictated. He went on with his letter. However, after the dictating was finished, he heard Fanny telephoning in the front room.

"Is that you, Tom? I just called up to say that my date for tonight is off and if you are still free. Oh, I'd rather go home and change first. Oh, well, if you insist. At five, then."

At five o'clock, as the girls were preparing to shut up shop for the day, Tom Cottar breezed in with an engaging grin on his ugly face. He had eyes only for Fanny; clearly he was hard hit. It occurred to Lee that after all Tom and Slim Markoe were of much the same type, only Tom's glance was as open as the sky, whereas Slim's, even when he was laughing and carrying on with a girl, was always masked. In short, Tom was straight and Slim was crooked.

Tom and Fanny departed laughing, and Judy's eyes followed them enviously. Judy had no date tonight; she went home alone. For a long time afterward Lee continued to sit tipped back in his swivel chair with his feet dangling, smoking and mulling things over in his mind.

CHAPTER SEVENTEEN
THE MYSTERIOUS SYMBOL

AT ELEVEN O'CLOCK on the following morning, Lee Mappin entered
the building of the *Sphere*, and inquired his way to the office of
Houson Bell, better known to the world as Beau Gramercy. The
Beau, as befitted his fame, actually rated a private office, though
it was but a narrow slit, and Lee found him seated behind a big
desk dictating his flowery stuff to a beautiful young stenographer.
He had a special chair built a little higher than ordinary, so that
when you came on him at his desk he looked like a man of average
size. You couldn't see it, but there was a tall footstool under the
desk for him to rest his little feet on.

"My dear Lee!" he cried. "What a delightful surprise!" It was
characteristic of the Beau that however extravagant his language
might be, his long face never cracked a smile. "Excuse me if I don't
rise. I seem to be hemmed in here!" He looked distractedly from
side to side, though there was nothing to prevent him from getting
up if he wished to. He sent the stenographer away with his blessing: "This is the famous Amos Lee Mappin," he said to her, "so
take a good look at him as you go."

"Sit down!" he went on to Lee. "Smoke up! To what do I owe
the pleasure of this call? Or is there no reason for it? That would
indeed be flattering!"

"I'm afraid I'm interrupting you," said Lee.

Beau Gramercy waved his hands. "Perish the thought! Time was
made for slaves!" He wore a beautiful piece of jade on the little
finger of his left hand and a bloodstone intaglio on the third finger

of his right. It was a mistake because the rings called attention to the age of his hands.

It was the first time Lee had been there, and he looked around him curiously. The Beau's little Homburg hat lay on top of a filing case with a pair of yellow gloves beside it, and in the corner stood the ebony stick with a gold knob that was almost as well known around town as its owner. Lee had missed it lately. The most conspicuous feature of the room was the tall ranks of filing cabinets extending along each side from the desk to the door. Lee noted (a) that they were made of steel, (b) that they were equipped with locks.

"Good God! What do you keep in all those files?" he asked.

"Reputations!" said the Beau.

"I thought as much. Dynamite!"

The little man shrugged expressively. "If I should ever get fired out of my job—"

"You never will," put in Lee.

"No, I don't think I shall. I know too much. But if I should ever feel like retiring, I will write a book and Tell All!"

"It would create a revolution!"

The Beau raised his hand delicately. "You flatter me, Lee!"

"You will never retire either," said Lee.

"Ah, I see you know me! It is true I'm attached to my job. It feeds my malice so pleasantly. Years ago when I was young, the society reporter was looked upon as a little lower than a servant, and snubs and slights were my daily fare. I swallowed them and now my time has come. Within the past few years the entire structure of society has been remade, and I helped to remake it. The people who insulted me years ago are themselves objects of ridicule now, and the present leaders of society are my creatures. I made them and I can unmake them. I am flattered, I am feted, I am showered with gifts. Being human, I rather enjoy getting my own back." He broke off to ask, "Are you still working on the Doria case?"

Lee nodded.

"But I thought that was cleared up. Poor old Dexter Brocklin! He was always a pitiful creature, but everybody feels sorry for him now. They'll never convict him."

"Probably not. The case is not closed for me, until I can lay hands on the missing hundred grand."

"The serial numbers of the notes have been circularized, I assume."

"Naturally."

"And none have turned up?"

"Not a sign of one."

"How awkward for the thief! To have all that money and not be able to spend a cent!"

Lee glanced at the files again. "I suppose you keep a dossier of every person prominent in society."

"It amounts to that," said the Beau.

"Might I be permitted to examine the dossier relating to Jack Vynson?"

"But, my dear fellow, of course! And you are the first person I ever allowed to look inside my files. Have you got anything on Jack?" he asked eagerly. "By God, that would please a lot of people! Vynson is one of the best hated men in town."

"Why?"

"Well, he's crooked and he's arrogant. A crook has to be good-humored to get by."

"Why don't they kick him out of their society?"

"Well, his name still has news value."

"I haven't a thing on him," said Lee. "There is only his unexplained association with Doria. Ever since Doria came to town they have gone around together; they have been referred to as intimate friends. Yet when I suggested it to Vynson, he angrily repudiated it. He all but cursed the dead Doria."

"That's characteristic of his world," said Beau Gramercy. "When a man is down, they all rush to kick him."

"How have you endured that world so long?"

Beau Gramercy turned the jade ring. "Oh, it's my job to explore it," he said. "I take it for granted." He touched his breast. "But I don't allow it to sully my inner life!"

Lee studied him, wondering if the manikin *had* an inner life. Most likely it was a fantasy.

The Beau slid out of his chair like a child, and going to the file, unlocked a drawer and pulled it out. One after another he brought three thick folders and placed them on the desk.

"Good God! What a mass of stuff!" said Lee.

"Well, it covers a period of 12 or 18 years, back to the time when Vynson first began to be spoken of around town. Mostly newspaper clippings, you see; my stories and the stories of others when they stole a beat on me. Together with photographs. I also file the innumerable anonymous letters I receive, but I never use the information until it is confirmed through other sources. Oddly enough, the information in such letters usually turns out to be correct."

The Beau went on, "I'm sure you'll understand, my dear Lee, I could not possibly allow you to take any of this stuff out of the office. These collections constitute my all, my stock-in-trade, my very life. And you might be in a taxi accident or a fire."

Lee said, "Of course I understand that, Houson."

"You may sit here and read it until I close up at one o'clock, and I'll be happy to have you come back as many mornings as you please."

"Thanks very much."

A folding table and a chair being fetched in and placed by the door, Lee set to work. Meanwhile Beau Gramercy resumed his dictating. But the principal part of his job was to receive visitors and telephone calls. The visitors were of types not often seen around newspaper offices: pretty debutantes, glamour boys and smart matrons. Beau Gramercy was a social thermometer—Lee could gauge the exact social importance of each visitor by the warmth of his greeting. When it was a really distinguished person (in the Beau's eyes) he would hook the stool out from under the desk with his toe and stand on it. With his long-waisted coat this gave him the effect of a man of good height. Every visitor must have seen through the trick, but the little man continued to take a childlike satisfaction in it. His conversations with the visitors were always carried on in earnest whispers. They brought him information.

Meanwhile Lee was turning over the clippings relating to Jack Vynson's career. He was soon able to distinguish at a glance

between what might prove useful to him and the mere fluff of the
society columns. In the beginning there were continual references
to the youth's extraordinary good looks, and the photographs of
that period bore it out. He was also said to possess unusual "magnetism." There was not a word that threw any light on his origin.
His name was mentioned in connection with one woman and another, and three years after he had first appeared, he married Myra
Fitch, one of the great heiresses of the day. There were columns
describing the magnificent wedding in St. Patrick's Cathedral which
Lee turned over hastily.

The newspapers then were more decorous than they are today—
they dealt in hints and innuendoes, and Lee had to read between
the lines. Apparently success had come too easily to Jack Vynson.
Having realized his ambition, he began to go to pieces. There were
several drunken escapades, and he became so promiscuous in his
amours that even the loose standards of the prohibition era were
outraged. His good looks and health both began to suffer, as the
photographs clearly showed, Apparently he had obtained a handsome cash settlement upon his wedding. This he ran through
quickly, and thereafter he was dependent on his wife's bounty. It
was hinted that the allowance she made him was not large, and he
was therefore put to all kinds of shifts to satisfy his expensive
appetites. During the last years of prohibition he was referred to
as the gilt-edged bootlegger, and when liquor was first permitted,
he became a champagne salesman for a while.

His wife would not divorce him because of her religion, and
Vynson dared not sue for a Mexican or a Paris divorce because that
would cut off his only certain source of supplies. His reputation
was now such that no other woman would have married him except a congenital idiot. Vynson still occupied a suite in the enormous Fitch mansion; it had its own entrance on a side street. This
"husband's door" had been the joke of New York at the time it was
constructed. It was said that husband and wife had not spoken in
some years. There were no children.

As time passed, there were veiled references to even darker sins
on Vynson's part, at which the columnists seemed to lick their lips.

Apparently his reputation had now become so bad that it was a social asset. He was enveloped in the glamour of wickedness. There were many references to the part he had played in introducing René Doria to café society. Lee had read most of that before. But he came upon one item which seemed to have possibilities. This was a reference four years earlier to a visit Jack Vynson had paid to Hollywood. Lee made a note of the date.

Lee finally closed the folders and sat thinking over what he had read, struck by a curious resemblance between Jack Vynson's story and that of his apparent pupil and successor, René Doria. Not in external events, for Vynson after a brief period of social success had married his heiress, whereas Doria, after a longer social career, had been killed on the eve of his marriage. The resemblance lay in that each of these men, so dissimilar in other respects, had revealed the same flair for publicity. All the little anecdotes of their savings and doings had that special quality which is called news value. It was this, rather than their good looks or their "magnetism," which had brought them fame in the big city. Lee noted that of late Jack Vynson occupied more space in the social columns than his present status seemed to warrant.

It was now nearly one o'clock. Beau Gramercy slid briskly out of his chair. "I'm going to take you to lunch at '21,'" he announced. "I owe you a good lunch, and anyhow I want to let the world see that I possess one intellectual friend. You can continue your studies here tomorrow."

"I have finished," said Lee.

"What did you learn?"

"Nothing that I didn't know before."

Beau Gramercy had made "21," and a table was reserved for him every day in such a position that he could see all who came and went. The comedy of the slightly higher chair and its attendant footstool was repeated here. The Beau came early and stayed late, because he preferred to be seen sitting down.

All through the meal people came hastening to his table. The tiny notebook was kept busy. Lee insisted on eating doggedly throughout the vivacious chatter (the food was superlatively good),

but of course he had to respond to introductions. Some of the val-
ues of this new society struck curiously on his old-fashioned mind.
One handsome young initiate, it turned out, was a tailor, and a
lady, very weirdly gotten up, was a fortune-teller. The man who,
next to Beau Gramercy, received the most attention in the place,
was an entertainer who sang bawdy songs at another restaurant in
the evening.

"Have you never heard him?" said the Beau, rolling his wicked
old eyes appreciatively. "My dear fellow! He stops at nothing, nothing! You see," he went on, "in modern society birth cuts no ice!"

Nor breeding? queried Lee in his mind.

"Nowadays a person has to do something or be something in his
own right to become a social success. It is much more amusing."

"Much," said Lee.

During the meal, Jack Vynson entered the restaurant and strode
scowling past their table without deigning a glance. Beau Gramercy
was deeply affronted. "Sulky brute!" he muttered.

When they had finished eating, Lee left the little man seated
on his throne with all the courtiers kow-towing to him, and proceeded to the Conradi-Windermere. In this hotel of hotels Miss
Vida Cadbury occupied a fine suite at the expense of the management.
Naturally she was an honored guest because she brought so much
business to the hotel. All her lavish entertainments were held there.

Lee found her in her "studio" surrounded by secretaries. These
she dismissed with a wave, and came waddling forward with both
hands outstretched. "My dear Lee! How nice of you to pop in like
this!"

Vida had herself well in hand this afternoon. Naturally she had
not attained to her present eminence as Director-General of smart
New York without having to face many a difficult moment on the
way. She was ready for anything. Lee apprehended that he had a
powerful personality to deal with. He suspected that her surprise
was only a stall—she had been expecting him. Vida led him to the
most comfortable chair in the room, and pressed a button. A softly-
stepping manservant entered, and as if by magic the makings of
highballs appeared on a table beside him.

Lee waved it away. "Just had lunch," he said. And added, "With Beau Gramercy. Remarkable character!"

Vida smiled stiffly.

"I had been down to his office earlier," Lee went on, "to consult his private file."

Vida's eyes leaped back to his face. "What for?"

"In connection with the René Doria case."

Vida's face became masklike again.

"If you're not going to partake I am," she said. "Mix me a weak Scotch and soda."

Lee obeyed. When she took the glass from him she added more Scotch. Lee watched her hands. They did not tremble. "You said weak," he remarked.

"Weak, yes, not wishy-washy." After settling herself in a low chair she went on, "What's the Beau got to do with the Doria case?"

"I thought I might find evidence in his file."

"And did you?"

"Yes and no. Nothing conclusive."

"Lee, are you playing with me?" she asked.

"Playing with you! Whatever do you mean?"

"Why did you come from Beau Gramercy to me?"

"For help."

"Well, go on."

"Jack Vynson was the one I was looking up."

Her eyes pounced on his again. "Anybody else?"

"No. The Beau guards his file like a dragon."

"So Jack Vynson is under suspicion?"

"In my eyes. He and René were thick as thieves."

Vida held up her highball and looked through it. "I don't see what I can tell you that you don't know already. Years ago Jack Vynson used to hang around me like they all do, hoping to get something out of it. Now he no longer needs me, and he's too old for my purposes."

"Your purposes?"

"I'm supposed to furnish brisk young men."

"Did you introduce him to Myra Fitch?"

"No. But wait a minute, maybe I did. Introductions are merely perfunctory. How can I be expected to remember? If I didn't introduce them somebody did."

"Were you in charge of the arrangements at the wedding?"

"Good God, Lee! What are you insinuating?"

"Well, that's part of your job, isn't it? Weddings. Were you familiar with the marriage settlement?"

"Damn it! I'm not a matchmaker!" she said angrily.

Lee took a pinch of snuff. "Why of course you are," he said. "I know of three cases where you helped to promote a marriage. It's a very useful service."

"Well, I didn't act for Jack Vynson," she said.

When Lee got home his first act was to check the date of Jack Vynson's visit to Hollywood four years before against certain notes he had made on the Doria case. He discovered that Vynson's visit coincided with René Doria's abrupt walking out on his motion-picture contract and return to New York. So it was Vynson who brought him back!

Lee then visited his own file, which was somewhat different from Beau Gramercy's. Lee's great preoccupation was with crime. The obvious had no interest for him, but of all cases which present unusual or romantic features, he kept a complete newspaper record, and unsolved crimes were his particular dish. What he had read of Vynson's life had struck a vague note of recollection in his mind that tormented him because he could not fix it.

He finally found what he was looking for in the Stockley case of 18 years ago—suicide or murder? Ralph Stockley was the son of a once prominent family of Connecticut that had become impoverished and had dropped out of the social race. The young man came to New York to make his fortune, and though he brought no letters of introduction, he was so good-looking and his manners so winning, that he was taken up by the best people. These were the days when the Four Hundred still ruled; café society had not been heard of. There was some mystery as to how Stockley had succeeded in entering the inner circle, but enter it he did. He attended all the debutante parties and exclusive balls; he dined at the best houses, and in the course of time he became engaged to Clara Portman, the daughter and heiress of one of the original oil magnates.

Young Stockley appeared to have been a very decent fellow. The parents of his prospective bride were strongly attached to him, and since he had no money of his own, Mr. Portman wished to make a settlement on him. But Stockley refused it—he could always get a job that would keep him in pocket money, he said. A week before the date set for his wedding, he was found shot to death in the little apartment that he shared with another young man. There were powder marks in his skin, and the gun lay beside his hand, so that at first it looked like suicide. But the young fellow was so happy in his approaching marriage, there was no conceivable reason why he should have killed himself.

Various suspicious circumstances came to light. The young man's skull was crushed in, which might have been due to a blow previous to the shot, or to his fall afterward. His friend had been called away from the flat by a phony telegram. The friend swore that Ralph had never possessed a gun. But if it was murder, there was no clue to Ralph's assailant; as far as his closest friend knew, he had no enemy. So the case had remained unsolved to this day. Lee had filed clippings telling of Miss Portman's marriage to another man a year later. Her father had died in the interim. The second man proved to be a common adventurer, and after making away with a large part of his wife's fortune, he had disappeared.

Lee was struck by the parallel. He thought: It is more than a coincidence. This is another piece of my puzzle, but I don't know where it goes: 18 years ago Jack Vynson had not come to New York; indeed, at that time he could not have been more than 17.

Lee called up Loasby at Headquarters. "Inspector, have you any recollection of the Stockley case?"

"No," said Loasby, "18 years ago I was a Lieutenant on the desk in the 33d precinct. Why?"

"That case bears an extraordinary resemblance to the Doria case."

"What!" cried Loasby. "You're hipped on the mystery angle, Lee! This case is as plain as the nose before your face."

"Maybe," said Lee calmly. "But do something for me, will you? Find out who was in charge of the investigation of homicides 18 years ago, and if he's still on the force."

"Sure, anything to oblige you, Lee."

Half an hour later he called Lee back. "Inspector Matthew Connolly was in charge of the Stockley case, Lee. It was never solved. Connolly was retired for age a few years ago, but he's still living." He gave Lee an address in the Bronx.

Lee immediately called a taxi and proceeded to the given address. The aged police officer knew all about Amos Lee Mappin and was immensely gratified at receiving a visit from him. Nothing pleased him better than to recite his old cases. He gave Lee an exact and painstaking account of the Stockley murder—all of which Lee had just read in his own file.

After hearing him out patiently, Lee said, "Inspector, in an important case there are often certain pieces of information which the police withhold from the press for good reasons."

"Surely, Mr. Mappin."

"Cast back in your mind and see if you can bring up any such facts in the Stockley case."

After considering a while, the old man said, "I mind one thing that struck me as very peculiar, Mr. Mappin, and I didn't say anything about it to the press, because I wanted to investigate it first. But I never did succeed in establishing what it meant, and I made up my mind it didn't mean anything, but was just somebody's idle scribbling."

"What was it?" asked Lee.

"Well, when I was called to the house upon the discovery of the body, my first job was to make an examination of the rooms. There was a desk in the living-room with a nice clean blotter on it, a green blotter, and somebody had taken a pencil and drawn a circle on the blotter, and put four dots inside it in the form of a square. It looked like a symbol, but I wasn't able to connect it with the murder."

Lee took off his glasses and polished them hard. He was a little excited. "That is exceedingly interesting, Inspector. You will hear from me later. In the meantime, please say nothing about my visit."

CHAPTER EIGHTEEN
THE KILLER

ON THE FOLLOWING MORNING (Friday) the reports of Stan Oberry's operatives for the previous day were put in Lee's hands. They conveyed nothing of importance. The story of Jack Vynson's day was the record of one who had nothing to do but kill time. He had spent upward of an hour with Slim Markoe in the 63d Street house; he had lunched at "21" and lunch had lasted until it was time to go for cocktails to the apartment of a Mrs. Stovall. This lady was a newcomer from the West, with an unlimited drawing account. The inference was that Jack Vynson consented to show himself at such parties for a fat fee. He had dined at the Restaurant Passy with another lady not in her first youth, and ended the day at El Zingara. He returned home at three o'clock pretty drunk but still able to navigate. He lived at the Hotel Vandermeer.

From the report of the man who was installed in the next room to Slim Markoe, it appeared that the conversation between the two on Thursday was confined to the subject of Slim's deportment.

But at two o'clock on Friday, Oberry sent Lee this man's report for that same day, with a note saying that the operative considered it of sufficient importance to be rushed through. And when Lee read it, he agreed.

After the usual lesson in how to talk, walk, eat and wear one's clothes, Vynson said to Slim:

"We think the time has come for you to meet the girl."

Slim answered, "Wouldn't it be dangerous so soon?"

"Not if nobody knows about it. It is more dangerous to put it off. She might marry anybody on the rebound. One meeting will be sufficient for the present, and it's up to you to see that you make a lasting impression. Then later when you run into her on shipboard the battle will be half won."

"Who's going to introduce me to her?" asked Slim.

"Nobody. An accidental meeting is better. More romantic. She is suspicious of everybody who is introduced to her formally."

"But how the hell can I run into a dame like that accidentally on purpose?"

"What do you suppose you've been taking riding lessons for? She's nuts on horses. You're to motor up to Braemar Manor this afternoon. Braemar is a hotel in Westchester County, very popular during the fall season. Your name is Egerton Brinsley; one of the best suites will be reserved for you, parlor, bedroom and bath. You ought to have a smart servant, but we haven't got a man at the moment that we can trust. Baddely is the ideal man for you, but somebody might recognize him. You'll need to take sport clothes, riding togs and evening dress. They have good saddle horses for hire at the hotel.

"The girl's estate is only two miles from Braemar. Its called Eastover. She rides every morning from 10:30 until lunch. A groom always follows her. She never ventures off her own place but as that consists of a couple of thousand acres of woodland with bridle paths in every direction, she has plenty of room. All the gates to the place are guarded. You've got to find your own way in, and contrive to meet her when she's riding. You apologize to her for trespassing—that gives you an opening. Tell her you didn't know any of the family was in residence, and the place looked so good to you, you were tempted to put your horse to the fence. The rest is up to you. With a neurotic, inhibited girl of that type the virile, red-blooded line is the best."

"Are you telling me?" put in Slim.

"If you want to take Saturday just to scout around, and put off the meeting until Sunday, that's all right. But there must be no slip-up—you won't get a second chance. You've *got* to pull it off. Saturday afternoon you can take a golf lesson—it will come in useful in the future. Saturday night there's a dance in the hotel. You can go to it and you can pick up a girl if you want, but for God's sake, don't dance around grinning like a hick. Act superior and reserved; don't say much; keep 'em guessing about you. Understand, this will be your final test. You'll be under observation while you're in the hotel, and it depends on you whether you'll be dropped, or taken right into the concern."

Vynson had repeated these instructions until he was sure that Slim understood every point.

As soon as Lee had digested the report, he reached for the telephone. Calling the Brocklin house, he got the butler on the wire. There was now a good understanding between Lee and Wilton.

"Wilton, is Miss Brocklin in town?"

"No, Mr. Mappin. She and Mrs. Thorne have gone up to the country place, Eastover, for the sake of the privacy. It made Miss Brocklin nervous the way people hung around this house and stared at her when she went in and out."

"I can understand that," said Lee.

"Miss Brocklin drives into town every afternoon to see her father," said Wilton. "I can have a message conveyed to her."

"That won't be necessary. I'll call you again."

Lee hung up, and lighting a cigar, paced the floor with his hands behind him while he debated his best course of action. There was nothing to be gained by going up to Westchester immediately. By showing himself at Braemar Manor he might be recognized before he succeeded in spotting his men. If he let the plot start working before he intervened, he would have more evidence with which to convict the gang. Meanwhile, he must take the police into his confidence.

He taxied down to Headquarters. Inspector Loasby's ruddy face paled when he heard what Lee had learned from the retired police officer. "Eighteen years ago!" he exclaimed. "The same symbol! Circle and four dots! Lee, do you think we have made a mistake in arresting Dexter Brocklin?"

Lee smiled at the plural pronoun, but forbore to rub it in. "I'm afraid we have."

"Good God! This may break me!"

"I wouldn't worry about that, Inspector. The evidence against Brocklin was so strong it was a natural mistake. If you succeed in nabbing the real killer, the mistake will quickly be forgotten."

"Slim must be re-arrested immediately," said Loasby. "We have positive evidence that he is planning to skip his bail."

"Wait until tomorrow," said Lee. "Tomorrow night you should call on all your resources even if it means planting 100 men in Westchester."

"I'll mobilize 200," said Loasby.

"I'll warn the girl," said Lee, "but not until *after* Slim has seen her. We mustn't let the gang suspect that any hitch has occurred in their program. Don't take any action until you hear from me tomorrow. If you start mobilizing too soon, there is danger of a leak."

"Right," said Loasby.

On Saturday morning Lee taxied directly from town to Eastover, avoiding the hotel. On this expedition he was forced to leave Fanny Parran behind because she was too well known to Slim and Vynson. His other girl, Judy Bowles, was instructed to register at Braemar Manor during the afternoon. Lee wanted the cover that would be afforded by a woman companion at the dance. He timed his arrival at the Brocklin country house for 12:30, and sent his taxi away because he didn't want to advertise that there was a visitor by letting it stand in front of the door. The driver was instructed to return in three-quarters of an hour.

At Eastover, an impressive château in the French style, there was another corps of servants. The butler had never seen Lee before, but he was impressed by his name. "Miss Brocklin is riding, sir."

"Well," said Lee, "I'll wait."

The butler showed him somewhat dubiously into a small reception room and went away. Lee seated himself by a window which commanded a view of the drive. The man evidently reported to Aunt Clara, for that lady presently came in, stout and short of breath.

Lee was associated in her mind with two painful scenes; she disliked him exceedingly, but tried to hide it. "Good morning, Mr. Mappin. Peggy is out riding. If you will tell me what you want to see her about, perhaps I can save you a tedious wait."

"Oh, she can't be long," said Lee. "She will be returning for lunch. I don't mind waiting."

Aunt Clara did not much care for this answer. "Well, anyway, you can tell me what you have to tell her. I am the closest to her of anybody on earth."

"Of course you are," said Lee politely, "and I'm sure she'll tell you herself after I have gone, but my communication is for her ear alone."

Aunt Clara stiffened and gave Lee a poisonous glance He saw that she had made up her mind to stay where she was. She made small talk to which he gave the polite answers, meanwhile watching through the window out of the corner of his eye. After a while, two riders appeared in the drive where it issued from the woods. Lee could recognize the man as Slim Markoe. The two were walking their horses slowly, and their attitudes suggested friendliness. Slim has been successful; he would be!

They pulled up their horses, and Lee guessed that Peggy was telling the man that he must go back now. The groom rode past them and came to the house where he dismounted, waiting for his mistress. Peggy gave Slim her hand, and he held it for a moment, looking into her eyes, then rode away. Peggy cantered up to the house, wearing a half-smile that made her insipid, pretty face look almost beautiful. The groom helped her to dismount, and went around the house leading both horses.

Peggy came directly into the reception room, slim and graceful in her boots and breeches. Mrs. Thorne bounced up, "Here is Mr. Mappin to see you."

Lee was no favorite of Peggy's. "How are you?" she said coolly. "What is it about?"

"I must speak to you alone," said Lee.

"Well, I *must* say!" exclaimed Aunt Clara indignantly. She flounced out of the room, and the girl made sure that the door was closed tightly.

"Well, Mr. Mappin?" she asked, languidly pulling off her gloves.

Lee was not disposed to spare her. "This man you have just left—" he began.

"You have been spying on me!" Peggy interrupted.

"No. I knew yesterday about this intended meeting in your park."

"It was an accidental meeting. You couldn't have known!"

"Not accidental on his part," corrected Lee. "He was obeying instructions."

"I don't understand you!"

"He introduced himself to you as Egerton Brinsley. That is the name he was told to assume. I don't know what his real name may be, but he is known to the police as Slim Markoe."

The girl started and paled.

"That name is known to you, I see," Lee went on. "As a matter of fact, this man is the dark horse that the District Attorney has been holding in reserve as a witness against your father."

"Then why does he seek me out?" she demanded. "If he testifies against my father I wouldn't have anything further to do with him."

"He will not testify against your father. Before the trial opens he will disappear. Without his evidence the District Attorney has no chance of obtaining a conviction. Your father will be acquitted. You will then, as you have publicly announced, take him abroad to forget the whole ugly business. On the ship you will run into Mr. Egerton Brinsley, who will pay ardent court to you—and your riches. He is a very attractive fellow. That's why he was chosen—"

Peggy stared at him in horror. "I don't believe you!" she murmured.

"My dear young lady," said Lee earnestly, "what possible reason could I have for lying to you?"

"Everybody lies to me!"

A feeling of pity for her welled up in his breast. "I came to warn you, my dear. I'm sorry I was so blunt. This man is doubly dangerous, because of the sinister figures behind him."

"What do you mean?" Her lips merely shaped the words.

"Whatever cash settlement he may induce you to make on him, either before or after marriage, he is to divide with those who have groomed him for this."

Peggy's face was all screwed up like that of a small child. Her clenched hands were pressed together. She suddenly turned, and flinging open the door, vanished. Lee heard her running up the stairs.

He stood looking out of the window. Nobody came. After a bit his taxi drew up in front of the house, and he let himself out of the front door. He ordered the driver to return to New York.

At Headquarters, Lee consulted with Inspector Loasby, and they completed their arrangements for the coming night. Lee dressed and dined at home, and drove up to Westchester again, arriving at Braemar Manor at ten o'clock, just about time, he figured, when the dance would be getting into swing. The great hotel with its wide-spreading wings had too many entrances to please him; however, it was Loasby's job to see that they were all covered.

Lee checked his hat and coat, and after a brief search found Judy Bowles gracefully disposed in an easy chair against the wall of the broad corridor leading to the ballroom. It was Lee's self-pleasing custom, whenever one of his girls was required to attend a social function in the line of duty, to present her with a new dress. Judy looked positively regal in a billowy gown of purple chiffon with her sleek black hair rolled and drawn back in the style of Victoria Regina.

He dropped in a chair beside her. "Have you seen anybody answering to the description of our friend?"

"You couldn't mistake him," said Judy, "he's unique. I saw him first this afternoon when he came in from the golf course. He tried to pick me up then, but I thought it was too soon, and I ignored his signals. I learned from the register that his suite is number 224. I tried to get an adjoining suite, but they were taken. The best I could do was 229 which is down the hall a little. By opening my door a crack, I could watch his door He came out at seven o'clock, dressed for the evening, and I supposed he had gone down to dinner. But he did not dine in either of the restaurants. Yet I don t think he was going out to dinner because he didn't have hat or coat. Just a few minutes ago he got out of the elevator and he didn't have hat or coat then, but he certainly looked like a man who had dined. I think he must have dined with somebody in a suite upstairs. He just passed me on his way to the ballroom. He wanted to pick me up again, but I looked the other way because I was afraid I might miss you."

"I'll start a little inquiry about his dinner date," said Lee. "Wait here for me."

Two of Inspector Loasby's men, elegant young men who could pass as guests of Braemar Manor, had been stationed in the main lobby to act as liaison officers between Lee and the force outside the hotel. Lee approached one of these, and the two greeted each other as pleasant acquaintances.

Lee accepted a cigarette. "Have you got in touch with the chief house detective?"

"Yes, sir, he's a former police officer. We can count on him."

"Good. Tell him I have learned that Mr. Egerton Brinsley dined in a private suite at seven o'clock, and ask him to find out what suite it was and who is in it. It ought not to be difficult, because there cannot be many people in a place like this who would choose to dine in their rooms on Saturday night."

Lee returned to Judy and they entered the ballroom together. The music was playing, and the floor was thronged with dancers. Down each side of the long floor were arched openings, with tables in each. Finding a vacant table, Lee had it pulled back a little so that he could sit hidden from the dancers by a pillar. On his right the beautiful Judy sat in full view of the floor. It was hot and he ordered rum Collinses.

Lee was content to sit back smoking, depending on Judy for a report of what was going on.

"I can't see him anywhere, Pop. I'm sure he's not dancing now." The music stopped and a babel of conversation was released. After a little the band started to play again. "Now I can see him across the floor. He has spotted me, Pop! He's making a beeline across the floor! Do you want me to dance with him?"

"Let me have a word with him first."

A moment later Slim was bowing over the table. "Will you dance?" he asked Judy. His style was pretty good, considering the shortness of his tuition.

Judy looked at Lee, and Slim, following her eyes, recognized her partner behind the pillar. His color changed but he kept command of his features. "Ah, Mr. Mappin!" he said.

"Sit down for a moment before you dance," suggested Lee.

"Thank you very much, sir, but—"

"Sit down!" said Lee in a quiet tone that the young man was forced to obey. He dropped in the chair facing Lee and having Judy on his left. Lee went on, "The game is up, Slim."

Slim continued to smile pleasantly. "I don't understand you, Mr. Mappin."

"All your movements and conversations during the past few days have been reported to me—including your ride this morning."

"So what?" asked the smiling young man. "There is nothing criminal in my actions. Every young fellow has the right to do the best he can for himself."

"Under an assumed name?"

"Oh, that was my lawyer's suggestion. He wants me to avoid all publicity until after my case is tried."

"Is it every young man's right to line up with a murder gang?"

Slim looked at Lee blankly.

"There's no use trying to make out you don't understand me," said the latter. "You are not a fool."

Slim glanced out across the floor with easy assurance, but Lee noted that his hands were trembling though he was pressing them on the table.

"Whom did you dine with tonight?" asked Lee.

"I dined alone."

"That's not true."

"I play my own hand," said Slim. "If I had any confederates I wouldn't betray them."

There was a silence. Lee was idly drawing little circles on the tablecloth with a pencil, and putting four dots in each. Slim's glance was attracted to what he was doing. The young man caught his breath; his eyes seemed to start from his head. With an agonized effort, he dragged them away.

"If they are watching you now," said Lee softly, "after having been seen talking to me, your life will not be worth a dime."

Slim fetched out a laugh. "You're talking nonsense, Mr. Mappin." Fine beads of perspiration broke out on his forehead. He wiped his face, saying lightly to Judy, "Lord, it's hot in here!"

Lee, quietly smoking and studying him through narrowed eyes, persisted. "Your safest course now would be to put yourself in the hands of the police. There are two officers in the lobby within call, and many more outside the building. I can guarantee you protection."

"How many times have I got to tell you there's nothing in it!" said Slim. Under Lee's steady gaze his morale crumbled. "For God's sake, don't keep me sitting here!" he murmured. "It's torture."

Lee shrugged. "Go ahead and dance," he said. "I've given you your chance."

Slim and Judy stood up. Slim slipped his arm around her and they joined the throng of slowly turning dancers. As soon as he got away from the table Slim recovered himself. He danced, gazing down at his beautiful partner with a half-smile, and apparently as oblivious to his surroundings as any young man on the floor. Lee, sitting forward, watched them to see if there were others in the ballroom paying more than ordinary attention to the couple. Perhaps there were such, but Lee could not discover them.

The couple had made a complete circuit of the room and were half around again when they stopped dancing near the entrance opposite where Lee was sitting. He could not see what was taking place, there were so many people between, but he immediately got up and started to circle the floor. There was such a crowd, it was hard to get through and he lost a couple of precious minutes. He finally met Judy coming toward him.

"He's gone," she whispered. "While we were dancing a young man cut in. I declined to dance with him, but Slim insisted on handing me over. I didn't think you would want me to hang on to Slim and make a scene, so I let him go."

"You did right," said Lee. "He won't get far."

They got out as quickly as they could without attracting attention. One of the young policemen in evening clothes was lounging in the corridor. He said, "He went up in elevator number two."

"Get word to the Inspector that the alarm has been raised," said Lee, "then come back."

The officer slipped out through the nearest entrance. Out in the lobby the other tail-coated policeman came sauntering up. "Where's the house detective?" asked Lee.

"He's in the pantry waiting for the waiter who served dinner upstairs."

When elevator number two next returned to the ground floor Lee said to the operator, "The slim, blond young man that you carried up five minutes ago, do you recollect him?"

"Yes, sir."

"Where did you take him?"

"Second floor. He's in number 224, sir."

Lee said to the police officer, "Find the house detective and bring him up to 224." The young man hurried away. To Judy, Lee said, "You wait down here for me, my dear."

"Pop, you mustn't go up alone!" she faltered.

He smiled at her. "I'll wait for the other officer."

The young man he had sent out of the building presently returned, and he and Lee had themselves carried to the second floor. As they proceeded through the long, softly carpeted corridor, the officer took out his gun. He was looking forward to his first important capture and his eyes were shining. When they came to the door of 224 the key was in it.

"We have him!" he whispered gleefully.

"I'm not so sure!" Lee hesitated with his hand on the doorknob. Finally, as with an effort, he let the door swing in. The room was brilliantly lighted. The young policeman gasped. Slim Markoe lay face down, sprawling on the floor with his arms flung wide. There was a wound on the back of his head and blood was running through his blond hair—not much blood. But there was an ugly round depression in his skull.

The officer ran into the adjoining bedroom. It was empty, also the bathroom. Lee closed the door into the corridor. When the officer reappeared, Lee said:

"You can put up your gun."

They dropped beside the body. Slim was dead. "Not 10 minutes ago," stammered the officer, "he walked past me."

"Turn him over," said Lee.

"Look!" cried the officer in amazement.

Somebody with a swirl had drawn a circle on the dead man's shirt front, using a greasy red pigment like lipstick, and had placed four dots inside it in the form of a square. "The same childish mummery!" said Lee contemptuously. He was more interested in several colorless wet splashes that appeared on the shirt front below the red marks.

"That's funny," said the officer.

"I think I can account for those marks," said Lee.

There was a sound at the door. The second officer entered bringing the house detective. "Oh, my God!"

"Where did they dine?" asked Lee.

"In number 168 on the first bedroom floor."

"Let's go there," said Lee. "This fellow is beyond help."

They locked the door and took the key: 168 was in a different wing of the hotel. As they hastened down the stairs and through seemingly endless corridors, the house detective said, "Dinner for three was ordered served in 168 at seven o'clock. Two waiters carried it up. They were received by a tall, dark-complected man about 37 who looked like a heavy-drinker."

"I know him," put in Lee.

"The waiters could hear two other persons talking in the adjoining bedroom, but they didn't see them. When the table was set, the dark man told them they wouldn't be needed and they left. When they were rung for an hour later, the trays with all the dishes had been put out in the hall."

They reached the door of 168 and the house detective opened it with his passkey. This man was no tender innocent, but a low cry of horror was forced from him when he looked into the sitting-room.

On the floor sprawled the body of a man in evening dress in almost the same position as the other, and bleeding from a head wound. His skull had been crushed in similarly by one terrible blow. This was a heavier man with an older, mottled complexion.

"Jack Vynson," said Lee.

"My God!" murmured the house detective. "This is the work of a fiend!"

"It was inevitable," said Lee. "We had the goods on this man, and through him the trail would have led straight to his boss."

On Vynson's shirt front appeared the same insignia of the circle and four dots. He was still breathing.

Lee said, "He will die without regaining consciousness, but anyhow, fetch the house doctor, quick."

One of the young officers ran out.

"This must have happened within the past 10 minutes," said the house detective excitedly. "The killer can't have got far. We must go after him!"

"There's nothing we can do," said Lee. "Every possible precaution has been taken."

Vynson's day clothes were found in the bedroom, but in neither room was there any clue to the identity of the third person who had dined there. When Lee had satisfied himself of it, he said, "I'm going to County Headquarters to meet Inspector Loasby. I will report these two murders. Nothing must be touched until the police take charge."

"Tell the Chief to send only plainclothes men," begged the house detective. "The guests mustn't be alarmed!"

Lee picked up Judy downstairs and they set off for the county police office in a taxicab. He didn't tell her what had happened until they were clear of the hotel, and then only half of it.

"They got Slim, my dear. He's dead."

"Oh, Pop!" she faltered. She began to weep and her head fell against Lee's shoulder. "Oh, Pop, how awful! Only half an hour ago I was dancing with him! He held me so close!"

There was a good bit of excitement around the county police station; a score of cars lined up in the street, and inside the main office, a crowd of New York detectives standing about. They made a lane for Lee to pass through.

"Did you get your prisoner?" he asked.

Several voices answered. "In the Chief's office."

When Lee opened the inner door, he saw Loasby, the County Chief, and two detectives lined up with their backs toward him, and at first he could not distinguish who was sitting beyond them. But the seated figure recognized him and sprang up.

"Lee Mappin! Thank God! He can vouch for me!"

The officers stepped aside and the odd, gnomelike figure of Beau Gramercy was revealed in his natty evening topcoat, silk hat, white gloves. He was cool, but there was an uncanny glitter in his eyes.

"Tell them that they have made a mistake, Lee. Tell them that I am Beau Gramercy and that I was attending the dance at Braemar Manor in my professional capacity!"

Lee fronted him in silence. The tiny man's topcoat was open and he was seen to be wearing a gardenia in the buttonhole of his jacket. Lee drew the flower out with care and held it up so that the police officers could see the neat holder of black glass in which it was held. He said:

"This is an important bit of evidence, Inspector. Take care of it. Notice that there is no water in the glass. It spilled out on Slim Markoe's shirt front."

The Beau ran up his heavy eyebrows like an actor. "What nonsense are you talking, Lee?"

Lee paid no attention to him. "Where's his stick?"

"I wasn't carrying a stick tonight," said the Beau.

Loasby addressed one of his detectives: "You nabbed him? Did he have a stick?"

The mail was confused. "I didn't see any."

The second detective spoke up: "He had a stick, all right. While McArdle was holding him he quietly dropped it and gave it a little kick behind him. I picked it up." From under his coat he produced the well-known ebony stick with a gold knob.

"Good work!" said Lee. "This stick has killed three men. Perhaps more."

CHAPTER NINETEEN
THE LEGACY

A SEARCH OF BEAU GRAMERCY'S APARTMENT on the following day brought to light, among other pieces of evidence, a key to René Doria's apartment in 46th Street. Lee also picked up a bottle of perfume for men called "Tweed" which he considered of importance. Furthermore, in a safe deposit box the police found $100,000 in marked bills. Beau Gramercy, no doubt, had intended it to lie there until the Doria case was forgotten. He could afford it, for he was found to be a very wealthy man.

Westchester County was disposed to turn the prisoner over to the New York authorities in order to save the expense of a trial, and on a subsequent day Lee Mappin, Inspector Loasby and the District Attorney met to discuss the case. Lee's talk on this occasion later formed a large part of the District Attorney's opening address to the jury when the man was tried:

"This case begins nearly 40 years ago," Lee said, "when young Houson Bell, the descendant of two old New York families, was thrown on the world penniless. Not trained to do anything useful, it was natural he should try to cash in on his social connections by becoming a society reporter. Society reporters were despised in those days, and the slights and snubs he had to put up with drove the iron deep into the young man's soul. A powerful personality and an overweening vanity were imprisoned in that tiny body.

"The obvious solution would have been a rich marriage, but no heiress would look twice at a little shrimp like him. So his perverted mind formed the scheme of finding and pushing forward

209

better-favored young men to play the part denied to him. The psy-
choanalyst can explain how this frustrated man obtained a vicari-
ous satisfaction in the triumphs of the handsome and full-blooded
males that he promoted—in other words, his creatures. And when
one of them made a strike, Beau Gramercy shared in the profits. It
was a game for huge stakes.

"He had the creator's jealousy of his own puppets. It roused
him to a murderous rage when they disobeyed him. The first case
of which I have notes is that of Ralph Stockley—18 years ago this
handsome and agreeable young man was launched in New York
society through somewhat mysterious means, and in the course of
time he became engaged to a Miss Clara Portman, a great heiress
of that day. Stockley's backer seems to have misjudged his man:
he refused the cash the girl's father offered to settle on him. And
so he was murdered, in precisely the same manner of René Doria,
Slim Markoe and Jack Vynson. Later, another candidate married
Miss Portman, got hold of her fortune and disappeared. The cut
must have been enormous.

"Five years later, Jack Vynson turns up. Beau Gramercy, becoming powerful in New York society, was in a position to make
his puppets famous. The clippings show that he did this with extraordinary cleverness. Beau Gramercy invented all the anecdotes
of Vynson's sayings and doings, and circulated them—mostly
through women. They soon found their way into the gossip columns. In his own column Beau Gramercy took a different course;
he appeared to abuse Vynson, but always in such a way that it con-
tributed to the glamour surrounding the young man. Beau
Gramercy and his protégés were never seen together in public.
Vynson seems to have given him no trouble. In time he married
the great Fitch fortune and there was another big cut.

"Vynson ran through his share and his rich wife practically cast
him off. He then became Beau Gramercy's assistant in bringing
forward new young men. Gramercy has other agents and spies.
All the evidence suggests a smoothly working organization. It's
up to the police to find them. One of them was the man Baddely,
who worked as René Doria's servant and spied on his actions.

Gramercy's rather childish trick of signing his murders with the circle and four dots was done with the purpose of striking terror into the hearts of his other creatures.

"Eight years ago Beau Gramercy, or one of his agents, picked René Doria up as a penniless extra hanging around the lots in Hollywood. René, with his extraordinary good looks, was precisely the instrument that Gramercy required. Once he had received the gloss of good breeding, this lusty fellow was irresistible among the hothouse flowers of society. René appears to have first kicked over the traces four years ago. He accepted a motion-picture contract and went out to Hollywood to act. Jack Vynson fetched him back. After that he seems to have been docile enough. He began to pay court to Peggy Brocklin, and finally their engagement was announced. Her fortune was the biggest prize of all, and there were no parents or trustees.

"Rene was now preparing to defy his master again. On the day before he was killed, his bride-to-be presented him with half a million dollars as the first installment of his wedding settlement. The fact that he immediately invested $400,000, proves that he had no intention of splitting with Beau Gramercy. The other $100,000 was for Rose Bosi. René seems to have been genuinely attached to Rose, and planned to rejoin her after he had shaken off his rich wife.

"Just at what moment Beau Gramercy began to suspect René, I can't say, but he had the information about René's previous marriage in his hands for nearly two weeks before he used it. The final murder plan appears to have been extemporaneous. Gramercy liked to pull his stunts on the spur of the moment. Owing to Dexter Brocklin's bitter opposition to the marriage, Gramercy had it in for him, too, and no doubt figured that if he could separate father and daughter, the latter would more readily fall for his next candidate. At any rate, this is what happened on the night of the murder:

"Beau Gramercy reached the apartment on 46th Street before René and let himself in with his own key. When René came he was hidden in the closet off the living-room: when the door of the closet was first opened next morning, there was a distinct smell of 'Tweed' on the air. While René and Mrs. Vosper were cooking and eating their supper—this part is only my guess—Beau Gramercy made a signal to Jack Vynson in the street, and Vynson telephoned to Dexter Brocklin, as you know.

"I am convinced that Dexter Brocklin's story of what happened while he was in the apartment is literally true. René disarmed Brocklin and sent him away with his tail between his legs. So Beau Gramercy's first plot to have the angry father kill René failed. But Brocklin's gun was still lying on the floor, remember, and the opportunity was too good to be passed up. When René was left alone in the apartment, Beau Gramercy stepped noiselessly out of the closet and struck him down with the gold-headed stick. He snatched a scarf off the piano and wrapped it around his head to catch the blood.

"He then laid René's head on the steel floor of the fender and, picking up the gun in a gloved hand, put a bullet in his skull. He threw the gun down the dumbwaiter shaft and shoved the body after it. He stuck a few of René's hairs on the knob of the fender to make it appear as if René had cracked his skull by falling on it. You will find, however, that the depression in René's skull fits the knob of Beau Gramercy's stick, not the fender. He then picked up the money and went home, taking René's gun with him. This plan missed success by the narrowest of margins. Certainly, if Beau Gramercy had not happened to drop his gardenia and later, the little glass that held it, Dexter Brocklin would have been convicted of murder. Slim's story of what he saw in the Doria apartment is true, too. He didn't get in until the Beau had left.

"Some days after the murder, Beau Gramercy saw Slim Markoe for the first time. I happened to be with him. It was in the magistrate's court, and when the Beau saw the stir among the women spectators when Slim was brought in, he decided Slim was the man for him. For Beau Gramercy's purposes, Slim was one in a million. This necessitated a change in his plans. Dexter Brocklin was to be allowed to escape conviction—though everybody would still believe he had killed René Doria.

"Slim was released on bail and his training commenced immediately. Beau Gramercy was now playing a very complicated and dangerous game; it was the sort of thing that appealed to him. He was pushed for time because Peggy Brocklin had publicly announced her intention of going abroad to live, and he had to catch her fancy with an American boy before she was snapped up by a titled foreigner. Slim was to have been planted on the ship that carried her across the ocean.

"That brings us up to the double tragedy at Braemar Manor. The Beau must have been watching Slim Markoe in the ballroom. Such an old hand would know how to see without being seen. He saw Slim talking to me, and guessed from the young man's agitation that the game was up. My mere presence in the place was enough to warn him. He watched Slim dancing—he saw his hasty retreat from the dance floor. Slim, I take it, ran up to his room to get his coat and hat. The Beau followed him there and struck him down.

"He then, with his customary coolness, proceeded to the suite where Vynson was waiting, and, when his back was turned, silenced him forever. Vynson had become dangerous. The Beau left the hotel by a side entrance, and if Inspector Loasby's men had not been on the job, he would have got clean away, too, for up to that moment we had nothing on him. The gold-headed stick and the marked money are going to send him to the chair."

Tom Cottar took Fanny to dinner at André's, a little, old-fashioned restaurant on Frankfort Street. It was always crowded in the middle of the day, but at night it had a quiet and cozy atmosphere, and the food was marvelous. Tom favored it because he liked to talk. They could always go on to some other place to dance.

Fanny was wearing a new hat of green suede. Tom studied it with a droll glint in his eyes.

"I don't care whether *you* like it," she said. "I do."

"But it suits you! The angle at which it turns down balances the angle at which your nose turns up."

"My nose does *not* turn up!"

Tom laughed delightedly, but there was an imploring look in his eyes. After a while, he said very casually, "Did you see my story of the Doria case this morning?"

"Yes."

He waited for more, and when it was not forthcoming, asked with an even greater casualness, "What did you think of it?"

"It was all right."

"Is that all?"

"Pop didn't think much of it,"

"Why didn't Pop like it?"

"It played him up too much."

"Pop's a funny little cuss," remarked Tom.

Fanny's brows drew together. "I don't like the way you say that."

"It's no more than you say yourself."

"Sure. Pop *is* a funny little cuss. I can say it because I love him, and because I admire him."

A note of bitterness came into Tom's voice. "I admire Pop myself, but I get tired of having him shoved down my throat. Whenever I am with you it's Pop this and Pop that. One would think he was the only man on earth!"

A dimple appeared in Fanny's cheek. "Whereas you know of another man that should not be overlooked."

"Sure! Meaning me. I'm only human. What would happen if we got married?" he suggested offhandedly.

Fanny affected to shiver delicately. "Don't speak of such a thing. It would be hell on earth."

"Maybe not."

"It would, too—or else one of us would become a poor, broken-spirited slave and the other an insufferable egoist."

"You overlook one factor."

"What's that?"

"Sleeping together."

"What's that got to do with it?"

"Quite a good deal."

"I suppose that's the way you count on taming a woman."

"I don't want a tame wife. I look forward to quarreling with my wife to the end. Those are the marriages that stay fresh. Quarreling without rancor. Hell with interludes of heaven."

Fanny bridled and preened like a little hen. "Well, don't start in by abusing my friends."

"I could love Pop with all my heart—under certain circumstances."

"What circumstances?"

"Ah, you know. Don't make out you're a dope."

"There are several possible explanations."

"I could love Pop if I were sure of you."

"No man will ever be sure of me!"

"I mean, if I were sure that you gave a damn for me."

Fanny lowered her eyes. "I give several damns for you."

"Will you seal it when we get out of here?"

"I won't kiss you in the dark street because you'd never let go. I'll kiss you here across the table. But, mind, it doesn't mean anything."

They leaned toward each other and their lips met. The fat old waiter bustling up to the table with their scallopini grinned happily.

"Oh, boy!" said Fanny. "Here's the food!"

SHORTLY BEFORE the departure from this life (hastened by process of law) of Houson Bell, better known to the world as Beau Gramercy, one morning Lee Mappin received a plain envelope in the mail which contained three little flat keys folded within a blank sheet of paper. There was not a word to identify the sender or to throw light on his purpose in sending the keys. Lee put them carefully away, confident that the explanation would transpire one day or another.

Some days after the execution, a letter came from the attorneys of the deceased, quoting a paragraph from their client's will: *And I hereby devise and bequeath the personal file in my office and all its contents to my friend Amos Lee Mappin, Esq. The keys are already in his possession. Lee Mappin, of all the men I know, is best able to appreciate the material I have been gathering for so many years. He is to use it in any way that he sees fit.*

Lee scratched his bald pate. "Well, I'll be damned! Malicious to the grave—beyond the grave!"

When his property was delivered to him, Lee took out the folder marked *Vida Cadbury*, and slipping it in a briefcase, picked up his hat and taxied over to the Conradi-Windermere. He found Vida at home. Her eyes widened when she saw what he was taking out of the briefcase and she began to breathe fast.

"It appears that I am Beau Gramercy's literary executor," said Lee.

"What—are you going to—?" she stammered. Then she perceived that Lee was offering her the folder. Snatching it from him, she pressed it to her broad bosom. "Have you read what is in it?"

"No."

Lee noted that her eyes did not stand still but darted swiftly from side to side as if she were trying to see around his eyes. "I actually believe you are telling the truth!" she murmured incredulously.

Vida dropped the briefcase on her desk and laying her head upon it, wept unrestrainedly. Lee inspected the *objets d'art* around the room.

"I never did anybody any harm," she wailed. "This is a rotten business I'm in, but I never did any harm—not knowingly! I wasn't like Houson Bell! The worst I did was to keep my mouth shut."

"You have known all these years what he was up to?"

"I didn't know anything, I only surmised it. I knew by a process of elimination that it *must* have been Houson. People come and go fast in our world, and things are quickly forgotten. Only Houson and I went on year after year, each playing our own game. He was afraid of me because I had such a long memory. Then he got hold of some letters of mine; he stole them—foolish letters, Lee, not wicked—and he was no longer afraid of me. What could I do? I live by publicity, and the wrong publicity would have destroyed me!"

Still weeping, she opened the folder, and thumbing through the newspaper clippings, drew out three old letters written on a thick lavender paper in an angular hand. Lee noted with inward amusement that it was *not* Vida's own hand. She lighted the little candle on her desk that she used for melting sealing wax, and burned the letters one after another. Her tears ceased to flow.

"Now I can sleep o'nights," she murmured.

Going to Lee, she picked up one of his hands and fondled it between her soft plump paws. Tears started again. "I'll never forget this, Lee! Never! You're a good man. I didn't think there were any more!"

Lee repossessed himself of his hand. There was a twinkle behind his brightly polished glasses. "Law, Vida! Are we going soft in our old age?"

COACHWHIP PUBLICATIONS

COACHWHIPBOOKS.COM

ISBN 978-1-61646-255-8

WHO KILLED THE
HUSBAND?

HULBERT FOOTNER

ISBN 978-1-61646-256-6

Coachwhip Publications

CoachwhipBooks.com

1

HULBERT FOOTNER
THE ADVENTURES OF
MADAME STOREY

ISBN 978-1-61646-236-9

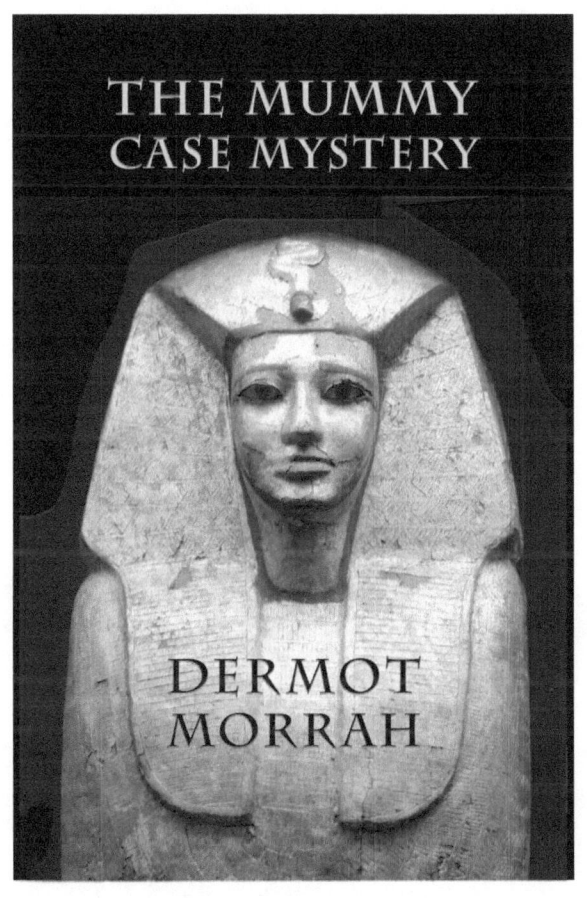

THE MUMMY
CASE MYSTERY

DERMOT
MORRAH

ISBN 978-1-61646-250-7

COACHWHIP PUBLICATIONS

COACHWHIPBOOKS.COM

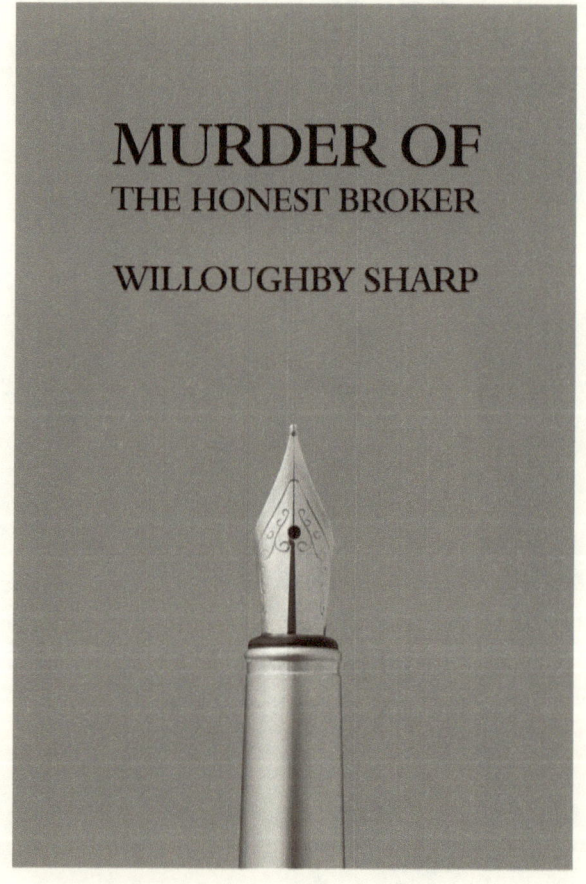

MURDER OF
THE HONEST BROKER

WILLOUGHBY SHARP

ISBN 978-1-61646-211-6

COACHWHIP PUBLICATIONS

ALSO AVAILABLE

THE QUINNY HITE
MYSTERIES

CHINESE RED · HERE LIES THE BODY

RICHARD BURKE

ISBN 978-1-61646-247-5

www.ingramcontent.com/pod-product-compliance
Lightning Source LLC
Chambersburg PA
CBHW020401030726
47496CB00007B/2255